23
A.

-
F
S

Alafair Burke was born in Fort Lauderdale, Florida, the daughter of mystery novelist James Lee Burke. Raised primarily in Wichita, Kansas, where her mother was a school librarian, she traces her fascination with crime to BTK, a serial killer who was active in the area during the 1970s. After graduating with distinction from Stanford Law School, she served as a deputy district attorney in Portland, Oregon, where she prosecuted domestic violence offences and served as an in-precinct adviser to the police department. Burke currently lives in New York City and is a Professor of Law at Hofstra Law School. A bestselling crime author, she has served as a member of the board of directors of the Mystery Writers of America and as President of its New York chapter.

You can discover more about the author at alafairburke.com

THE EX

Olivia Randall is one of New York City's best criminal defence lawyers. When she gets a phone call informing her that her former fiancé has been arrested for a triple homicide, there is no doubt in her mind as to his innocence. The only question is, who would go to such great lengths to frame him — and why? For Olivia, representing Jack is a way to make up for past regrets, and the hurt she caused him. But as the evidence against him mounts, she is forced to confront her doubts . . .

Books by Alafair Burke
Published by Ulverscroft:

JUDGMENT CALLS
MISSING JUSTICE
CLOSE CASE
DEAD CONNECTION
CITY OF FEAR
LONG GONE

ALAFAIR BURKE

———————————◆———————————

THE EX

Complete and Unabridged

CHARNWOOD
Leicester

First published in Great Britain in 2016 by
Faber & Faber Limited
London

First Charnwood Edition
published 2017
by arrangement with
Faber & Faber Limited
London

The moral right of the author has been asserted

A catalogue record for this book is available
from the British Library.

ISBN 978–1–4448–3244–0

Published by
F. A. Thorpe (Publishing)
Anstey, Leicestershire

Set by Words & Graphics Ltd.
Anstey, Leicestershire
Printed and bound in Great Britain by
T. J. International Ltd., Padstow, Cornwall

This book is printed on acid-free paper

For Lish Whitson and Joel Summerlin

June 17, 2015

TRANSCRIPT OF RECORDED INTERVIEW WITH JACKSON HARRIS

10:27 AM — recording starts
NYPD DET. JIMMY BOYLE

BOYLE: Okay, I've turned on the machine, Mr. Harris. Just to make clear, are you here at the First Precinct voluntarily?

HARRIS: Yes.

BOYLE: And you're willing to speak to me of your own accord?

HARRIS: Sure.

BOYLE: Terrific. As you know, we're tracking down folks who were at the waterfront this morning. We've spoken already, but if we could just get it down on tape real quick since we're talking to so many people. Can you tell me in your own words when and why you were there?

HARRIS: Sure. About seven AM. I was meeting a woman named Madeline.

BOYLE: And you don't know Madeline's last name or phone number.

HARRIS: No, just her e-mail address.

BOYLE: You said you'd only seen her in person once, at the Christopher Street Pier two Saturdays ago. Pretty girl, huh?

HARRIS: Sure.

BOYLE: But you said it was more than that. You said it was 'surreal' — I think that was your word?

HARRIS: You need this part?

BOYLE: The more detail, the better chance we have at identifying her. Since she was meeting you, she may have been in the area, too.

HARRIS: Okay, yeah. I was on my morning run, and I see this woman in a party dress, sort of a pale pink color, strapless. But she's sitting right on the damp grass. The sun was just beginning to rise. And she's barefoot, drinking champagne straight out of the bottle. Yes, the whole thing was sort of surreal.

BOYLE: And you mentioned a basket?

HARRIS: She had some kind of package on the ground next to her. When I got closer, I could see it was a picnic basket. I think she noticed me looking at her, because she held up her bottle like a toast when I ran by. Oh, and she was reading.

BOYLE: And you said it was the book that really intrigued you.

HARRIS: Well, I'm a writer. So a beautiful woman in last night's dress, drinking champagne, with a book. What's not to like?

BOYLE: But you didn't actually talk to her?

HARRIS: Oh, God, no. But then I mentioned this woman to a friend.

BOYLE: Charlotte Caperton?

HARRIS: Yeah. I should've known she wouldn't let it drop. Charlotte's kind of a busybody when it comes to running my life. Anyway, she's the publisher of this website, like an online magazine all about the city. It's called the Room.

BOYLE: Oh sure. Can't call yourself a New Yorker and not know about the Room.

HARRIS: So the next thing I know, Charlotte's posting a missed-moment article online.

BOYLE: And that's one of those 'I saw you on the 6 train' kind of things, right?

HARRIS: Or in my case, 'I was the out-of-breath middle-aged jogger who saw you on the pier.'

But Charlotte made it sound less pathetic.

BOYLE: And is that normal? Does your friend write personal ads *every time* you see a pretty woman?

HARRIS: There's no *every time* in my case. My wife — well, she's gone, and there hasn't been anyone else. I've got a teenage daughter. I'm not exactly a player. So, yeah, Charlotte figured it was a big deal that I even mentioned this woman. That maybe I was finally ready, whatever that means. Anyway, I guess a lot of people read the Room, because a few days later, this woman Madeline responded to the post. Turns out the book she was reading was one of my favorite novels. We started e-mailing back and forth, and last night, she proposed that we meet in person. I feel bad taking your time with this corny story given what's at stake.

BOYLE: I guess I'm curious. I'm single myself. The whole OkCupid, Match, Tinder game. And you've got to admit, this is pretty —

HARRIS: Incredible, I know.

BOYLE: And you mentioned you also had a basket with you this morning at the waterfront?

HARRIS: Really, I'm not sure why we need to get into this. It's a little embarrassing.

BOYLE: Look, our conversation here is just one

tiny part of figuring out who was where and when. So, you know, if another witness mentions seeing a man with a basket, we'll know — yeah, that was Jack Harris. Onward.

HARRIS: Sure, okay. Yes, Madeline's e-mail said, you bring the picnic basket, I'll bring the champagne. So that's why.

BOYLE: And explain to me again why you were supposed to meet at the football field. Seems like the meet-up spot would be Christopher Street Pier where you first saw her in the grass. It's only a couple of blocks away.

HARRIS: She suggested the sports field. There's a scene in the book I mentioned that's set there. Meet at chapter twelve — sort of a puzzle.

BOYLE: Sounds complicated. And then after all that, she didn't show up?

HARRIS: Not that I saw. When I got there, a few people were milling around, but no one who seemed to be looking for me. I left when it started to pour.

BOYLE: Did you e-mail her asking where she was?

HARRIS: No. Not yet, at least.

BOYLE: If it were me, I'd want an explanation after such a dramatic lead-in.

HARRIS: It's like reality set in with the rain. The whole thing seemed silly.

BOYLE: What happened to the basket?

HARRIS: I left it outside the field with a note.

BOYLE: I see. Where outside the field?

HARRIS: On a bench on the path leading to the street. I figured she'd see it if she showed up later.

BOYLE: What exactly was in the basket?

HARRIS: Wow, you really want the details. Um, a few croissants and some grapes. And the note.

BOYLE: Where'd you get the paper for the note?

HARRIS: I always have a reporter's pad in my pocket. Tools of the trade, I guess.

BOYLE: When did you hear the shots?

HARRIS: I didn't know they were shots until later, when I got home and heard the news. Other people around me — we were all wondering what the sounds were. Like firecrackers. They seemed distant, so it was hard to tell.

BOYLE: Okay, but where were you when you heard them?

HARRIS: Charles Street. On the opposite side of

6

the West Side Highway. I'm surprised the sound carried so far.

BOYLE: Believe it or not, they've got acoustic sensors that can pick up gunfire two miles away. So, just to sum up, there's no reason you went to the football field other than to meet this Madeline woman?

HARRIS: No.

BOYLE: You don't know anyone else who would've been at the field this morning?

HARRIS: No. Other than Madeline, of course. I can give you her e-mail address.

BOYLE: Okay, so it's just a coincidence that Malcolm Neeley was one of the shooting victims?

HARRIS: I'm sorry. What —

BOYLE: You know the name, right? Of course you do. Malcolm Neeley was one of three people shot this morning at the football field, just yards from you and your little picnic basket. Care to explain that, Mr. Harris?

HARRIS: Wait, that doesn't make sense.

BOYLE: You said yourself: The story sounded a little surreal. You even said 'incredible' at one point.

7

HARRIS: You don't . . . you can't possibly think I did this. [No response]

HARRIS: I need a minute to think.

10:36 AM — recording stopped

1

White noise is magic, right up there with tinfoil and Bluetooth and Nespresso pods. White noise makes the sounds of the city disappear. The horns, garbage trucks, and sirens all vanish with the touch of an app on my iPhone. When white noise fills my room, I can be anywhere, which means I'm nowhere, which is the only way I can sleep.

And then the phone rings.

★ ★ ★

Relying on muscle memory, I managed to answer without opening my eyes because I knew the room would be filled with light I was not ready to face. 'Olivia Randall.'

'Hey.'

I knew from the voice that it was Einer, our assistant-slash-investigator. A deeper voice behind me murmured something about what time it was, and I felt a heavy forearm drape across my hip. I rolled forward to face my nightstand, away from the voice in my bed. 'Hey,' I said in response.

'Don thinks you're taking the morning off because of Mindy,' Einer said. 'He says you're resting on your laurels, but I think he's jealous of all the attention.'

I forced myself to open my eyes. The clock in front of me told me that it was 11:17 AM, nearly

9

halfway through a normal person's workday.

Next to the clock was a half-empty bottle of grappa. Grappa? The odd shape of the bottle triggered a memory: a client — referred by a law school friend who, unlike me, made partner at Preston & Cartwright — handing me a bottle, inexplicably shaped like the Eiffel Tower, to thank me for getting a glove compartment full of parking tickets dismissed in one fell swoop. I told him that a tip wasn't necessary, but he missed the hint that it was insulting. Into the kitchen cabinet went the bottle. And then another memory: the forearm across my hip reaching into the cabinet last night: 'Grappa! I love grappa.'

I forced myself to focus on Einer's words. Morning off because of Mindy. Right: Mindy, the twenty-four-year-old former child starlet I saved from prison yesterday by suppressing the cocaine that had been found in her impounded Porsche while she was collecting a ten-thousand-dollar club-promotion fee in the Meatpacking District.

My fee was more.

'Tell Don I have no laurels to rest on,' I said, leaning back against the padded headboard of my bed. Don's my law partner. He's also my mentor, plus an honorary dad or an uncle or something. Most important, right now he was probably wondering where I was. I could still hear the white noise, even though the app was closed now, as I wracked my brain for a credible story I hadn't used recently. 'A client from a couple of years ago called early this morning. His son got picked up on a DUI coming home from a house party in Brooklyn. He thought he had slept it off but was still drunk from the night before.' The voice next to me muttered, 'He's not the only one.'

'It took a little longer than I thought to keep him from getting booked.'

'Good, I think Don will be happy to know you're not in the neighborhood. He won't admit it, but that old softie worries about you like crazy.'

I didn't get the connection between the two sentences, but here's the thing about being a liar: you develop an instinct for when you've missed a step and need to fake it. 'No cause for worry,' I said. 'You weren't calling to check on me, were you?'

'No, there's some kid who keeps calling. Won't leave a name. He or she or whatever is threatening to come to the office if you don't call back. And when it comes to kids, that's a serious threat by my standards.'

'Nice to know we've got an iron spine at the front desk, Einer. Just give me the number. And tell Don not to worry. Just a stupid DUI.'

I opened my nightstand and pulled out a pen and one of the many notebooks I always keep nearby.

I had half the number entered in my phone when I felt the hand at the end of the forearm across my hip beginning to explore. Really?

I threw back the blankets, rolled out of bed, and started gathering items of clothing from the floor. 'It's late. Your wife's flight lands in an hour.'

The phone rang only once.

'Hello?' The voice was eager. Clear, but low. I could tell why Einer had been uncertain about gender. Probably female. Not a little kid, not a woman.

'This is Olivia Randall. You called my office?'

'Yeah. I'm worried about my dad. He's not answering his phone or his texts.'

Great. Had we reached the point where kids call lawyers the second their helicopter parents go incommunicado? I was tempted to hang up, but if I did, with my luck, her father would turn out to be someone important.

'I'm sure your father probably just stepped out for a little while, okay?'

'No, you don't understand. The police were here. He left with them. He said everything was fine, but then the police returned, like, immediately.' My mind wandered back to Einer's comment about Don being relieved to hear I wasn't near the office. 'They had the super with them, and they knocked on the door and told me I needed to leave the apartment.'

'Did they say why?' I asked, beginning to strip the sheets with my free hand.

'No, but I asked them if I was under arrest. They said no, and then they started being nice to me, calling me *sweetie* and stuff — asking if they could contact a family member for me to stay with or something. So at that point, I stopped asking questions and told them I had debate team practice and was supposed to spend the night with my aunt.'

'So you're calling from your aunt's house?'

This conversation was starting to make my head hurt. Everything was making my head hurt.

'No, I don't even have an aunt. But I figured I could do more on my own than if they put me in a foster home or something.'

'So you're in foster care?' I tossed the top sheet onto the floor of my closet.

The girl on the other end of the line made a growling sound. 'Oh my God. The police were here talking to my father. Now he's gone. And there are cops at our apartment who basically kicked me out. I'm pretty sure they have my dad for some reason. In which case, I don't have anywhere to go, in which case they might throw my ass in foster care. So I made up an aunt and called you instead.'

If I had to guess, the girl's father had probably been arrested, and she spotted my name in the euphoric tweets from my latest celebrity client, Mindy Monaghan. I started into my usual blow-off speech, about how I wasn't taking new clients, etcetera. She responded by demanding that I get down to the First Precinct to help her father.

'How do you know he's at the First Precinct?'

'I don't, not for sure. But the police cars parked outside our building have a one painted on the side of them.'

Bingo. That would be the precinct number. 'I can e-mail you a list of referrals — '

'No, you *have* to help him. It's the least you can do after the way you treated him.'

'You're saying I know your father?' Too many clients think that just because you represent them for one thing, you're their lawyer for life.

'My name is Buckley Harris. My father's Jack Harris.'

★ ★ ★

Jack Harris. The name hit me in the gut so hard that I tasted last night's grappa at the back of my throat.

Her voice pushed away the competing thoughts — images from the past — working their way into my consciousness. 'I heard them talking about gunshots or something. So I assumed it was about my mom. And then I saw the news online, so now I'm totally paranoid, thinking it has something to do with that.'

After what had happened to her mother, I wouldn't blame the girl for being paranoid. But, once again, I wasn't getting the connection between one sentence and the next. What news?

'I'll go to the First Precinct and find out what's going on. Do you have somewhere to go in the meantime?' It was June. Were kids still in school? I had no idea.

'I'm headed to Charlotte's now.'

Now there was a name I hadn't heard in a very long time.

The second I hung up, I made my way to the living room. My briefcase was on the sofa, exactly where I had let it drop while Ryan was pulling off my suit jacket last night.

I slid out my laptop, opened it, and Googled 'New York City gunshots.'

Someone had opened fire this morning on the

14

Hudson Parkway. The number of injuries and fatalities was unclear. And my ex-fiancé, Jack Harris, might or might not be at the First Precinct for reasons that might or might not have something to do with it.

★　★　★

As I approached the front desk at the First Precinct, a uniform nudged his buddy, followed by a quick whisper. Maybe they recognized me, either as a relatively successful defense attorney or perhaps from precinct gossip. (Though I was by no means what the cops would call a 'Badge Bunny,' you can't spend ten years on the criminal court scene as a single woman without a thing or two happening.)

Or, more likely, I had the look of someone who didn't belong in a police station. To any half-decent police officer, it would be apparent from my tailored suit and expensive shoes that I was either a prosecutor or a defense lawyer or a reporter or a high-maintenance victim: trouble whatever the story.

At forty-three, I knew by now that my natural expression when I was thinking — intense, brow furrowed, lips pursed — could be intimidating to most people. The Internet called it RBF: Resting Bitch Face. And, no question, I had it. But lucky for me, I also know how to turn that frown upside down. *First impressions*, as my mother always warned me.

'Hi.' As I gave the huddle of officers my best smile, I felt my hungover skin yearning for hydration. I told them I was looking for a Jack Harris.

I hoped for blank stares. Instead, the desk sergeant asked if I was Harris's lawyer. I held the smile.

'I am,' I said coolly. 'I also know Mr. Harris well personally. He's a man of some significance in New York City. If he's here, I assume you have an explanation.'

Police like to say that they're straight shooters, all about the justice, color blind, fair and balanced, yada yada. But the truth is that they're used to both victims and perpetrators who are poor and powerless. When someone rich and powerful collides with the criminal justice system, it's a big fucking deal. No harm in flashing your feathers early and often.

But the desk sergeant who spoke up was unfazed. 'You say you know Jack Harris? Well, I'll be honest, I might've thought I did, too. It's a damn shame what he's gone through. Yesterday, I would have rolled out the red carpet if he walked in here. But now?' He made a *pssshht* sound.

Once again, I was a step behind, but I knew I wasn't going to get information out of a glorified receptionist.

He picked up the handset of the nearby phone.

'I'm sure you know, Sergeant, that under New York's right to counsel laws, you *must* immediately inform Jack Harris that a lawyer is here for him.'

He jiggled the phone in his hand. 'Who d'ya think I'm calling? Ghostbusters?'

16

★ ★ ★

The man who emerged minutes later from the stairwell was immediately identifiable as a multigenerational cop. Young but confident. The pale skin, red hair, and freckles of an Irish kid from the city. The introduction he offered sealed the first impression. His name was Jimmy Boyle.

'Wow, that's a real name, or did the NYPD give it to you as a promotion?'

'One hundred percent authentic. Not James. Not Jim. Jimmy Boyle on the birth certificate.'

I told him I needed to see my client, and he told me that's what he'd heard. I followed my gut and asked if Jack was here because of the Hudson River shooting.

Jimmy Boyle nodded. All business. 'Likely to be three counts.'

That would be of murder, I surmised. Three counts of murder against a guy I could only imagine being arrested if he accidentally walked out of a Whole Foods with a raisin granola bar. Buckley Harris's worst fears about her father's situation were quickly becoming a reality.

I asked Jimmy Boyle if we were talking about the same Jack Harris. 'The one I know couldn't possibly — '

'Nice try, Counselor. You'll hear the details eventually. But Harris? From hometown hero to bad guy zero, just like that.'

17

2

As I followed Detective Boyle up two flights of stairs, through a squad room, and down a narrow hallway lined with interrogation rooms and holding cells, I tried to prepare myself mentally.

I hadn't seen Jack in person for nearly twenty years, only pictures. The Sunday Styles announcement when he and Molly née Buckley got married ('Mrs. Harris, 25, is a substitute high school teacher. She graduated from Boston College. She is the daughter of Pamela and Daniel Buckley of Buffalo, New York.') The author photos on three different novels, all typical fare for male literary writers — no smile, intense stare: the opposite of Jack. The annual Christmas card pictures on our friend Melissa's refrigerator — pictures that would eventually turn up in all those 'remembering the victims' retrospectives after Molly died.

I knew from all those photographs that Jack, like the rest of us, had aged. A little extra weight softened the angles of his thin face, and a few lines added character to his green eyes. Some flecks of gray lightened what was still a full head of messy brown waves. But despite the subtle changes, he looked in pictures like the boy I'd first met when we were eighteen. If anything, he was one of those people who'd grown more attractive with time.

The man I glimpsed through the one-way glass when Boyle paused outside an interrogation room was not what I had expected from all those photographs. Think of every beauty tip for looking one's best: good sleep, plenty of water, no stress. Getting arrested means the opposite of all that. Jack looked tired and disheveled. Sweat marks pitted his plain white undershirt. Don called it getting hit by 'custody's ugly stick' — fear, exhaustion, bad fluorescent lighting: it wasn't pretty.

Jack flinched at the sound of the interrogation room's door opening. His eyes brightened as he recognized me.

I tried to reassure him with a quick smile, then turned to Boyle. 'We'll need a private room, please.'

'It's private once I shut the door, Counselor. The recording equipment's off.'

'Look at it this way, Detective. When your hard work and savvy investigative skills lead you to some nugget that could have been gleaned from the conversation I'm about to have with my client, do you really want me claiming that you got it through a Sixth Amendment violation? Judges know how easy it is to monitor these rooms with the touch of a button. And let's face it, these days a lot of them aren't big fans of the NYPD.'

I could see Boyle picturing a courtroom scene in the distant future. 'No skin off my ass. Give me a second.'

Jack started to speak once Boyle was out of view, but I raised an index finger to my lips. He

19

was staring at me like I might not be real, his eyes searching mine for something — comfort, an explanation, an apology, what? The room, already small, seemed to shrink with every second that passed in silence, and I finally had to look away. Two minutes later, Boyle reappeared, instructed Jack to stand, and handcuffed his wrists in front of him.

'Really, Detective?'

'You're the one who wants him moved from this comfy room with a big sturdy lock. Can't have it both ways, Ms. Randall. Or did you forget that your boy's the suspect in a triple homicide?'

★ ★ ★

There were no one-way windows or recording instruments in sight in the conference room Boyle ushered us into. I thanked him as he closed the door. He rolled his eyes.

Jack was still looking at me in disbelief. 'How did you know — '

'Your daughter called me.'

'But how did she — '

'She pieced it together and got worried. From what I can tell, you raised a clever girl.'

There was an awkward pause, and he looked at the door that Detective Boyle had just shut. 'They really eavesdrop?'

'He needs to know you've got a lawyer who's not going to make his job any easier.' Boyle would be back here any minute to say the clock was ticking on the next transport to MDC. After the standard spiel about attorney-client privilege,

I got straight to the point. 'They seem to think they have something on you. What is it?'

He muttered something so low that I could barely make out the words. *Howard Johnson.*

'The hotel?' I asked.

'No. Your first mock client interview in law school. The professor gave you a fake case file, a robbery. The client's name was Howard Johnson, and you were practicing on me. We were on that lumpy futon in the living room, don't you remember? And you got so mad at me for laughing every time I said my name was Howard Johnson. We kept starting over and over again until you told me to change my name to something else so you could get through the questions, exactly how you wrote them.' Jack was staring into the table, seeing a scene that had played out twenty years earlier. 'So I started throwing out alternatives: Mel Content, Jerry Atric, Drew Blood. You didn't see the humor until Seymour Butts. You don't sound like a stressed-out first-year law student anymore.'

Jack was suffering not only the physical, but also the cognitive tolls of custody. For some people, this part was almost like going into shock. There was no time to reminisce. I had to shake him out of it.

'Jack, you're under arrest, apparently for murder. There were shots fired at the football field at the Hudson piers today. People died. Did they explain any of that to you?' From the quick news searches I'd done on my phone during the cab ride to the precinct, I had yet to see any identification of the victims, or any mention that a suspect had been arrested. 'Listen to this question carefully: what would make the police think you did this?'

I had learned the careful phrasing from Don. As worded, the question allowed for distance. It gave the client a chance to tell me what evidence the police might have, but still allowed me ethically to let the client take the stand and offer an entirely divergent story.

'I — I heard the shots by the West Side Highway. I didn't even know they were shots. Then I got home and heard the news. Obviously, I was rattled. I mean, after Molly. That I had been so close to another shooting — '

Back when Molly was killed, I had thought about reaching out. But how? A phone call? A sympathy card? Does Hallmark have a special section for, 'Sorry I haven't talked to you since I shattered your life, and now I'm sorry you lost the woman who pieced it back together?' Probably not.

As Jack described how he ended up in an interrogation room wearing a sweaty undershirt, I could picture every step, starting with Jimmy Boyle's knock on Jack's apartment door. Boyle told him they were canvassing for witnesses, like it was standard door-to-door protocol. The police were looking for 'folks' who might have seen something. If he could come down to the station, that would be helpful. And Jack was Jack. He was as helpful as they came.

I interrupted to double-check whether the police gave him the option of 'helping' from the comfort of his own apartment.

22

'Um, yeah, I guess so. But Buckley was home, and I could tell she was worried. You know how kids are.' Actually, I didn't. 'And, well, things with Buckley — she's a tough, brave girl in a lot of ways, but she's sensitive about certain things. The way she lost her mother — it damaged her. So the thought of police coming to her home and asking about anything gun related — you can imagine that it's upsetting. So when the detective said maybe we could talk at the station instead, I figured it was because he saw me distracted by Buckley.'

'So you agreed to come in?'

'Basically. But I said at least half an hour ago that I needed to get home, and he just keeps saying they need a little more time.'

I pressed my eyes closed. Jack really was still the same: kind but gullible. The police had played him. 'Your daughter was worried for a reason, Jack. You're not a witness. You're a suspect. And that detective seems pretty confident that they have a case against you. What have you told them?'

'This morning — Oh God, Olivia, talking to you, of all people, about this. It's embarrassing.'

'Well, right now, I'm all you've got, and Boyle will be back here to process you soon.' Booking. Transport. A holding cell. This was no time for him to be shy. 'I can't help you if you don't start talking. So let me ask the question again: *what would make the police think you did this?*'

When he was finally done answering my carefully phrased question, he slumped back in his chair and looked up at the acoustic-tiled

23

ceiling. 'Jesus, they're never going to believe me.'

I managed to keep my response to myself. *Damn straight they won't.*

* * *

I pressed Jack to tell me exactly how much of this information he had given to the police.

'All of it,' he said.

'Seriously? The party dress and the basket and the book?'

'The detective said he was curious. He said he was single, too. Every time I asked him why he needed all these details, he seemed to have an explanation.'

Boyle had pressed for details because they now knew Jack was locked in — on tape — to a complex explanation for being near the site of the shooting. And complicated stories don't sound as true as simple ones.

Jack was saying he never should have mentioned the woman to Charlotte. 'She runs that website, the Room. And she loves romance posts. Jesus, I even said the woman reminded me of Molly — that, for the first time, I was open to the idea of another shot at happiness.'

Not a second shot at happiness, but *another* one. Molly was already the second, because I was the first. Twenty years later, and still so much guilt.

'I should have realized,' Jack was saying, 'that Charlotte would take me literally and try to find the woman. And when Charlotte sets her mind to something . . . the next thing I knew, she's got

24

this post on the Room's home page. I was mortified. She didn't use my name, but she may as well have with all the biographical details. I actually forgot about it, but then Charlotte got a response a few days later. We started e-mailing, and I was supposed to meet her today. I swear, that's all I know.'

And he had fed every detail to the police, who would twist and turn the information to suit their needs.

'This woman Madeline's the one who picked the football field as the meeting spot? The e-mails will back that up?'

'Absolutely. Well, with a few connections of dots. Once she responded to the post, I asked her what book had her so engrossed. It was *Eight Days to Die*. It's one of my favorites.' I had never heard of it, but, then again, I wasn't a big reader these days. 'So last night, when she suggested that we meet in person, she said meet at chapter twelve. Flip to that chapter of *Eight Days to Die*, and there's a scene at the football field.'

His bizarre, complicated story about Missed-Moment Madeline had taken on one more absurd layer, but as long as the woman backed him up, we could show that it had not been Jack's idea to place himself at the sports field that morning.

I asked him exactly what happened when he got there.

'Nothing. No big dramatic moment. I saw a few people on the far end of the field, but no woman who seemed to be waiting for me. I wondered for a second if I was on some kind of *Candid Camera* show. I mean, was the entire setup someone's idea of a cruel joke? I felt pretty stupid. Then when it started pouring rain out of the blue, I took it as a sign. Enough of this, back to real life.'

I pointed out that he hadn't completely given up. He had left the basket and the note.

'I guess part of me wanted to believe she'd come through. But I don't know what any of that has to do with the shooting. Or why Malcolm Neeley was there. I swear, when the detective said his name, it was like, *thwack*. An anvil descending from the sky in a cartoon, right onto my head. It still doesn't feel real.'

Yet he didn't ask for a lawyer.

Everyone thinks he's somehow going to convince the police he's innocent as long as he doesn't lawyer up. Dumb, dumb, dumb. I asked Jack where his shirt was, even though I suspected I knew the answer.

'When we first got to the station, he said they were running tests on everyone who'd been near the waterfront. He said it would be quick. They swabbed my hands.'

'You didn't think it was weird when they asked for your *clothing?*'

'You don't have to talk to me like I'm an idiot, Olivia.'

One of our first fights had begun with the identical sentiment: I didn't have to treat him like an idiot. 'I'm not treating you like an idiot,' I had said. 'You're actually *being* an idiot.' And then instead of defending himself, he told me I

26

was *emasculating* him. I said something even meaner.

Now, I simply said, 'Jack: your shirt.'

'The shirt came later. After I told him that I needed to get home, he said we could clear some things up if he could run another test on my shirt. Whatever I need to do to prove I'm innocent, I will do. How long do those tests take?'

I held my tongue.

Gunshot residue. GSR tests were a one-way street for law enforcement. A positive test made the suspect look guilty. A negative test could be explained away by some soap and water.

'I wish you'd tell me this isn't that bad,' he said. 'I assume the missed-moment post is still floating around online. The police can read my e-mails, whatever they need. I know it's kind of nutty, but that doesn't mean I shot anyone. How could they even think that?'

'Jack, it's Malcolm Neeley. How could they *not* think it?'

He looked like he was about to cry, but then regained his composure. 'You know the irony? When I first saw Madeline on the pier with some kind of package next to her, I thought, maybe she's a runaway bride who has fled her hotel room with a frantically packed go bag, ready to catch an early train out of Penn Station. And then there it was. *Penn Station* — a reminder of the reason I don't look at and wonder about and conjure up entire imagined backstories for women I don't know. Something always sneaks up and reminds me that I don't have *normal* anymore. The minute I thought about Penn Station, I should have run away and never looked back.'

3

Every generation of Americans had at least one day where they all could remember where they were when they heard the news. Pearl Harbor. The Kennedy assassination. Nine-Eleven.

And then there were some dates that left the same kind of mark, but in a smaller and more regional way. Columbine in Colorado. The federal building in Oklahoma. The marathon in Boston. A bell tower in Texas. Riots in Los Angeles. A club fire in Rhode Island.

For New York City, the most recent of those searing, scarring events was the Penn Station massacre. Until that morning three years ago, we moved like cattle through the turnstiles and corridors of our crowded public transportation systems, complaining about delayed trains, bumped briefcases, or a fellow passenger in dire need of a shower. But then a mass shooting broke out in the heart of the city during peak commuting hours. What seemed unimaginable suddenly felt inevitable.

Thirteen people dead, not to mention the wounded, or the shooter who fired a final bullet into his own jaw at the first sight of police coming his way, which was less than two minutes after the first sound of gunfire. Roughly one shot every 2 seconds for 108 seconds was the gruesome estimate later bandied about by the media.

These weren't the only shocking details to come out in the aftermath. The killer wasn't a foreign jihadist, as most of us assumed when we first heard about an attack in Penn Station. He was a local. And he wasn't even a man yet. Just a boy, fifteen years old, all of five feet seven and 127 pounds. His name was Todd. Todd didn't need physical size to inflict that kind of damage, not when he was armed with a Bushmaster rifle and two .40-caliber pistols, all three weapons semiautomatic.

In the same way I had not been able to stop myself from watching the constant replays of planes heading toward the Twin Towers, I had been glued to my television for consecutive days afterward, afraid to leave my apartment in the midst of warnings about feared copycat attacks.

How did a fifteen-year-old boy have access to those kinds of weapons? outraged and bewildered New Yorkers wanted to know.

After another twenty-four-hour news cycle, we began to have an answer to that question. Todd's mother, still clinically depressed despite three hospitalizations, killed herself when he was just eight years old. Todd's older brother was nearly out of college at the time. Todd's father, determined that his younger son be treated 'normally' — despite multiple assessments from teachers and counselors that he was anything but — resisted mental health treatment or anything that would label his son as 'sick' like his mother (his word, not the doctors').

He moved his son from school to school, in search of a place that was willing to ignore

Todd's behavioral and psychological problems. At the time of the shooting, Todd was enrolled at the Stinson Academy, apparently a last stop for rich screwups in the world of elite private schools. Instead of seeking help for his increasingly alienated and angry son, the father used his considerable wealth to encourage activities that father and son might enjoy together, at least in the few minutes a week the father could spare for his son: Yankees games, an occasional round of golf, and guns. Lots of weapons. Lots of ammunition. Lots of hours at the shooting range near their country home in Connecticut.

Todd did not leave a note, a diary of his plans, or a video-recorded manifesto like so many other mass shooters, but police did find drawings: baby dolls hanging from nooses, rabbits angrily mounting each other, men in capes being eaten by dragons. But no explanation was really needed. Mental illness, social isolation, guns: all the ingredients in a familiar and deadly recipe.

And then in the next news cycle, the photographs of the victims started to emerge. Thirteen lives lost, their faces and short bios filling half a page of the *New York Times*. A forty-six-year-old cancer researcher. A twenty-one-year-old Korean exchange student. A sixty-six-year-old Vietnam vet who'd survived Agent Orange. A forty-year-old teacher. A ten-year-old Alabama boy visiting New York City for the first time.

Todd had chosen them indiscriminately — white, brown, and black; male and female;

young and old; rich and poor. A small but representative New York City melting pot, their fates bound together only by the misfortune of being within a bullet's reach from Todd that horrible morning.

My gaze had circled back to the photograph of the teacher. I froze at the immediate recognition but checked the name anyway. 'Molly Harris, 40, New York City, substitute teacher,' the text beneath the photograph read. I had seen her face on Melissa's refrigerator for more than a decade's worth of Decembers: Jack; Molly; their daughter, Buckley, moving from baby to toddler to girl to tween.

I scoured the Internet, rereading the media coverage with a new focus. According to multiple survivors, a middle-aged woman in a blue dress was seen speaking to Todd right before she became the first of his victims. Todd froze as the woman fell to the ground. Some witnesses said that his face was so distraught that they failed to notice the gun in his hand. And then the pause was over, and he began shooting.

A *Daily News* article identified the woman in the blue dress as a mother and teacher. 'Those who knew the woman have suggested that, in light of her training in how to respond to school violence, she may have tried to talk him out of his deadly intentions.' I reexamined the *New York Times* tribute. Molly had been the only teacher. Instead of running or ducking, Jack's wife had died trying to save complete strangers.

Within weeks, it wasn't just the faces of the slain on news pages and television stations.

Family members came forward to speak of their loved ones. From a shared and unwanted bully pulpit, they called for reforms like increased security on mass transit, better mental health services, and increased regulation of firearms. And some were even willing to say aloud what many people had been wondering from the beginning: *what the hell was that father thinking?*

And then a year ago, after train ridership had returned to pre-shooting levels and victims' names had faded from public consciousness, those survivors — led by 'the husband of the heroic teacher' — went further and filed a wrongful death lawsuit against the shooter's father, just before the statute of limitations was set to run out. Last month, newspapers barely noticed when a New York County trial court dismissed the families' lawsuit for failure to state a claim of action.

And now this morning, the city had suffered another report of shots fired, followed by terrified New Yorkers fleeing for safety. And, once again, this time, not everyone had made it out alive. Only three dead, according to Detective Boyle, not thirteen. But for immediate purposes, what mattered most was the identity of one of the three: Malcolm Neeley.

I didn't need to do any research to know that Malcolm Neeley had been a multimillionaire, an investment banker to some of the wealthiest and most powerful people in the world. He was the kind of *rich* that made celebrities look poor. Yet few people knew his name — until his fifteen-year-old son, Todd, opened fire in Penn Station, killing thirteen people and wounding eight others.

He'd made it through the wrongful death lawsuit only to be killed this morning. And now the hero-teacher's husband was in custody, and the closest thing he had to an alibi was a woman he didn't even know.

4

On the other side of the conference table, Jack's eyes were closed and he was whispering to himself that he couldn't believe this was happening.

My mind jumped back to our sophomore year in college. Jack banging on my door, breaking down into tears once he stepped inside my dorm room. His father had died of a heart attack. Charlotte was on one of her weekend trips to somewhere fabulous. *I can't believe this is happening.* That's what he kept saying over and over again as he sobbed with his head in my lap. His mother had died of cancer when he was still in high school. He and his brother, Owen, would now be on their own.

I stroked his hair until he fell asleep and then sat there on the bed, my back against the wall, for the rest of the night. When he finally woke up, he told me he didn't know what he would do if I weren't in his life. Until that moment, I had no idea how much I meant to him.

Leaning forward now, I touched one of his handcuffed wrists for emphasis. He needed to focus.

'What else could the police possibly have?' I asked. 'Other than your statement.'

He shook his head, sounding dazed. 'I told you. I have no idea. I mean, I get how it looks. I did try to sue Malcolm Neeley. But I wasn't the only plaintiff. The lawsuit was on behalf of all the families, a united front.'

I was probably one of the few people who had followed the failed lawsuit in the news. At one point, I had even looked up the attorney's phone number, tempted to offer help.

Jack may not have been the only plaintiff, but the media certainly had chosen him as the face of the lawsuit. It was a role that suited him. He was a successful literary author with three acclaimed novels, now raising a daughter on his own. His wife had been the hero who tried to talk Todd down. The most in-depth stories even managed to throw in the fact that Jack's brother, Owen, was an NYPD cop who died in a car accident shortly after Jack graduated from college.

He was the poster child for hard knocks.

'Jack, if those handcuffs haven't made it clear, you're under arrest. They don't do that unless they have probable cause. They must think they have something more than your problem with Malcolm.'

'I had more than just a *problem* with him. It's because of that man that my wife is dead.'

I shushed him. 'That's the kind of stuff a prosecutor will use to bury you in front of a jury.'

'A jury? It's going to get to that?' His voice cracked. 'Sorry, Olivia. I hated that man — if you could even call him that — but, I swear to God, I did *not* do this. Find Charlotte. She's got keys to my apartment. She can bring my laptop, and I'll show the police the e-mails. Madeline

36

will back me up. I was only there this morning to meet her.'

'Jack, if I had to guess, the police are probably searching your apartment right now. And trust me, they'll scour every byte of your computer.'

'Well, good. They'll see that I'm telling the truth.'

I'd seen this before — someone so certain that the truth would set him free. I still had no idea what evidence the police had against Jack, but I could read the tea leaves. He wasn't going home tonight. But I couldn't bring myself to tell him that. We both had learned the hard way that I was incapable of breaking bad news, at least when it came to Jack.

I started rattling off the names of some excellent lawyers, but he was shaking his head. 'No, I don't want that. I want you.'

'Jack, I came here because I assumed it was some mix-up I could get straightened out right away. But this is serious.'

'Yeah, no shit.'

'Let me find you someone, okay? Without our . . . baggage.' I had always wondered what it would be like if I ever ran into Jack again. Once, I went so far as to schedule a coffee appointment at a café next door to one of his signings, hoping he might spot me through the window as he passed. Would he come inside to say hello, or pretend he hadn't recognized me? I didn't stop monitoring the sidewalk until long after his event would have ended. Now we were finally in the same room, and he was in handcuffs. All those conversations I had imagined would have to wait. 'I'll make sure they see you through this.'

'It's too late for that. You're here, and you said yourself they're going to be back any second to transport me. God knows how long it will be before they let me see a different lawyer.'

'I'll tell the new lawyer everything you've told me, okay?'

'No!' He slammed the tabletop with his fists, the sound amplified by the clank of his handcuffs against the faux wood grain. Even when I had been horrible to Jack, he had never once yelled at me. I jumped from my chair on instinct, and he immediately apologized for the outburst. 'I'm begging you, Olivia. I know you're used to representing people who can take this in stride. They get booked and processed and detained. They get strip-searched and deloused and use the toilet in front of their cell mates. They wait it out for trial and trust you'll do your thing along the way. But I can't wait, okay? I have Buckley. She's only sixteen years old, and she's already lost one parent. You know I didn't do this, but some other lawyer won't. They'll just put me through the system. I need to go home. Olivia, please, you've got to get me out of here.'

The last bit of light fell from his face. Even after hours in custody, the thought of his daughter having to live without a parent aged him another decade.

I rose from my chair, turned my back to him, and banged loudly on the conference room door to indicate I was ready. Behind me, I heard Jack choke back a sob.

Detective Boyle cracked the door open. 'Just

in time for transport, Counselor.'

'Do you have any idea what you've done, Detective? Your next move had better be a phone call to someone with the power to unlock those handcuffs and escort Mr. Harris back to his apartment, apology in hand, or you'll be on the front page of the *Post* as the nitwit thug who locked up the Penn Station widower. If you're lucky, you'll spend the rest of your career investigating subway cell-phone grabs.'

Boyle reached out and patted me on the head. 'Your tough-talking defense attorney bullshit's adorable.'

I hadn't expected that. But I did know what he was anticipating in return: offense and outrage. Instead, I took a seat and calmly crossed my legs. 'Then call my bluff. Or play it safe and call ADA Scott Temple. Tell him exactly what I said to you, and then see what happens. Things will be interesting either way, Detective, I promise.'

★　★　★

Jack was tapping the table so loudly that my head was starting to throb, my hangover resurfacing. I knew that every minute that passed without him getting moved to MDC was a good sign, but Jack was growing more anxious by the second.

I pulled a notepad from my briefcase and slid it across the table with a pen. 'Your computer information. All your e-mail accounts and passwords. Your Web provider. Any social media pages. Everything.' It would keep him busy, or at least his hands from that incessant tapping.

When he nudged the pad back in my direction, I blinked at the sight of a tidy list in neat, round, perfect, familiar print. Even with the cuffs, he was like a human Cambria font.

Jack@jackharris.com
Jacksonharris@gmail.com
Jharrisbooks@aol.com
Facebook.com/jackharrisauthor
@Jackharrisbooks

Wow, Jack on Twitter. Somehow I had missed that in my late-night drunken cyberstalking over the years.

'Passwords, too,' I said.

'It's the same for everything, down at the bottom of the page.'

Volunteered to go to the station. Didn't lawyer up. Consented to a GSR swab. And one password for every account. He was still the same, naive Jack.

At least the password wasn't 'password.'

He had written:

jack<3smollybuckley

★   ★   ★

It took a second to register. Less than, like the math symbol, followed by the number 3. The two shapes together formed a heart. Jack loves Molly and Buckley.

'It was an easy way for all of us to remember

our passwords when we first set up the accounts. Molly's was Molly loves Jack and Buckley. And so on.'

'Sweet,' I said, because it seemed like something I should say.

'The Olivia I knew would be more like — ' He made a gagging gesture with his finger and laughed quietly. 'Hey, I don't know why I feel the need to say this, but I'm not some blubbering fool who falls in love with a pretty woman at the park. Or, despite all appearances, some imbecile who gets railroaded by police saying they're on a routine canvass. I mean, how many times have I wondered what you would think of me if we ever saw each other again, and here I am, some pathetic pushover.'

So he had wondered, too. 'None of that matters right now, Jack.'

'No, I guess not. But I do want to thank you — for coming here, and for staying. I mean it. I don't know what I'd do if I didn't have someone who knows me — who knows I couldn't have done this — on my side. You scared me with that 'call my bluff' business, but I think whatever you said may have rattled him.'

I had given Jimmy Boyle two choices — process Jack as he planned, or call ADA Scott Temple. At that moment, I placed the odds at fifty-fifty.

Once the room fell silent, I was the one getting nervous. I pulled out my cell phone and called the office. Einer picked up, as I expected. 'Good afternoon, Ellison and Randall.'

'Einer, it's Olivia.'

41

'Hey, mamacita.' For reasons that remained a mystery, Einer Ronald Erickson Wagner, raised by law professors in Connecticut, had decided to co-opt myriad distinctly non-WASPy linguistic styles. 'You coming in today? Don was asking.'

I did not want to think about what Don would say when he found out about our new client. 'I'm following up on that kid's call. You got a second?'

Einer was a jack-of-all-trades, but the fact that Don and I were almost completely dependent on him for any computer work that went beyond basic e-mail and Google explained why we put up with his many eccentricities. I gave him an extremely truncated version of the facts: a missed-moment post on the Room, followed by some e-mail messages back and forth. I asked him to find the original post, the e-mails between Jack and Madeline, and, most important, whatever information he could track down about Madeline.

'Sounds like the beginning of a rom-com. This is what that kid was yammering on about this morning?'

'Just do it, okay? Oh, and while I've got you — ' I said it like there was no connection whatsoever. 'Any arrest in that shooting downtown yet?'

'Nope. I've been flipping channels and refreshing constantly for any updates, but so far there's no real news. Only three shot, at least one dead, reporters waiting for confirmation about others.'

We now lived in a country where *only* three shot was good news. 'Nothing else? Witnesses? Rumors?'

42

'Nah. I mean, they've got the usual interviews — the sounds of gunshots, people running. But without any concrete information, they're already resorting to talking heads debating gun laws and whether New York City is getting more dangerous.'

So Jack's name wasn't out yet. That was good. Once his name was leaked, the news reports would create their own momentum and I'd have no hope of stopping the train. 'Great. Call me about those e-mail messages as soon as you've got something.'

Another call came through before I'd even disconnected. I didn't recognize the number on the screen but answered anyway. 'This is Olivia.'

'Did you find my dad?'

'Yes,' I said neutrally. I didn't want to upset Jack any further than necessary. 'I'm working on that now.'

'Is he okay?'

'Just fine. I'll know more soon. You found a place to wait?'

'Yeah, I'm at Charlotte's. You know her, right?'

'Yes,' I said, 'from a long time ago. I'll call you back as soon as I know more. I promise.'

Jack looked up at me as I clicked off the call. 'Another client in trouble?'

'Something like that.'

★ ★ ★

My cell phone rang again within minutes. It was the office. 'Einer, you're a star. You found something already?'

43

It wasn't Einer. I heard a familiar gravelly voice, heavy Brooklyn accent firmly in place. 'Can you please tell me why I just saw Jack Harris's name on Einer's computer screen? Imagine my surprise when he tells me it's for our new client. Something about a phone call earlier today?'

I signaled to Jack that I needed to step into the hallway outside the conference room. 'Don, I was planning to tell you, but this was urgent.' I lowered my voice to a whisper. 'He's under arrest. It's serious.'

'So tell the man to sit on his rights and call him a different lawyer. Why do you have Einer sifting through e-mails?'

'It's a long story. But there's a computer trail that could go a long way to clearing Jack.'

'*Clearing* him? You sound like Perry Mason. We don't *clear* people. What is this, a DUI or something? There are other lawyers.'

I found myself chewing my lip. When I was fired — *correction*, when I was told I would not make partner — by Preston & Cartwright, Don was the one who gave me a job, even though I had never actually been in court and had never handled a criminal case. He took me in because he loved his niece Melissa, and I was Melissa's best friend.

'I can tell you're still there, Olivia. And don't you dare try telling me you're losing your signal. I've known you far too long to fall for that move.'

I had to tell him it wasn't just a DUI. 'Jack's daughter called the office this morning. It's about the shooting at the waterfront. One of the victims was Malcolm Neeley. And Jack has already admitted that he was nearby.'

'Ay yay yay.' That was Don's way of saying 'total cluster fuck.' 'Have they booked him?'

I explained that Jack clearly wasn't free to leave the precinct, but hadn't been transported yet to MDC. 'I asked the detective to get an ADA down here.'

'To talk to Jack, or to talk to you?'

It was an important distinction. If a client had something to offer, you got an ADA to work out a cooperation agreement pre-charge. But that's not why I had bluffed Detective Boyle into calling ADA Scott Temple.

'To me.'

I've pulled some questionable stunts in the name of zealous representation, but I had never — not once — looked an ADA in the eye to vouch for a client's innocence unless I knew to a certainty that the police had fucked up. So if ADA Scott Temple got a phone call from a homicide detective saying I insisted on speaking with him, the message would be clear. I was spending some hard-earned capital.

The fretting noises got louder. 'Why would you do something so reckless?' Don sounded like he wanted to crawl through the phone line and wring my neck personally.

'Don, I have a feeling.'

'A *feeling?* Dear girl, you pick today of all days to suddenly have feelings?'

'Oh come on, I've heard you say a cop feels hinky. Or a new client feels like the real deal, truly innocent. This isn't just me believing an old friend.' I heard Don scoff at the choice of the word 'friend,' but I pressed on. 'His side of the story is just too bizarre to be fabricated.'

'Are you listening to the words that are coming out of your mouth? You're basically saying it sounds too much like a lie to be a lie. You need more than that kind of logic to vouch for a client.'

I could still hear Don's words as I ended the call. *Why would you do something so reckless?*

I'd given him a bogus answer about a gut feeling, but I knew precisely why I was sticking my neck out for Jack. It was the look on his face when he mentioned Buckley. That was when his situation had become real. Neeley was dead. Jack was under arrest for murder. In just one instant, he had realized that life as he knew it would never be the same.

It reminded me of his expression when he'd walked into our apartment and realized we wouldn't be getting married after all. And that changed everything in ways Don could not possibly understand.

5

I had to hand it to Boyle: the detective had a sense of humor. As I had hoped, he had called Scott Temple at the DA's office, supposedly only 'out of curiosity,' and now Temple was on his way to the precinct. The spot Boyle had selected for me to 'cool my heels' was a bench outside the detective squad that already contained two occupants at either end. The gentleman on the left was a man who smelled like pee and bong hits. On the right was a guy telling me that the NSA could upload the thoughts in my brain to a secret satellite station in space. I decided to stand.

It wasn't long before I heard labored footsteps from the stairwell, slow and heavy. Out stepped a winded Scott Temple. He used the palm of his hand to wipe off a drop of sweat from his cheek. His face looked flushed, though with his blond hair and fair skin, it could have been the fluorescent lighting. 'Did you hear we may be sitting ourselves to death?' he said between breaths. 'I eat like a baby bird — vegetables, steamed fish, freakin' quinoa. But I sit in a chair all day. Some fatty stuffing his face with a maple bar just sprinted past me to the fourth floor. A maple bar! I mean, who eats like that?'

'Guys who don't sit in chairs all day,' I offered. 'Thanks for coming, Scott.'

'Been a long time since I got called out to a

precinct. It's usually to hammer out a cooperation agreement, but Boyle seemed to have
another impression. You're trying to stop a guy
from being booked? On a triple homicide,
Olivia? Come on. Not even you can pull that
off.'

'You're handling the case, though, right?'

He nodded. A shooting in a tourist-popular
part of town. At least one powerful victim.
Maybe others as well. It was as high profile as a
case could get. I had been close to certain which
ADA would be assigned. The one with the pretty
face and surfer-boy hair, the one who ate like a
supermodel to stay attractive for the jury.

And lucky for me, this particular ADA had a
special reason to trust me. Seven years ago,
Scott's sister was arrested buying heroin from an
undercover police officer in Long Island.
Increasing dosages of prescription painkillers
had eventually led to street drugs. Scott needed a
lawyer who could steer her case through a
first-time-offender probation program and make
sure that no one ever made the connection
between a drug-addicted Long Island housewife
and the little brother who was making a meteoric
rise through the Manhattan district attorney's
office. In the world of prosecution, a family
member with a drug problem meant accusations
of hypocrisy and claims of corruption. It was a
career ender.

I had kept his secret as if he were my own
client.

'He didn't do it, Scott. Jack Harris is
completely innocent.'

'He's not innocent, Olivia. Jack Harris shot three people this morning.'

I didn't expect Temple to personally unlock Jack's handcuffs based solely on my word, but I was sure he'd hear me out. I asked how he could possibly be so certain about his case after only a few hours.

'You know I can't tell you that.'

'Come on, Scott. Give me *something*. How did the police even wind up at Jack Harris's door this morning? Some kind of anonymous tip? You know how reliable those can be.'

'Now that's a question I can answer. We got surveillance video.'

My eyes widened involuntarily. 'Of the shooting?'

He made a don't-be-stupid face. 'No. It's from the Pier 40 parking garage.'

I confirmed that he meant the big ugly brick building just north of the football field.

'That's the one. Got a tape of a guy in a blue-and-gray-checked shirt, walking alone, fast, like he's determined. And he's carrying some kind of case. Or that's what we thought at the time. Now we know it's a picnic basket.'

'And you just happened to recognize him as Jack Harris of all the people in New York? Those are some good cameras.'

He gave me the face again. 'Turns out your new friend Jimmy Boyle's got a photographic memory. By the time he rolled on to the scene, Neeley had already been identified by the ID in his wallet. Even the initial responding officers were saying, 'Hey, this could be revenge for what his son did at Penn Station.' Especially with the lawsuit just getting dismissed.'

'Jack Harris isn't the only person who filed that lawsuit.'

'Do you want information or do you want to argue? We get the surveillance tape from the garage. Boyle sees it and he's immediately, 'That's the teacher's husband.' Turns out that if you pull up tape of the presser Harris did with his lawyer right after the civil suit against Neeley was dismissed, he's wearing the same blue-and-gray-checked shirt. Boyle didn't miss a beat.'

In another case, I could destroy Temple's logic. I'd send Einer down to Lord & Taylor to buy eight shirts that looked identical in a grainy surveillance video. I'd call the manufacturers for data on how many were made. But it was all moot given Jack's admission that he'd been at the waterfront this morning.

'You need more than proximity to the scene to charge someone with murder.'

'Motive, means, and opportunity. Trial summation 101, Olivia.'

'Except I don't hear anything going toward means. Where's the gun?'

'That basket he's carrying in the video seems to me like a discreet way to carry a weapon through downtown. And we already pulled footage from his apartment's elevator. He leaves at 6:40, basket in hand. Back at 7:25, no basket. Where did it go?'

'Jack told Boyle exactly where he left it and why. Go find it. Check out the note inside. Find this woman he was supposed to meet. Conduct a

50

proper investigation.'

'No jury's going to buy that ridiculous explanation. His secret soul mate just happens to lead him to a spot right next to the man he's been consumed with for the past three years? Quite the coincidence.'

'This isn't some misdemeanor you can wrap up on instinct, Temple. You're accusing someone this city has come to see as a hero. How's it going to look when I've got this missed-moment woman on the courthouse steps for her first press conference: Madeline and Jack, love at first sight. Then all of New York will sigh wistfully as she explains how she would have shown up this morning if not for — something at work, or a sick child perhaps. It was all just a misunderstanding,' I added dramatically. 'I hear people love that shit.'

'It's not going to happen, Olivia. The girl doesn't exist. You realize that, right?'

'But if she does? You'll be apologizing to the Penn Station widower, and the entire country will know that you wasted valuable time that could have been used to find the real shooter.'

'So you're just trying to help me out now, huh?'

'I'm trying to help my client, who did not do this. Saving his ass happens to mean saving yours, too. It's a win-win. You know me, Scott. I wouldn't have asked Boyle to call you if this weren't legit.'

I held his gaze and then widened my eyes, the facial equivalent of an exclamation mark. He shook his head. If we were at a bar with martinis, he would have been twirling his toothpick. He was mulling over the evidence and seeing it all disappear, piece by piece. This was good. It meant they didn't have it wrapped up tight.

They couldn't, after all. This was Jack. There was no way he had pulled that trigger.

I pushed once more. 'Come on, you know Boyle doesn't have this thing locked and loaded. You really ready for this to hit the news? Do you even have the GSR results?'

'Give me a second.' I could see him pulling out his cell phone as he walked down the hall. He was calling the boss.

He didn't reemerge for twenty more minutes. When he did, Detective Boyle was walking beside him toward the squad room. They were whispering intensely and the conversation continued next to a desk that I assumed was Boyle's. They were arguing.

As Temple turned in my direction, Boyle slammed himself hard into his chair, rolling backward a foot.

'We're going to wait for the GSR results before booking him,' Temple said. 'I called for a rush.'

'If he's clean, you'll release him?'

'No, I didn't say that. But I told Boyle to hold off on the transport for now. We'll take it from there, okay? But, I swear to God, Olivia, if you burn me on this, if we release him today, and he flees — '

'I know, your office will never trust me again.'

'No. My office will never trust *me* again, and I'll devote every moment of my unemployment to making your life a living hell. That's how much this matters. Now, I'm heading back to the courthouse until we hear back from the lab. A very upset Detective Boyle will be escorting Harris to a holding cell. Try not to gloat, okay?' Once he was out of view, I allowed myself to smile. The gamble had paid off.

Once those tests were back, Jack could go home. Maybe we'd even sit down and talk after all these years.

★ ★ ★

Thirty minutes into my wait, I had already ignored three voice mail messages from Don, pleading, imploring, and then pleading once again that I get back to the office immediately. My legs beginning to tire, I finally gave up and assumed a seat on the bench outside the detective squad. By now, the man rambling about the NSA had been led away, and his fragrant neighbor had managed to air out.

I waited until exactly two PM and then called the main number for the firm. Don would be at the courthouse by now for a pretrial conference he'd been dreading all week.

'Good afternoon, Ellison and Randall.'

'Einer, have you looked up that computer stuff I called about?' I turned my back to my fellow bench occupant.

'Just finished. I think I've got diabetes from reading it all. 'I'm just a girl, sitting in front of a boy, next to the filthy Hudson River, asking him to love her.' Cue a shirtless Matthew McConaughey before he lost all that weight and won an Oscar.'

'What's the gist?'

'Just like you said, there was a missed-moment post that went up on the Room ten days ago. The author of that post was Charlotte Caperton, the Room's publisher. I'll send you a link now. A woman named Madeline responds, saying, I think that was me. Charlotte then forwards that message to Jack Harris. Then some e-mails back and forth between Jack and Madeline — typical online dating triteness, not an ounce of sex talk. That's why Tinder's more my speed.'

'The e-mails, Einer.'

'Right. Then last night, she suggests meeting at chapter twelve this morning. What's that, a café or something?'

'No, but what else?'

'He says, see you there. And that's it.'

'So how do I get hold of this woman?'

'I guess e-mail her.'

'You don't have a last name? Nothing?'

'No, that's sort of the point of a certain kind of e-mail account, Olivia.'

'It's important, Einer.'

'Of course it is. Like everything. By the way, Don was apoplectic when he walked out of here. What's the deal with this new client?'

I resisted the urge to point out that he'd learned that word from me and still wasn't certain what it meant. 'It's fine. I'll deal with Don. Just send me all those e-mails.' I was already picturing how grateful Jack would be once I cleared all this up.

* * *

54

The first e-mail from Einer had no subject line. The body of the message was a link, which I clicked.

The Room
June 7, 2015, 8:07 am

Good morning, Roomers. As you know, we here at the Room try to balance our beloved sarcasm and snark with a healthy dose of heartwarming romance. And ain't nothing that warms Auntie Charlotte's heart like a Missed-Moment post. If I took all the hours I spend finding you the best missed connections on the Interwebs and devoted them to my own personal life, I might have someone in my bed other than Daisy the Ugly Pug.

But this morning, I have an extra-special post for you. It's written in the third person, which I'll explain below.

Here goes:
He saw her on the grass by the Christopher Street Pier Saturday morning, 6:30 am. He was kicking off the day with his usual morning run. She was barefoot in last night's party dress, drinking champagne from the bottle. He looked in her direction, and she raised her bottle in a toast. He noticed that in her other hand, she held a book. He wants to know more.

Come on, fellow romantics. That's a specific time, date, location, and description. We can do this! Are you the woman in the grass? Do you know who she was? Here's why you should come forward.

The 'he' in this post is a catch: an acclaimed novelist, a graduate of Columbia University, and an all-around good guy. He has a huge heart. And I happen to love him more than anyone else in the world (and that includes Daisy).

He may kill me for posting this, but if we Roomers can connect him to this mysterious woman in the grass, maybe the sacrifice will be worth it. Let's get those e-mails rolling in!

I closed the Room post on my screen and returned to my e-mail account. The subject line of Einer's next message was 'Fwd: What did you DO?' I clicked on the message to open it. The introductory explanation was to me from Einer:

O, here's the back and forth b/w Jack & Charlotte, publisher of the Room. Read from bottom up to read in order. (Please tell me you would know that without me telling you.) — E
Begin forwarded message:

I did as Einer had instructed, scrolled down to the earliest message, and read from there.

_____

FROM: jacksonharris@gmail.com
TO: charlotte.caperton@roommag.com
DATE: June 7, 2015 8:46 AM
Subject: What did you DO?

B just texted me to see if you had another best friend who went to Columbia and writes books. A missed moment? When I figure out a way to get you back, you will wish that I had killed you. Can I persuade you to take it down?

FROM: charlotte.caperton@roommag.com
TO: jacksonharris@gmail.com
DATE: June 7, 2015, 8:58 AM
Subject: RE: What did you DO?

You know I have no other friends. You, Buckley, Dog. Admit it: You wouldn't have told me about her if you didn't sort of want me to do something. If we find her, it'll at least make a great story, maybe more. Besides, think of it as a blind item to get you some free publicity.
As for Buckley, she just told me yesterday that she thinks you need a girlfriend!

FROM: jacksonharris@gmail.com
TO: charlotte.caperton@roommag.com
DATE: June 7, 2015 9:04 AM
Subject: RE: What did you DO?

Don't try to throw Buckley under the bus for this. I know for a fact that the thought of me with a woman totally 'grosses her out.'

FROM: jacksonharris@gmail.com
TO: charlotte.caperton@roommag.com
DATE: June 7, 2015 11:12 PM
Subject: RE: What did you DO?

I can't believe I'm asking this, but any word?

FROM: charlotte.caperton@roommag.com
TO: jacksonharris@gmail.com
DATE: June 7, 2015, 11:19 PM
Subject: RE: What did you DO?

Nothing credible yet but lots of shares and tweets.
We're gonna find her. I feel it. Go to bed.

Sent from Charlotte's iPhone. Mention typos at your own risk.

FROM: charlotte.caperton@roommag.com
TO: jacksonharris@gmail.com
DATE: June 10, 2015, 3:27 PM
Subject: RE: What did you DO?

What did I do, you asked? Found the woman in the grass, that's what I did! Booya.

Got a whole bunch of prank responses (as usual) but hers is legit, down to the details. Here's the copy and paste:

58

Dear Charlotte, I just saw your Missed-Moment post on a friend's Facebook page. Little did the friend know that I'm the woman you're looking for. At least I think I am. Check with your mystery man: I have long dark hair and was wearing a bridesmaid's dress. Oh, and I had a basket with me. Just so he knows I noticed him, too: if he's the guy I smiled at, he was wearing a T-shirt that said 'World's Okayest Runner.' How great is that? If he wants to reach me, I'm at mlh87@paperfree.com. My name's Madeline.

Here are my thoughts, Jack, whether wanted or not: 1) She uses excellent punctuation. 2) You really shouldn't wear that shirt in public. 3) The fact that she liked said shirt means you could be perfect for each other. E-mail her, goofball.

FROM: charlotte.caperton@roommag.com
TO: jacksonharris@gmail.com
DATE: June 10, 2015, 6:27 PM
Subject: RE: What did you DO?

Me again. It's been exactly three hours. Did you reach out to Madeline? Do it, Jack, or I may do it for you. And who knows what I might say? (Maniacal laugh.)
xox

I found myself smiling. Here I was, thinking of Jack as the guy to feel sorry for. His mother died when he was in high school, followed by his father our sophomore year in college. Then everything that happened with us, plus Owen, plus the aftermath. Then he starts a new life with Molly, only to lose her so violently.

But he still had Charlotte, who I knew from experience would stop at nothing to look after Jack. He had someone to e-mail at midnight. And he had a daughter who was probably the one to buy him cheesy T-shirts that were right in his humor wheelhouse.

I of all people had no reason to feel sorry for someone who had all of that.

★ ★ ★

I clicked on the final e-mail message from Einer. It was a forward of all the exchanges between Jack and Madeline.

A quick scroll revealed that there was a lot to read, so I jumped back to the top for the important stuff.

Just like Jack had sworn, Madeline was the one to suggest the meet-up at the football field. She had set the time, the date, and the location. She was the one who told him to bring the picnic basket. She'd bring the champagne.

All good.

I was starting to read the messages from the beginning when an incoming text message appeared at the top of my phone's screen: *Are you at the precinct? Have you seen my dad?*

I ignored the text and continued to skim. Jack's first e-mail to Madeline explained that the

60

silly T-shirt was a gift from his daughter. Most men wouldn't lead with the kid, but Jack never did have much game. He asked her what book she had been reading when he spotted her at the pier. She told him *Eight Days to Die.*

Okay, he responded. *I may need to verify that you're actually real, and this isn't Charlotte punking me.* Eight Days to Die *is far and away my favorite book from last year. What are the odds of that? I've stopped recommending it to people, because they insist that a person with only eight days to live is 'too sad,' but it's one of those clean, simple novels that proves heart-breaking stories can be life affirming.*

Oh dear. Einer wasn't kidding about the diabetes. Really, Jack? A published author and you can't do better than that? The next time Melissa pushed me to try online dating again, I'd have to remind her of why I quit in the first place.

Another text message popped up at the top of the screen: *Is my dad under arrest or not? Not knowing is driving me crazy.*

Followed by, *P.S. This is Buckley Harris.*

How in the world could she even text that fast? I wouldn't be giving my cell phone number to any more teenagers.

I scrolled to the final addition to the e-mail chain, Jack's response to Madeline's invitation to meet in person: *See you there.*

I had to smile at his response, so spontaneous and unquestioning. Some of my best times with Jack had been spur-of-the-moment ventures.

My thoughts about the past were interrupted

by yet another text message. *If you're trying to protect me . . . DON'T! I can handle it. Just tell me what is going on!!!!*

So many exclamation points. I texted a quick response: *Cautiously optimistic that we'll have your dad home soon. Be patient. I promise to call when I know more.*

I had just hit Send when my cell phone rang. Buckley, I assumed, demanding more detail. But the number on the screen was the outgoing number for the district attorney's office.

It was ADA Scott Temple. 'The lab called. Two hours, just as they promised. Jack Harris's hands are clear, at least of GSR.'

Even though I'd been expecting this, I felt a wave of relief wash over me. 'That's great.' I assured him that Jack would not leave the jurisdiction while they continued to investigate, and began piling on ways of backing up the promise: turning over his passport, electronic monitoring, the works.

'Save all that for the bail hearing, Olivia. Boyle's processing him now for transport.'

'Then why have I been stewing on a bench here all day? Is this some kind of joke? What was the whole point of waiting for the GSR testing?'

So much smugness and indignation. It was a posture I struck well. Outrage can work wonders to shame people when you're right, and they're wrong.

But here's the thing: you better be right.

'Look, Olivia, it's not my business, but you called me for a reason. I respect you, and I listen to you when you stick your neck out. But you're wrong on Harris. I don't blame you. The Penn Station widower thing may have clouded your judgment.'

'My judgment's just fine.' Even I knew I sounded defensive.

'His hands were clean, but we tested his shirt, too. The GSR test came back positive. Sorry, Olivia. Your guy's guilty. He played you.'

6

I still had my phone in hand as I marched through the squad, calling out for Detective Boyle. A younger female detective rolled back her chair and rose to meet me in the middle of the room. 'Whoa, whoa, whoa. You can't just be storming through here.'

Boyle appeared at the back of the squad room, his hands pressed on either side of the doorway leading to the hall containing the interrogation rooms. He was intentionally blocking my view.

'Ramos is right, Counselor. This is our house, not yours.'

I saw the movement of officers in uniform behind him. The white cotton of a T-shirt. It was Jack. They were moving him.

'I need to talk to my client. You are interfering with his right to counsel.'

'Nice try, but I know a little bit about the law. We were done questioning him long before your arrival, Ms. Randall. I did you a favor letting you back there the first time. You don't get to ride in the car at his side.'

'Just five minutes, Detective. He has a daughter. I need to know where — '

'Most everyone we'll arrest this week has kids. Just because his is white and rich doesn't make him special.'

I ran to Detective Boyle and craned my neck

to get a better view of Jack being led down the hall. 'Jack!'

Boyle exchanged an amused look with the female detective and shook his head.

I wanted to push Boyle out of the way but knew there would be nothing more I could do once I made it past his guard post. I called out loudly but calmly, 'Jack, don't say anything to anyone — not police, not prosecutors, definitely not other prisoners. Do you hear me? Not a word.'

I managed to catch one final glimpse of him as he struggled to look back at me as two flanking officers led him away. I had never seen anyone appear so terrified and utterly confused. His knees seemed to buckle when I said the word 'prisoners.'

The last Jack knew, I was working on getting him freed. I had walked out of the conference room to take a phone call. Now he was being processed into the system with no explanation of what had changed.

★ ★ ★

Outside the precinct, the typical end-of-day Tribeca traffic was at a standstill on Varick Street. Trucks lurched forward a few inches at a time, honking horns as if the sound might somehow blast a clear path through the line of cars fighting for a spot in the Holland Tunnel. A stocky man in a Mets tank top stood next to a cooler, selling bottles of Poland Spring water to drivers at a buck a pop. A street vendor told me that my outfit could use one of his necklaces. A man who passed me on the sidewalk made an 'mmm-mmm' noise and suggested it was 'too damn hot for all those clothes' I was wearing.

I could see and hear all of it, but none of what was happening outside my head mattered. My phone was buzzing in my hand — dueling calls from Don and Buckley, according to the screen — but I kept walking.

I had to make a decision: Door A or Door B. Door A is what Don would want: call another firm, bring them up to date, get them to represent Jack. Door B: stay on the case.

Lawyers say it doesn't matter whether a client's innocent. It's not our job to know. We fight zealously no matter what. What a bunch of crap.

I'm not good at everything. Or, to be more honest, I'm pretty bad on some fairly major metrics. I'm selfish. I feel entitled to things always going my way. I despise hearing about other people's problems, because I don't like most people, especially people who would be described as normal. They say ignorance is bliss? I think bliss is for the ignorant. But before he met me, Jack was normal and good and blissful, and made the mistake of loving me anyway. And he got burned for it.

I am extremely good at one thing, though. I am good at tearing apart a prosecution. And from what I already knew, Jack needed someone good.

I owed this to him. And maybe I owed it to myself as well.

★ ★ ★

I pulled up a number on my cell phone and hit Enter.

'Café Lissa.'

The woman at the other end of the line was the Lissa of Café Lissa. We met when I was eighteen years old through the luck of the draw that was Columbia University's roommate matching system. A quarter century later, Melissa Reyes was still my best friend and quite possibly the only person I had ever met who truly understood me.

'Hey there.'

'Hey, I was hoping to hear from you. You've been incommunicado since a very late text last night about bumping into Ryan at Maialino. I'm afraid to ask.'

'It's the same old thing. It's . . . whatever.' Anyone else, if they actually knew that story, would start in with a lecture. But like I said, Melissa understands me. 'Can you make a point of checking to see if Don's swinging by the café tonight? He's not real happy with me right now, and I need to talk to him.'

Don, in addition to being my law partner, was Melissa's uncle. Her mother's brother, to be precise. And, like me, Don could be found at Lissa's multiple times a week.

'Sure, but won't you see him before I do? What's going on?'

'I can't explain now. But it's important.'

True to form, Melissa didn't hesitate. 'No problem. I'll get him here.'

67

Once I hung up, I started typing a new text message to Jack's daughter, Buckley. *Where are you?*

★ ★ ★

I shouldn't have been surprised that Charlotte's apartment was in a luxury building on Central Park South. Even in college, she made no effort to hide the fact that she benefited from family money. She was one of the kids who could whisk away a friend to Paris for a weekend or show up with enough weed for the entire dorm. Her room, down the hall from Melissa and me, was a single, despite supposed campus policy that all freshmen have roommates. Rumor was, her grandfather was on the board of trustees. When Jack and I first moved in together to a place off campus, she showed up with a four-thousand-dollar espresso maker that took up half the counter space in our galley kitchen because she couldn't stand my 'Mr. Coffee mud drip diner sludge.'

These days, at least she earned some of her money on her own. Charlotte launched an online magazine back when people used to ask, 'Who would *possibly* rely on information from the Internet?' The Room was part gossip, part politics, part news, focusing on life in New York City. The revenue started off slowly, with an occasional paid advertisement from an Eighth Street shoe store or yet another midtown pizza stand claiming to be the 'original' NYC pie.

The big splash came a few years after Jack and

I broke up when the Room began encouraging people to send in their local celebrity sightings. All tips were compiled on a map. With just one click, any member of the public could find out who was where, wearing what, and with whom — preferably with photos, the less flattering, the better.

A media star was born.

I was with Jack for five years, which meant I was with Charlotte Caperton for five years, because for reasons I never quite understood, she was his best friend. They certainly weren't cut from the same cloth. Jack only knew her in the first place because his father was the caretaker for the Capertons' summer place in Long Island. Somehow two little boys from Glen Cove — Jack and his big brother, Owen — and a little girl from the Upper East Side became joined at the hips, playing Marco Polo a few times a year in a luxury pool overlooking Long Island's north shore. Charlotte and Jack never could remember which of them decided to opt for Columbia first, but where one went, so did the other.

Like a protective mother, Charlotte never did approve of me as an appropriate partner for her best friend. The only good thing I could say about her then was that at least I didn't need to be jealous. Charlotte was a 100 percent Gold Star Lesbian.

The lobby of her apartment building would be up to any discerning New Yorker's standards, even Charlotte's, with overstuffed furniture, gleaming white tables, and fresh flower arrangements the size of beach balls. I was in the process of confirming that the walls were lined with leather when Charlotte's attentive doorman ended his quick phone call and gestured toward the elevator at the far end of this luxury fortress. 'Miss Caperton is expecting you.'

As I stepped out of the elevator on the twenty-fifth floor, I saw her waiting for me at the end of the hall, the apartment door open behind her. For some reason, I'd been expecting an older version of 1990s Charlotte — super-short brown gender-neutral hair, oversize clothes, a self-proclaimed 'fat butch.' But she'd grown her hair out into a bob with blond highlights and was probably two jean sizes smaller than she'd been in college. She was wearing makeup and, if I wasn't mistaken, a Helmut Lang tank top I'd been tempted to purchase on my last Bloomingdale's trip. At her side was a tan pug looking warily with big black bug eyes at the new arrival.

'It's about fucking time.'

She hadn't completely changed. 'Nice to see you, too, Charlotte.'

★ ★ ★

The girl inside the doorway, though only a few years from being a beautiful woman, was still small enough to have been hidden from view by Charlotte's imposing frame. Once Charlotte stepped inside the apartment, I was able to get a good look at her. Even without context, I might have immediately known her identity.

Buckley Harris had her father's thin nose and

70

angular chin, and her mother's strawberry blond hair and a sprinkling of freckles. She was one of those kids who looked like a photo mash-up of her parents. Her shoulder-length hair fell in loose curls, and her light green eyes were enormous. To me she looked haunted, but maybe I knew too much about her life.

'You must be Buckley,' I said, extending my hand. 'I'm Olivia Randall.'

When she didn't immediately return the gesture, Charlotte nudged her. 'Sorry,' Buckley muttered. She did not sound sorry. 'I've been going crazy wondering where my dad is. When is he coming home?'

I suggested to Charlotte that perhaps she and I should talk alone. Buckley interrupted with a firm no. '*I'm* the one who called you. I can handle it.'

Charlotte closed her eyes. I'd known her long enough to guess that she was counting silently. Old habits, etcetera. When she opened her eyes, her voice remained calm as she led the way to her living room. 'Olivia, Buckley may look like Taylor Swift's little ginger-haired sister, but she's an old soul with the IQ of — I don't know, some person too smart for me to have heard of. And, Buckley, not everyone gets you, okay? Get over it. Now, both of you: sit. Why the fuck is Jack under arrest?'

I looked at Charlotte to make sure this was really how we were going to do this, and then launched in, telling Buckley that her fears were correct. 'The police think your father was involved in the shootings this morning at the

71

waterfront. If I had to guess, they'll be making an announcement any minute now.'

'*Involved?*' Charlotte asked. 'Like, how is he *involved?* They can't just go around holding witnesses, can they? Don't they need a material witness warrant? Some special order from a terrorism court or something?'

By now, Jack would be getting booked at MDC. He'd soon experience the shock of his first encounter with a real jail cell. He'd be wondering whether he'd ever sleep in a room alone again, on a mattress more than three inches deep, or use a toilet that wasn't made of metal, or take a private shower.

'They're not holding him as a witness.' I fixed my gaze directly on Buckley. 'They think your father did this. They think he was the shooter.'

Buckley looked five years younger as her face puckered with confusion, then outrage. She looked like what she was: a terrified little girl. A terrified little girl with one parent dead from a mass shooting, the other an accused killer. As if sensing her sadness, the pug managed to leap onto her lap. Buckley gave her a pat and muttered, 'Good Daisy.'

'I know it's hard to process. But this isn't the end of anything; it's the beginning. At this point, he's only under arrest.' I saw no point in telling them that a senior ADA had already made up his mind about Jack's guilt. 'From what I can tell, a large part of whatever evidence they have right now is based on motive. One of this morning's victims was Malcolm Neeley.'

Buckley sucked in her breath at the mention of

his name. She and Charlotte simultaneously launched into the same arguments I had raised at the precinct — that suing someone wasn't the same as wanting to kill him, that other people blamed Neeley for his son's actions just as much as Jack did.

I cleared my throat to interrupt. 'There's a complication.' I didn't want to run the risk of them learning about the GSR evidence on the news. In dry, clinical language, I explained the process for testing for gunshot residue on a person's clothing. 'I'm told the test came back positive.'

Buckley fell back against the sofa, all the fight in her suddenly gone. Charlotte threw me a sharp look. So much for wanting me to give it to the kid straight.

★ ★ ★

The granite island in Charlotte's kitchen resembled the set of a cooking show, covered by an array of fresh ingredients, already chopped and measured, waiting to be assembled. I wondered if she'd done the preparations herself or had a chef for that.

'You realize you basically just told that girl you think her father's guilty?'

I could tell she wanted to yell, but didn't want Buckley to hear us from the den. 'You're the one who said she was an old soul.'

'That's because I didn't think you'd pull a total mind fuck on her. I treat Buckley the way I do to make up for all the tiptoeing everyone else has done around her since her mother died. She needs at least one person in her life who doesn't act like she's made of glass.'

'Jack said she could be sensitive.'

'No shit, Olivia. Some kid shot her mother at random. Kind of shakes your faith in the world, don't you think?' Perhaps realizing there was no point to this conversation, Charlotte shifted the conversation back to Jack's arrest. 'So someone actually killed that asshole Malcolm Neeley?'

'According to the police. And I don't see why they'd lie about it.'

'And two bystanders?' she asked.

'At least the way they describe it.'

'How can they know he was the target and not one of the other two? Or it could have been totally random.'

'Except for the fact that Jack just happened to be in the area at the time of the shooting and had gunshot residue on his shirt.'

'Well, obviously those stupid test results are wrong.' She picked up a dice of radish from one of the carefully arranged Pyrex cups and popped it in her mouth. 'Isn't that the kind of thing you do now? Get stuff like that thrown out? I can pay you, by the way. Your full fee. I want to help Jack however I can.'

'It's not about the money, Charlotte. I would hope you'd at least trust me on that.'

'Really? I should *trust* you?'

'As a lawyer. Yes, you should, or I should leave right now.'

She shrugged. 'My point is, we'll get an

expert. A whole team. Poof — gone goes the bogus test result.'

'It's not that easy.' I knew the standard ways to challenge the evidence — where police did the testing, how they handled the clothing, chain of custody, the involved personnel. But none of that would happen until trial. 'I really thought I had this nipped in the bud until those results came back. Charlotte, is there any way — '

'Hell no, are you kidding me? You know Jack. Not a violent bone in that man's body. After all, we know from experience how he handles things when his world falls apart.'

What she meant was, *when you made his world fall apart.*

She must have registered my discomfort. 'Sorry,' she quickly offered. 'My point is, we know for a fact that the only person Jack hurts when he feels lost is himself. He falls apart. It might've happened all over again when Molly died, but he had to hang in there for Buckley.'

'Speaking of Buckley, when she first called my office this morning, she told me that helping Jack was the — quote — least I could do after what I did to her father. How does she even know about me?'

Charlotte shrugged. 'Kids hear everything, especially that kid. Not even Molly and Jack were perfect. They argued like any other couple. My guess is your name came up — the omnipresent ex-girlfriend or something.'

'She knew more than that. *What I did to her father?*'

Another shrug. 'Trust me, she doesn't know

75

the whole story, or she wouldn't have called you. All she knows is that Uncle Owen died in a car accident. Once Jack got his shit together, he vowed never again to blame himself for what happened.'

Not when there was someone else to blame. I glanced down the hall to make sure that Buckley was still out of earshot.

'So just how much did Jack despise Malcolm Neeley?'

'Well, he definitely didn't sympathize with the guy. Or understand him. Jack is the most devoted father in the world. He'd do *anything* for Buckley. So imagine how he felt about this prick who *knew* his kid was a head case, but couldn't dare get him any help because, of course, no son of his could possibly be imperfect. Instead, he insisted on trying to butch the kid up, pushing him to follow sports and then — lo and behold — the kid likes guns. Yay! Let's encourage that. Great idea, asshole. So, yeah, Jack wasn't a fan. But all that means is he's got neurons firing in his brain. The lawsuit against Neeley wasn't even his idea. Some of the other families thought of it. He just ended up with more media coverage. You know, with Molly being the one who tried to stop Todd before he opened fire. Plus he's all squeaky clean and shiny and writes books that win awards. Not to mention the dead-cop brother. He made for good copy.'

'Speaking of you media types, I need to talk to you about that missed-moment post.'

She looked taken aback at the sudden change

in subject. 'How did *that* come up in conversation?'

'It's why he was at the waterfront today.'

'That's where he jogs.'

'I know, but that's not why he was there. He was there to meet Madeline — the champagne, picnic, book girl.'

'You mean he was actually going to meet her? I knew they were e-mailing, but he was being pretty hush-hush with the details.'

'They arranged to meet today. She picked the time and the place. Seven AM this morning, right at the football field.'

I waited while the implication set in. 'And Malcolm Neeley just happens to get killed there a few minutes later?'

I nodded.

'So that's an awfully big coincidence,' she said.

'Unless it's not.'

7

I asked Charlotte who Jack might have told about his plans for the morning.

She shrugged. 'If he didn't even tell me, I can't imagine that he mentioned it to someone else.'

'But Madeline could have told anyone. Jack used his real name when he e-mailed her.'

'And the person she mentions this to just happens to decide to frame Jack for murder? That doesn't make sense.'

No, it didn't, but working through all possible scenarios was the way I processed facts. 'If someone wanted to kill Malcolm Neeley, Jack was a prime candidate for a setup. Like you said, he made good copy as Neeley's number-one enemy.'

'Damnit. What if I made Jack too identifiable in the missed-moment post? Madeline could be a catfish.'

'A catfish is like a fake ID?'

'It's a lot more than that. It's the creation of an entire personality. You should see the number of supposedly gorgeous women on Twitter and Facebook who have a thing for fat, ugly geezers. But the person behind the profile is some ex-con in Lithuania. You know how many people have actually fallen in love — like, total, head over heels, quit their jobs and sell their houses to move across the country, in *love* — with someone who doesn't even exist? Sometimes it's just to screw with a person. Usually it's to take their money. But here maybe they're catfishing for a fall guy.'

'I don't think I'm following.'

'Okay, suppose someone wants to kill Neeley. They're thinking they can make it look like one of the Penn Station family members did it. Then they see the missed-moment post, realize I'm talking about Jack, and make up a woman named Madeline to rope him in.'

'And they just happen to know Jack's favorite book?'

'Easy,' she said. She walked over to a nook in the corner of the kitchen, and came back with an iPad. She used Siri's microphone to search for 'Jack Harris Eight Days to Die,' tapped the screen a couple of times, and pushed the tablet in my direction.

It was an author Q and A from the website goodreads, posted a month and a half earlier.

GR: Readers always like to know what their favorite writers have on their nightstands. Do you have any recent favorite reads?

JH: I always have a nightstand full of books, but I was blown away by last year's Eight Days to Die by a debut writer named Monica Harding.

I browsed the rest of his answer — how the book captured New York City so well, how it managed to be uplifting even though it was about a woman scheduling her own death, how his teenage daughter also enjoyed it, and how

79

they had spent an afternoon taking a walking tour of spots featured in the book.

With a quick Google search, 'Madeline' could have known what book she could claim to have been reading once Jack asked the question.

But then I saw a hole in Charlotte's theory. 'When Madeline responded to the missed-moment post, she knew what shirt Jack had been wearing. She also mentioned the basket. Those details weren't in the original post you published.'

'They weren't?'

I shook my head.

She whispered, '*Damn*,' under her breath. But I wasn't so ready to give up on her catfish theory. I was still thinking out loud. 'What if the actual woman he saw at the pier was also part of the catfish?'

'That's not how catfishing works. The whole point is, you don't need a real person. You just make one up.'

'Well, set aside the word 'catfish.' Maybe the woman he saw at the pier was also part of the setup. She gets all dolled up, trying to get his attention, with the long-term plan being to frame him for Neeley's murder. But then Jack pulls a Jack. He keeps on running. Doesn't stop to talk to her. Plan foiled. Until your post.'

I saw Charlotte's face fall.

'No, not like that,' I said. 'This isn't your fault. But are you following me? That makes sense, right?' Seduce Jack. Kill Neeley. Frame Jack. The seduction just took a different form than originally planned.

Charlotte nodded. 'Jack's a creature of habit. He runs that route every single morning. She'd know where to wait for him.'

Her comment raised another problem with my theory. 'But pretty women are a dime a dozen. How could anyone know that this particular one would get Jack's attention?'

Charlotte's face suddenly brightened. 'One of the pieces I wrote about Molly for the Room mentioned how she and Jack met. Jack saw Molly reading alone in a wine bar. Brainy, happy in her own head, confident enough to sit by herself, didn't need a man to define her.' With each new attribute, it was becoming increasingly clear that Molly had won over Charlotte's approval in a way I never had. I had followed enough of the media coverage about the shooting to know that Charlotte had played a role in shaping Jack's public image after the shooting. And I specifically remembered the piece she was talking about now. I remembered it because I remembered feeling pathetic for being jealous of a dead woman.

I focused again on the matter at hand. 'Did the woman in the grass' — that's what we were calling her now — 'look like Molly?'

She shrugged. 'I don't know. Jack didn't really say much about her physical appearance, just that she was pretty, I think. He was more drawn to her energy or whatever. It was a setup, I'm telling you. They mined the Web for info on Jack and used it to plant the perfect woman on his running route.'

'I don't know,' I said, shaking my head. 'It's so — elaborate.'

'That's nothing compared to some of the catfish stories we've covered. It would help if we could find the girl. My guess is, she's not involved. She's just the eye candy. They could have hired an actress, or a call girl. Can you get video footage from the city?'

'Maybe. I mean, there's no guarantee she'll be on camera, but, yeah, I can request it.'

I called the district attorney's office, asked for Scott Temple, and told him I was worried that he was cherry-picking the video evidence from the waterfront. 'Make sure you preserve everything. And not just from today. I want the last month, the entire south waterfront.'

Once I was off the phone, I summed up the other side of the conversation for Charlotte. 'He didn't make any promises, but at least he's on notice not to erase anything. A picture of the woman would help. It would show that Jack's not making this whole thing up.'

'I can do a lot with a picture. Pop that baby up on the Room, and the armchair detectives will go nuts. We'll have Madeline's identity in no time.'

Charlotte was so busy outlining her plans for a photograph we didn't have that neither of us noticed a third person lingering in the entrance to the kitchen. Buckley was staring at us, a laptop in her hands, Daisy the pug trailing her feet. 'You guys are making this way too complicated.'

'How much did you hear?' Charlotte asked.

'Enough to know that there's a much simpler explanation.'

★   ★   ★

Buckley set her laptop on the island while she explained. 'You said no one could have known all the details unless they were actually at the piers that morning. But that's not true. They just needed access to his e-mail.'

She tilted the laptop screen in our direction.

FROM: jacksonharris@gmail.com
TO: charlotte.caperton@roommag.com
DATE: June 6, 2015 11:47 PM
Subject: Weird thing

Hey. Too late to call, and I don't think I'd tell
you this anyway unless I wrote it all down.
Weird thing happened on my run today. Saw
this woman at Christopher St. Pier. She was
wearing a strapless gown and had a picnic
basket to herself at 6:30 in the morning. She
was carefree, sitting on the grass and reading a
book, which reminded me of Molly. And she
had long dark hair and was drinking champagne
right out of the bottle, which reminded me of
— well, you know who, but don't like it when I
mention her name.

My point is that I'm lying here in bed 18 hours
later and am still thinking about her. You always

83

remind me that there are — what's the number? 2.2 million age-appropriate women for me within New York City alone? I am starting to imagine the possibility that at least one of them might be worth meeting. Maybe you can even help me set up an online dating account. JK — don't you dare.

Oh, and get this: smooth operator here was wearing that T-shirt B gave me for Christmas. That's right: World's Okayest Runner. How can the ladies resist me?

Anyway, no matter who I might end up with in my life, my favorite women will always be you and Buckley.

'See?' Buckley said. 'It's all right there. Like you said, Dad's the perfect fall guy. If they hacked his e-mails, they'd have everything they'd need to respond to the missed-moment post.'

Buckley was sounding awfully proud of herself for coming up with a theory I had missed. I suspected it had something to do with her father's mention of someone from his past with long dark hair. I fit the bill.

'Told you she was smart,' Charlotte said. 'Now we just need to find out who was snooping in Jack's mailbox.'

'You might want to start by taking a look at that.' Buckley gestured toward the open laptop.

I blinked twice before speaking. 'You're telling

me this computer is your father's?'

Buckley didn't blink. 'Yeah, I picked it up when the police weren't looking.'

* * *

Einer showed up at Charlotte's front door twenty minutes later. Just as his first and last names would suggest, Einer was half Swedish, half German, making his puffy red hair all the more surprising. Though Einer's coif was always slightly Bozo-like, the day's humidity had left it looking like an oversize, carrot-colored Q-tip abandoned at the bottom of a suitcase for too long.

Charlotte and Buckley were with me in the entryway when I let him in, but he didn't bother with introductions. 'Are you trying to get us both fired? Don's been riding my ass all day, asking me where you are, making me promise to loop him in. I don't know what you're working on, or why Don's pissed, but I feel like one of those little kids caught in the middle of their parents' divorce.'

Coming up for air, he registered the presence of a teenager and the small dog smelling his pant leg, and looked at me as if I'd led him into an Ebola outbreak.

He followed us into the kitchen, where Jack's laptop was awaiting his magic touch. 'I need to know if someone hacked into an e-mail sent from this computer.' According to Buckley, Jack primarily used the desktop computer in his home office for writing. He generally used his laptop for research and e-mails. The idea was to associate one computer exclusively with his manuscripts to avoid online distractions. For now, we were assuming that Jack used his laptop to e-mail Charlotte about the woman in the grass.

Einer took a seat and started clicking away, his fingers flying across the keyboard, his brow furrowed. He threw me an annoyed look when Buckley got a little too close, peering over his shoulder.

I decided to distract her with a discussion I'd been postponing until now, hoping that Charlotte might be the one to raise it first. 'So, Buckley, are we going to talk about why you took your dad's laptop while the police were at your apartment with a search warrant?'

Even though her expression was fixed, one second she looked like an anxious little kid, the next an angry, defensive teenager. Her pale, thin face and wide, light eyes were so hard to read.

'You would've done the same thing,' she finally said. 'I mean, you're a famous lawyer; if I did something so wrong, you wouldn't have Ronald McDonald here doing his cyber thing.'

Einer waved over his shoulder. 'Don't mind me — right here within earshot. Been called that before, by the way. If you hear me sniffling, it's just me suffering high school flashbacks.'

I turned to face Buckley. 'You could have gotten into major trouble. Not to mention how it looks if a suspect's own kid gets caught snatching evidence. It looks like you think your father's guilty.'

Her bottom lip started to quiver. So far, I had chalked up Buckley's attitude to normal teenage angst, manifested as cocky smugness, but now I could see that the tough exterior masked a more sensitive core. 'It's not like that. I only took the laptop to be safe. Dad backs his manuscripts up to it. It's his *work*. At least, that's what I was thinking at first. And then, once I had it in my bag, I just left.'

'Is there something we're going to find on that laptop that's a problem, Buckley?'

'I swear, I was only thinking about his book. He's nearly done with it.'

Einer's fingers stopped clicking on the keyboard, and he sat back in his chair. 'Here's the deal: no sign of remote site software. But there's — '

'Dumb it down, please.' It was one of my frequent requests when Einer came to my rescue on the technological front.

'Okay, so the most thorough way to spy on someone is to install remote site software on his computer. Basically it lets someone clone the computer in its entirety — every keystroke is replicated remotely. Nothing like that here. But there are sixteen thousand ways to have accessed his e-mail, leaving no fingerprints on the hardware.'

'So basically, you can't tell from the laptop whether someone hacked him.'

'Correct. Your best bet is to contact his e-mail provider and find out when it was accessed and from where. He can then see if anything looks weird. Let me take a guess: you want me to get to work on that?'

'Please.'

'And one more thing,' Einer added. 'This one here may say she only grabbed the laptop for a book, but Ronald McDonald has a feeling the police might be interested in this.'

He hit a few keys and the screen filled with a gray window labeled 'Library.' 'This is the browser history,' Einer explained. 'It's a list of all the websites visited from this computer.'

I couldn't believe what I was looking at. It seemed like every other result involved the name Malcolm Neeley. Regular Google searches of both his name and his hedge fund, the Sentry Group. Clicks on results from his country club (placed third in a golf tournament two weeks earlier), the 92nd Street Y ('Leader's Circle' for donating more than fifty grand), a Princeton alumni report. There were even Zillow searches of Neeley's home address (current Zestimate=$8.2 M).

Einer clicked on the menu on the left side of the screen, pulling up the history for the previous month, and then the month before that, and the month before that. More of the same.

Charlotte, looking over my shoulder at the screen, asked Buckley, 'Did you know about this? Is this why you took the computer?'

'No, I swear. Besides, it's no big deal. If you looked on my computer, you'd find the same thing. Ask all the other victims. We all checked up on Malcolm, because we all hated him. The guy was an asshole, and he let his fucked-up loser kid kill all those people. He killed my mother.'

88

Buckley's whole body was shaking by the time she wiped away a tear. Charlotte wrapped an arm around the girl's shoulder and kissed the top of her head.

'Anything else?' I asked Einer quietly. He shook his head, and I gestured that we should leave.

I was reaching for the front door when he asked me, 'Are you really leaving that computer with those two?'

'Unless you think we need it.'

'The police, Olivia. They're the ones who will want it. They'll figure out it's missing. And you *know* that mama bear woman's going to scrub it. Or throw it off the GWB with her big strong arms. Did you see those guns?'

'The laptop's not our problem, Einer.'

'I hope you know what you're doing on this one.'

As we rode downstairs in the elevator, I shared his hope, because I was about to tell Don Ellison — the man who gave me a new career when my old one fizzled — why, for the first time in our law partnership, I was going to take a client whether he liked it or not.

8

I could hear the usual evening sounds of Café Lissa — a blend of raised voices and a killer playlist — before I even reached the revolving front door. As banks, drugstores, and big-box chains drove up the price of Manhattan's commercial real estate, small restaurants were closing in droves. But thanks to loyal neighborhood regulars, Lissa's dinner turnout rivaled that of any celebrity chef.

The wait at the bar was three people deep, and the Ramones were pumping from the overhead speakers. *Hey, ho. Let's go!*

Melissa was behind the bar, her preferred spot unless a crisis was unfolding elsewhere in the restaurant. Like me, she was forty-three years old, but somehow her tricep revealed no sign of a wattle as she shook a martini over her right shoulder. As she tipped the clear liquid into a glass, I heard her ask a bearded man whether he wanted an orange twist. He marveled at her recall, saying he'd only been in once, three weeks earlier.

That memory had earned Melissa a 3.84 GPA as a biochem major. Then a year into med school, she announced that her real dream was to open a restaurant.

I gave a quick nod to Melissa and then scanned the restaurant for Don. He was at his favorite table in the back corner, reading glasses helping him browse the *New York Post*.

'I see you're keeping an eye out on the enemy,' I said. 'You may as well have Fox News on replay in your bedroom.'

'That's the problem with your generation,' he said. 'You have too many options. Too much freedom to choose what you want to hear, what you want to read. It's good for the brain to listen to opposing points of view. The jurors who decide our clients' fates read the *Post*, if they read the news at all. You need to understand their world view.'

One of Melissa's bar backs, in a white oxford shirt and blue jeans, dropped off a martini I hadn't asked for. I raised it to Don's pint glass and gave it a clink. 'So, speaking of opposing world views — '

'I'm not stupid, Olivia. You avoided me all day, then had my niece call to make sure I'd be here tonight. Clearly there's something you think we need to discuss, and I suspect it involves that case you had a *feeling* about. Go ahead and say it.'

When I first started working for Don, he tolerated me only as a favor to Melissa, who was basically like a daughter to him. In his eyes, I was an elitely educated, big-law drone, brainwashed to think that real lawyers worked for the corporate clients who could afford to pay the best and brightest to do the highest quality legal work imaginable. At Preston & Cartwright, I once spent ten hours to draft two paragraphs of a thirty-page summary judgment brief. I dreamed of being a partner at a top-tier firm. If I made partner, it would validate all the personal sacrifices I had made to get there.

But then I reached the eight-year associate mark, and I didn't get the dream. I billed a gazillion hours. I approached the law in a 'steady, workmanlike manner.' But I had failed to 'develop meaningful relationships with mentors' or to 'take on a leadership role with the younger associates.' I had not 'demonstrated the potential for significant client development.' I was 'too blunt in my interpersonal communications.' I had memorized all of these words because I'd replayed them repeatedly in my head in the weeks and months that followed. In short, I could do the work, but no one liked me.

I should no longer consider myself on the partner track. That was code for take a year or two, but get out.

When Melissa told me that her uncle Don needed a junior lawyer, my first instinct was to think I was too good for the job. At one point, I had aspired to being a Supreme Court clerk or a law professor. I graduated from law school with one of the best résumés in the country. I was supposed to be a corner-office partner in charge of national litigation, not some errand girl for a solo practitioner catching criminal cases at the courthouse. But I was no longer straight out of school. I was a ninth-year associate. My résumé may as well have borne a giant stamp reading 'couldn't cut it.'

When I tried to make up excuses to decline Don's offer, Melissa had told me she'd 'punch me in the *pepa*' if I turned it down. I was no expert in Spanish slang, but she'd made her point. It wasn't like Melissa to ask her family to help her with anything. But she hadn't asked for herself. She'd asked for me. I had to accept.

To my surprise, Don had taught me more in my first year than I ever learned at Columbia or Preston & Cartwright. I owed it to him now to be direct.

'Here's the situation.' I leaned forward. 'Jack was booked. No eyewitnesses, but they can place him near the scene around that time. And one of the shooting victims was Malcolm Neeley.' Don continued to shake his head as I outlined what I knew about the evidence against Jack, not yet mentioning the GSR results.

'I can see why they made an arrest. It's all coincidental, but then his cockamamie mystery woman story completes a circle for the investigation.'

'What do you mean by a circle?'

'They respond to a shooting with three victims. One of them turns out to be a high-profile guy. Every theory is up for grabs, but it's only natural for the police to think, Hey, maybe this has something to do with the fact that Malcolm Neeley's son killed all those people. So then when they're watching surveillance video and just happen to spot a man carrying a basket who resembles one of the victims' family members — arguably the most well known of them all — of course that becomes the center of their attention. But, still, maybe there's some innocent explanation. Maybe it's not Jack Harris on the video after all.

Or if it was, maybe someone was with Jack at the waterfront and can vouch for his innocence. But instead of clearing matters up, Jack offers some cuckoo story about an anonymous woman, and that story further highlights the fact that Jack was near the scene of the shooting, alone, carrying a picnic basket before the shooting, and leaving the waterfront without it afterward. Prior to that story, this was one theory of an infinite number.'

I completed the thought for him. 'But Jack's statement closed the circle for them, bringing them right back to their initial suspicion.'

'Correct.' Don sat back in the brown leather booth and took another drink of his beer. 'Of course, we defense attorneys prefer to call this 'tunnel vision.' The police placed Jack near the scene, and then interpreted everything else through that lens. Happens all the time. But if Jack's lucky — or better yet, innocent — they won't find enough to convince a prosecutor to charge him.'

'They're going forward. When we talked on the phone today, I was pretty sure I was close to getting Jack released. But then the GSR tests came back.'

Don set down his mug roughly enough that some foam spilled onto the table. 'See? This is why you don't vouch for people. Residue on his hands?'

I shook my head. 'His shirt. It's still not good. But we've gotten past GSR evidence before.'

'Yeah, by arguing that the police were sloppy or worse. Pretty hard to believe they'd screw up

94

a case this important, this fast, against a rich white guy beloved by the entire city. Not how the system works, Olivia, and jurors know it.'

'Right. But I'm mapping out another theory.' I walked him through the possibility that someone had either orchestrated the encounter at the pier from the very beginning, or been monitoring Jack's e-mail looking for an opportunity to set him up for Neeley's murder. 'And we know that Malcolm Neeley has *many* more enemies than just Jack. For every person who feels sorry for him that he lost his son, another four blame him for the Penn Station massacre. So if someone was looking to kill Neeley, and somehow knew about Jack's plans to meet this woman today — '

'And then somehow managed to spritz him with GSR?'

'It's possible. I haven't had a chance to talk to him about possible sources of contamination. Or maybe the NYPD did something weird with the testing. Or whoever framed him passed him on the waterfront and — '

'Or he did it. The lawsuit against Neeley got dismissed. Jack could have snapped. It happens to people. You know that.'

Yes, I definitely did know that, especially when it came to Jack. But Jack's version of 'snapping' would never involve harming another person, and I didn't know how to get Don to see that.

'You think my judgment is clouded, but trust me, Don: I know him at his core.' The entire reason Jack and I didn't work out was because I knew him better than he knew himself. He thought I could make him happy for the rest of his life. I knew him well enough to realize that I'd keep disappointing him. 'He didn't do this. If nothing else, I can't see him taking the risk of leaving his daughter without a parent.'

Don held my gaze for several seconds before speaking. 'Look, I know I'm a hundred and seventy years old, and Melissa would probably accuse me of man-splaining for what I'm about to say. But the only thing I know about this man Jack is from when you've mentioned him on occasion over the years, never when you're at your best.' That was Don's polite way of saying that when I'm drunk, I have a way of blubbering about my past fuck-ups, with Jack traditionally at the top of the list. 'I gather he's some kind of great love, and you think you botched it. I know you feel guilty, but God knows you're not the first young person to have been a jerk to a boyfriend. You don't owe him anything.'

'But I do, Don. You have no idea just how much I owe him.'

★ ★ ★

Charlotte may never have liked me, but, ironically, I may never have met Jack if it weren't for her. She was the one who kept bringing her childhood pal around the dorm, making a point to linger near our open door when Melissa was home. Her desire to play matchmaker between Jack and Melissa was almost as obvious as the fact that neither of them was interested, or that Charlotte might have had her own reasons for liking Melissa.

Under orders from my parents to make my private education 'worth it,' I focused almost exclusively on my studies until the occasional episode of binge drinking left me open to the idea of companionship for the night. Jack's name was never among the potential candidates. He was cute and funny and shared my passion for *Twin Peaks* and the Smiths, but he was a little too clean-cut for my taste. Then one night when he walked me home from an especially boozy off-campus kegger, we ended up talking for two hours. I spent the night with him, sneaking out of his dorm the next morning in time for breakfast. I thought we both knew it was a one-time hookup, and, sure enough, his sweet, safe drop-ins continued, with no mention of our stumble into bed.

When I was packing up my dorm room for a summer internship in D.C., he dropped by with a mix tape, and my first day back on campus, he found me at the new dorm, asking what I thought. I lied and said it was great, but he could tell I had never even listened to it.

He came back the next day with a twelve-pack, and a few beers in, made Melissa and me promise to dance with him to the first song on a duplicate tape; it was 'Debaser' by the Pixies. We wound up in our own three-person mosh pit, slam-dancing around the room. When the song was over, he popped the tape from the stereo and declared that our 'musical education' would continue later.

As the school year continued, we fell into a pattern. Impromptu dance parties — sometimes in a group, sometimes one-on-one, but always one song at a time with that same stupid mix tape. They were great songs, too: 'Magic Carpet Ride' by Steppenwolf, 'Candy' by Cameo, 'Blue Monday' by New Order, 'Hot Pants' by James Brown, 'This Is Not a Love Song' by PIL, 'Mirror in the Bathroom' by the English Beat, 'Rock Your Baby' by . . . I don't know. A Sting song I would have hated if I hadn't found a certain amount of comfort in being held in my room for a slow dance.

That tape — and the ones that followed — had been a good move, the only one I ever saw Jack play. I started to look forward to his knocks on the door. Every pop-in was an adventure. I felt special and sought after. Over time, the music became less important than spending time afterward with someone who made me happy.

But I was still young and naive enough to believe that boys and girls — with their first taste of independence and college hormones raging — could be 'mostly friends.' Though I resisted labeling our relationship, that's how I chose to think of us: a friendship with benefits — nonmonogamous, at least on my part.

Then I heard rumors that Shannon Riley was showing up at Jack's dorm regularly after dinner, asking for help with her bio assignments, even though Jack sucked at science. After spotting Jack and Shannon traipsing around campus for the umpteenth time in weeks, I told Melissa that I was looking forward to Jack's 'little dalliance' running its course.

'Why do you care?' Melissa had asked.

'Because it's Shannon Riley. She's loud and obnoxious and always has to be the center of attention.'

'No. I mean, Olivia, why do you *care?*'

'Because Jack's going to end up hurt when Shannon decides to move on to someone else.'

Melissa had shaken her head and laughed. 'No, you care because you miss him. I've seen you perk up when there's a knock at the door. How you come home after seeing him like you're all high on something. It may have happened slowly, but I've seen how he's changed you. You love that boy.'

'Jack and I are good where we are.'

'You might be, but obviously he's not. You've been getting all the comfort of a boyfriend, without any of the responsibility. He comes when you call him, holds your hair when you're sick, and puts up with your shit. Meanwhile, you get to go on with your business. Honestly, I don't blame him for moving on. And you better watch out, because if I had to guess, once Shannon has him locked down, he'll stay that way for a long, long time. If you want him, you better take him.'

That night, I couldn't sleep. Melissa was right: I hadn't been looking for a relationship, and I may have been telling myself that Jack wasn't my type, but I didn't want to lose him. The next morning, I purposely bumped into him leaving the dining hall. On the way home, I got around to congratulating him on his new relationship.

'Oh, I guess you heard about that. Does it bother you?'

'Yeah, I don't like it. I miss seeing you.' He stopped walking and turned me to face him. I couldn't believe how happy he looked.

'Oh my God, you're actually turning pink. Olivia Randall is *blushing*. Why are you embarrassed?'

I have no idea how bungled my answer was, but I remember telling him about Valentine's Day when I was nine years old. My mother asked me why I didn't want to give a special card to one of the boys at school. I told her that feelings were *gross*. It was a conversation Jack and I would revisit many times in the years that would follow. What I had been trying to say to him was that, even at nine, I understood that feelings were what kept my mother with my father: *Olivia, don't you see that I love him?* Feelings led you to make bad decisions.

'And what bad decisions are your feelings for me leading you to?' Jack and I were standing in the center of the South Lawn, and I felt like everyone was looking at us.

I shrugged.

'But you're saying you don't want me to see Shannon anymore?'

'Right.'

There was an obvious next question, but he never posed it. Instead, he just kissed me. And when he took me back to his room, everything felt different. It was tender and loving, sober and unrushed. It felt absolutely pure.

For the next two weeks, we were as inseparable as two college students living with roommates could be. And then Jack showed up banging on my door when his father died. We may have fallen in love slowly, but being at his side in the days that followed pushed our relationship into hyperspeed. I met his aunt, uncle, and brother. I helped him and Owen select the urn. I missed a week of classes to get the house ready for the estate sale. I was there when the lawyer broke the news about the finances. I was the one who met with the realtor because they couldn't bring themselves to set a price.

Charlotte, Jack, and Owen may have grown up as the three musketeers, but the four of us became adults together. Even though Owen wasn't on campus, he saw us at least twice a week. By the beginning of junior year, Jack had poured his grief into writing, publishing a story about his father in the university's literary magazine. With the encouragement of two professors who believed he had 'real talent,' he was even working on a book proposal to submit to agents. Owen found a second family in the police department. Charlotte started to use her family's wealth for something more than frolicking. Even I had found a silver lining in the aftermath of Jack's father's death: apparently what my mother always called my 'cyborg' responses to emotion might make me a good lawyer. I liked feeling needed.

For the first three years, Jack and I were happy. Being with him felt easy and safe, the way I always thought relationships should be but never were. But I should have known that a fear of losing someone was not the best reason to kick off a serious relationship. Because five years later, it was me — not Shannon Riley — who broke Jack's heart.

★ ★ ★

We got engaged graduation weekend, but didn't set a date. We didn't need to. We agreed that I needed to finish law school first. For the time being, our change in status was only a word and a ring.

While I jumped into my studies, Jack fiddled around with stories that he never seemed to finish. He went to classes to get his teacher's certification. He even started to check out hotel ballrooms for our wedding.

I was thriving in law school without him — or at least that's how I felt — and all Jack could say was that he couldn't wait for law school to be over so we could get married and 'start our future.' His future felt like my end. What was supposed to be a word and a ring had changed everything. What used to be easy seemed boring. What had felt safe was now confining.

My sins started small. I stopped picking up after myself, put less effort into my appearance around the apartment, snapped at him on occasion. He seemed happy as ever, so I spent more time without him and was bossier when we were together. Before I knew it, it was like I was playing a game to see just how much Jack could take.

And, still, he waited for my every free second so we could spend it together.

The first time I cheated on Jack — truly emotionally cheated — was with the editor in chief of the law review, Gregg Bennett. I was a 2-L, he was a 3-L. It was during the big cattle call for law review submissions. We students got lobbied by professors from all over the country, trying to get their articles placed in a top-ten journal. It was like March madness for law geeks. Who would land Judge Posner's latest master-piece, sure to be cited by other scholars for years to come? Could we bluff Cass Sunstein into accepting by telling him we needed a decision in two days? Heady stuff for a twenty-four-year-old.

And no one got off on it more than Gregg.

I didn't set out to fall in love, at least that's what I would tell myself later. But I knew I enjoyed being around Gregg. Later, I'd realize that what I was really enjoying was not being with Jack.

And even though I knew that I was enjoying being around Gregg more than I should, I let it happen. Despite his engagement to a congress-man's daughter — or maybe because of it — we flirted to the point of making other staffers feel like they were crashing a date.

And sex with Gregg was everything it wasn't with Jack. There was nothing slow or sensitive about it. It was a hand under my skirt in the library. Getting pulled onto a table in the law review office when another staffer stepped into the hall. His hand over my mouth as he whispered to me from behind, 'You like this, don't you?'

But then after, I'd go home to that stifling

apartment at night. And hear Jack's daily 'miss you's' as I left in the morning with my backpack.

For months, I lied to everyone about everything: where I was going, why I ran late, who was on the phone. I lied so much that I didn't even realize that I was also lying to myself. It wasn't just my stupid little rules — never in our apartment, never with both of them on the same day, always taking off the necklace Jack had given me for my twenty-first birthday before being with Gregg, my promise to myself to break the news to Jack once classes were over. Those were the selfish things I would tell myself every time I lied to be with Gregg Bennett. The biggest lie I told myself was that my infidelity was somehow special.

It's not my fault I fell in love. The power of this particular lie is overwhelming. A few years ago, a newly married couple went so far as to highlight in their Sunday Styles wedding announcement the fact that they had met each other while still married to former spouses. The public lambasted the bride for whining about her feelings of being 'punished' for having failed to meet the love of her life earlier, but that's exactly how I felt while I was with Gregg. To avoid feeling like a horrible person, I elevated Gregg (he's my soul mate), derided Jack (I deserve someone who is more of a challenge), and turned myself into the victim (I met Jack too young, he's suffocating me). When I hear other people talk about how infidelity 'just happens,' I know how lame it sounds, but at the time, those words became my mantra.

104

I worked later and left home earlier. I gushed when Gregg landed a clerkship with the chief judge of the D.C. Circuit, which would make him a front-runner to land a Supreme Court clerkship.

And then when Gregg graduated, he dumped me. No, he didn't dump me. He just moved — to D.C., to his fiancée, to his real life. He had used me. And the thing is, I felt more *right* with him for months than I ever had with the man who loved me. One night the following summer, Jack saw me staring into space and asked if I missed Gregg. 'I mean, you guys were pretty good friends, is all.'

He knew. All that time, he had known. He just didn't want me to *know* that he knew. And now that it was over, Jack was still there. He even wanted to comfort me. I felt so guilty that I started to hate him for it.

I would look at him and imagine the scene play out in my head.

We need to talk.

I love you, but I'm not in love with you.

You deserve someone better.

I'd picture myself giving back the ring — his mother's engagement ring — and I'd hear him telling me, once again, that we belonged together, that he knew me better than anyone else, that we were perfect. I could almost hear my mother: *I knew it was too good to be true.*

No, I just couldn't do it. I couldn't marry him, but I couldn't be the one to say I wouldn't marry him. He would have to be the one to see that we were all wrong. I wasn't a good person, and I certainly wasn't good enough for someone as accepting and forgiving as Jack.

★ ★ ★

I was recounting bits and pieces of this history when Don interrupted. 'The case, Olivia. What does this have to do with Jack's arrest?'

'You need to know about the last time I saw Jack before today.'

Law school graduation was a month away. We had a wedding date eleven weeks out. The plan was to keep it simple — vows in Central Park with a reception to follow at a French restaurant on the Upper West Side called La Mirabelle. The honeymoon was more of a splurge, a week at Lake Como. My signing bonus at the firm would barely cover it all.

You know how gamblers keep adding good money after bad, unable to walk away with a loss? That was me. Nearly a year had passed since my thing with Gregg ended, but I found more where that came from. Hours spent at the library. Late nights at bars. Unexplained phone calls. I was never home, and when I was, I would bark at Jack constantly, all in the hope that he would be the one to walk away. I needed him to walk away. What did I need to do to make him leave me?

In my head, there was no alternative. Not after all this time. I became reckless to the point of inevitability.

Until that night, I had never brought another man into our apartment. But I crossed that final line in the biggest possible way. I knew Jack would be home any minute; his writers' workshop could have only so much to say about the dozen pages he'd managed since the last meeting. It was only his phone call from the corner that kept us from being caught in flagrante. *Need anything from Duane Reade? If I don't get some Q-tips, my ears might start to sprout.*

My companion made it to the staircase before Jack stepped off the elevator, but I hadn't even bothered to make the bed. If I had, I might have noticed the Seiko watch, unmistakably male, resting next to my pillow. I'm the one who'd slipped it from the wrist it belonged to.

Not even Jack could pretend to miss the clues. It was a cruel thing to do, I knew, but like Nick Lowe said, sometimes you've got to be cruel to be kind. Jack would finally see that he was too good for me.

I never stopped to think about what would happen next.

★ ★ ★

I had gotten to Jack's slamming the apartment door behind him when Don interrupted. 'I've got two ex-wives for a reason: I stepped out on the first for the second, and then the second stepped out on me for the friend of a cousin who she met at our Christmas party. I figure it was karma biting me in the butt, so we're even. You're not the first person to fuck up. You were young, and you weren't even married. Get over it.'

'Are you listening to me, Don? It's not just that I cheated. I intentionally set it up so Jack found the evidence.'

What I had done was actually far worse, but I couldn't bring myself to tell Don that part. I just couldn't. I had never told anyone except Melissa.

'Not to be a lawyer about this, but does your mens rea really matter? As far as the harm to Jack, it's all the same.'

'That's my point, Don. *The harm*. Jack was absolutely devastated. It wasn't until I saw his face that I realized that he really did think of us as forever. We were so young, and I was still in law school; being engaged just seemed like a word. But that's how he thought of us — his entire future. He ran out of the apartment like it was filled with poisonous gas. I waited for him to come home, but he didn't. I finally broke down and called Charlotte at three in the morning, and she told me that he had shown up at her apartment not much earlier than that, drunk and upset, with no explanation — or at least that's what she told me at the time. She was smart enough to figure out we'd had some kind of fight, but didn't press me for details. I was just relieved to know that he was okay and with a friend. I figured we'd talk the next day. I'd apologize. I'd say all the stupid things that people who cheat say when they get caught. And we'd do all the things that I had been dreading — figuring out who would keep the lease, dividing up the furniture and the CDs, all that messiness.'

'Been there, done that.'

Ramon, Melissa's headwaiter, came by to check on us for orders, but I indicated that we weren't ready. 'But that's not what happened. I spent the whole morning staring at the television, wondering when Jack would be ready to talk to me. And then the phone finally rang that night, and it was Charlotte. There'd been a car accident. Jack's older brother, Owen, had died.'

I could tell from Don's expression that Melissa had never told him any of this. Of course she hadn't. Melissa was better than a vault. 'I remember reading that in one of the profiles about Jack — his brother was a cop, right?'

'Yeah, NYPD, but he lived on Long Island, not far from where they grew up. Charlotte said they thought Owen fell asleep at the wheel on the LIE. Ran head-on into an embankment. He was DOA.'

'It's a sad story, Olivia, but I'm still not sure why we're talking about it.'

'Because I'm the reason Owen was in his car in the middle of the night, too exhausted to stay awake until he got home. He was in his car because when Jack found out I was cheating, he called his brother for support. Owen was in the city and met Jack at a bar. They stayed out because of me, because of what I did to Jack.'

'You can't put that on yourself, Olivia.'

'There wasn't even a funeral because there was no family left. For months, I had no idea where Jack even was.' How many times had I drunk myself to sleep, wondering where Jack had gone? 'Eventually Charlotte came to the

109

apartment to pack up Jack's things. She told me that he'd had a psychotic break. Major depression, catatonic, wouldn't move or speak or eat or drink kind of depression. He was in a psych ward.'

'Fine, I get it. He took some tough breaks. But again, not your fault.'

'Of course it is, Don. Simple cause and effect. A to B to C. Jack at our apartment. Jack calls Owen. Owen spends hours consoling him at a bar. Owen drives home and dies. Jack goes crazy.'

'And then Jack gets better, marries a woman, becomes a successful writer, has a child. He got a fresh start. You don't owe him anything.'

According to profiles I had read, Molly had supported Jack so he could stop teaching and finish his first novel. Jack was so grateful that he dedicated the book to her and began volunteering to teach writing workshops to troubled kids as a tribute to his teacher wife. She was the supportive woman I had never been, and, with her, he thrived.

But he didn't have Molly anymore. She was killed, and now Jack was accused of murdering the man he felt was responsible.

'Don, you've been telling me to get to the point. The point is, I'm taking this case. I'm a partner, not your employee. I choose my own clients — '

I heard a woman two tables over call out, 'Hey, turn that up! It's about the shooting.'

I watched as Melissa pointed the remote control at the television hanging in the corner above the bar. On the screen, the police commissioner took his place at the lectern while the mayor stood sternly at his side.

He delivered the kind of comforting preamble the public had come to expect after a mass shooting. There had been so many, I wondered if police departments shared notes.

'We know members of the public have been eager for details, and we have asked for your patience as teams of officers and detectives have been working on multiple fronts, both to notify and to support victims' families and also investigate the case and identify and capture the person or persons responsible. Tonight, I can report that, as we already stated earlier today, shots were fired shortly after seven AM. Three people were shot. Two of the victims were deceased by the time emergency vehicles arrived at the scene, and, unfortunately, just an hour ago, the third victim also succumbed to injuries. We can also release the names of the three victims: Tracy Frankel, age twenty; Clifton Hunter, age forty-one; and Malcolm Neeley, age fifty-seven.'

The commissioner cleared his throat as murmurs spread across the briefing room at the mention of Neeley's name. 'I can also report that we have arrested a suspect in connection with the fatal shootings. His name is Jackson Harris, he is forty-four years old, and is a resident of Manhattan. All evidence is that the perpetrator acted alone, and there is no remaining threat to the people of New York City.'

As the commissioner turned from the lectern,

the press erupted into a barrage of questions. 'Is that Jack Harris the writer?' 'Was this retaliation for the Penn Station shooting?'

Around us in the restaurant, fellow diners expressed similar thoughts. I heard a woman behind me say, 'Holy shit, guess that kid's father should have paid up on the lawsuit.' Within moments, the consensus at the table next to us was that Jack 'must have snapped.' There was that word again. There were *tsk* sounds, as if to say, 'That poor guy, what a tragedy.'

A three-minute statement by the police commissioner, and already, I could feel its impact: the entire city was sure that Jack did it.

I downed the rest of my martini. 'Are you going to say you told me so?'

Don's wince was barely perceptible, but I could tell I had managed to hurt his feelings. 'Of course not. You're not my underling anymore, and you're an excellent defense lawyer. You've earned the right to make your own decisions.'

'Don, I'll understand if you don't want any part of it.'

'That's not how we operate. Not ever.'

That wasn't technically true. Three years ago, Don used a claim of battered woman syndrome to defend a woman accused of child neglect. I refused to help him, and never explained why.

'We'd be even if you want to back out on this one —'

'No. I won't hear of it. If you're taking the case, we're taking the case. We stand by each other. We're partners.'

No one had ever said that to me before.

Ryan texted me a little after ten o'clock. *Where are you? Nightcap?*

Bed, I typed.

Not like you.

My thumb hovered over the screen. Who was Ryan to tell me what was like me?

Another message popped up. *Are you alone?*

Great, the guy who was next to me in this bed eleven hours ago assumed it was more likely that I was here with someone else than hitting the sack at a reasonable hour on a weeknight.

Did your wife get home okay? Bitchy, but I hit Send anyway.

Flight canceled. Not back until tomorrow.

At thirty-five, Ryan was eight years my junior. In what felt like a previous life, I was his supervising lawyer at Preston & Cartwright when he was a mere summer associate. I never gave him another thought once he flew the nest with all the other baby birds. Then two years ago, I got a voice mail. He wasn't making partner and had no idea what he was supposed to do. 'You probably don't even remember me, but I just need someone to tell me it's going to be okay.'

We met for drinks, a lot of them. It wasn't until the next morning, as he twirled my hair like it was the most fascinating substance he had ever encountered, that he told me about his wife, Anne. He said he'd known when he married her that they were making a mistake. 'I just couldn't bring myself to hurt her. She did nothing wrong. And then we had Brandon. And now I've done this. I've hurt all of us.'

I left him alone in my bed while he cried.

Six months later, a perky blond woman in a headband and cardigan sweater walked into Lissa's, sat next to me at the bar, and introduced herself as Anne. I had been keeping Ryan at a distance for weeks. I assumed she was there to confront me, but I was wrong. 'You don't know me, but trust that I would never say this unless I absolutely meant it: Ryan needs you right now. You make him feel better. I can't take him lying in bed all day. When he's back on his feet, things will be different.'

Now Ryan was back on his feet as a solo practitioner, closing real estate deals and writing wills, but things weren't so different. He and Anne had 'an understanding.' He didn't do anything to embarrass or endanger her. She visited her mother a little more frequently and understood when he had to work late.

My phone buzzed on the bed next to me with a new message. *Can I come over?*

Jack's bail hearing was tomorrow afternoon, and Don was helping, even though I knew he thought it was a terrible idea.

Go to sleep, Ryan. I turned off the light and closed my eyes.

9

I waited outside Jack's apartment building for Buckley, fanning myself with my folded copy of the *New York Post*. This morning's front page featured Jack's booking photo. He looked strung out. Above his photograph: FROM VICTIM TO VIGILANTE.

A black SUV pulled to the curb, and an attractive blond woman in a driver's uniform stepped from the front seat. She had to be close to six feet tall. Before she could reach the rear passenger door, Buckley hopped out, pulling her cross-slung messenger's bag over her head in one swift move.

She greeted me with 'Hey,' and began walking to the building entrance as she waved to the driver. 'Thanks, Barbie. I'll text you when we're done.'

I planted myself in her path. 'Your father's bail hearing is this afternoon. Not a good time to leave his lawyer waiting on the sidewalk for twenty minutes.'

Her pale eyes stared up at me. They were nearly translucent. I saw a tear begin to pool, and she used the back of her hand to wipe it away. 'I'm sorry. I normally take the subway, and didn't realize the car would take so much longer.'

'You know things aren't exactly normal.' Last night, I had told Buckley to shut down all her

115

social media accounts: Instagram, Twitter, Facebook, Vine, ask.fm. But it was only a matter of time before some enterprising online sleuth dug up an old yearbook photograph and went viral with it. She wouldn't be riding the subway for a while.

Her shoulders started to shake, and before I realized what was happening, she was on the verge of sobbing. 'I'm sorry. Honestly, of all people, I'm never late. I'm always on time. Always.'

I looked around to see if anyone was staring. I was annoyed about a teenager leaving me on the street, but I hadn't expected her to have a meltdown. I should have realized that eventually the stress of her father's arrest would get to her. I rested a hand on her shoulder, but then pulled it back. I wasn't family. 'Hey, it's no big deal.'

Her gaze dropped to the concrete beneath her feet. 'I see you looking at me like Dad raised a brat. Or maybe you think I'm spoiled or weird or something because of what happened to Mom. But I swear, I thought I'd be here early. Did I make it so you won't be ready for the bail hearing?'

I shook my head. 'No, of course not.'

'I should have at least apologized, I'm sorry. My dad says it's generational. He blames it on text messaging — the way people just wait until they're supposed to be somewhere and then type OMW, like it's all okay. He likes to respond, *Oh my word?* to mess with people.' She looked up with a shy smile. I could tell there was something else she wanted to say.

116

'What?'

'Nothing.'

She looked like she had a secret. 'No, I can tell it's something.'

'Just, the way you called me out. Charlotte said you could be — '

'Do I even want to know?'

She started to laugh. 'You know, passive-aggressive. But that was straight-up aggressive-aggressive. It was actually pretty cool.'

Crisis averted.

★ ★ ★

The doorman on duty greeted Buckley with a wide smile. 'How's my little rock and roller this morning?'

'Out all night with the band, Nick. You know how it is.'

When the building's elevator dinged, a middle-aged couple stepped out. They kept their gaze locked straight ahead as we exchanged places. Just as the doors were about to close, I heard one of them say to the other, 'That poor girl.'

I immediately changed the subject. 'So . . . Barbie?'

'I know. Ridiculous, right? Charlotte says feminism gives her the same right to keep eye candy around as any rich guy. I doubt Betty Friedan would agree. I heard what those douche bags said, by the way, but thanks for trying.'

'It's just two people,' I said.

'No it's not. I've been 'that poor girl' for a

long time now. I'm used to it.'

★ ★ ★

'You've *got* to be kidding me.' Buckley stood motionless in the middle of her living room.

I had warned Buckley to prepare herself to see the only home she had ever known redecorated by a search warrant.

I stepped over a tipped stack of books on the floor. 'Believe it or not, this is restrained. I had a client your age who was suspected of selling prescription Tylenol at school, and the police tore open the upholstery on the family sofa.'

'That's bullshit. Sorry. I cuss. Dad says I must get it from Charlotte, because he's like Flanders on *The Simpsons*. Totally G rated — he actually says 'pluck a duck' when he's mad. Mom was, too. They started a swear jar when I was nine, but gave up when it was clear I didn't have that many quarters.'

Jack and his fake cuss words. *Cheese and crackers. Monkey flunker*. And, yes, *Pluck a duck*. I thought it was endearing when we first got together. By the end, I wanted to stab him in the hand every time he'd dismiss my 'cursing' as an 'uncreative vocabulary.' I think being able to use one little four-letter word to convey a hundred different thoughts is pretty fucking creative.

Buckley used the toe of her hot pink Doc Marten boot to gather the shards of a vase that had fallen from the media table onto the hardwood floor. 'So where should I start?'

We were here so Buckley could give me a better idea of what police had seized from the apartment yesterday. They were required by law to file an inventory, but they also had a skill for vagueness. Bloody clothing matching the precise description of the clothes worn by an assailant became 'three items of apparel.' A drug dealer's journal, filled with customer names, numbers, and quantities, was a 'spiral notebook.'

'Just try to picture the way things were and fill in what's missing.' Chances are, I wouldn't get trial discovery for months. The GSR on Jack's shirt was bad enough. I didn't want any other bombshells at this afternoon's bail hearing.

'The only problem will be Dad's room. Like, I don't really go in there other than to put laundry on the bed.'

'What about his office?'

'We sort of share it.'

'Good, start there. If it's okay with you, I'll look around, too. Sometimes it also helps to know what police have left behind.'

'You said that like you expect to find something, like Dad's guilty.'

'That's not what I meant, Buckley.' Or hadn't it been? I'd been thinking about cases where police tore apart a living room only to miss the loose floorboard beneath the sofa. Or, more commonly, they overlooked evidence if they didn't realize its significance. So, yes, I must have entertained the possibility that there might be something to find. I told myself this was a good sign; I was letting my instincts as an attorney take over, even though I was dealing with Jack.

But that's not what I told Buckley. 'If I can compare what they took to what they left behind, it can help me figure out what the police might be thinking.'

I wasn't sure the lie made any sense, but she seemed placated and began reshelving books, one by one.

★   ★   ★

I left Buckley to her work in the living room and gave myself a tour of the apartment. Prewar. Three bedrooms. Probably close to eighteen hundred square feet. A palace by Greenwich Village standards. A console table in the hallway was identical to one I'd bought for our offices two years earlier.

When I reached Jack's bedroom, I closed the door behind me. The half of the bed closer to the door was more rumpled than the other. That was Jack's side when we were together.

Dresser drawers had been left open. I picked up some socks and T-shirts from the floor and tossed them on the bed. I moved on to the closet. Clothes on hangers, shoes neatly arranged on the floor.

Scanning the two-page property receipt again, I confirmed that no apparel had been taken.

The shelf above the hanging rod was too high to reach, but it looked like items had been pulled off and then shoved back into place haphazardly. I recognized a white square in the middle as a bread machine, the kind of storage that made sense only in New York City.

120

In the far corner of the room, a nightstand drawer was partially open. Half tubes of night creams and lip balms, an old bottle of Chanel No. 5 layered in dust. How do you throw out your dead wife's perfume? On the other side of the bed, Jack's nightstand was close to empty — reading glasses, loose change.

I found a small step stool in the back corner of the closet, stepped up cautiously, and began pulling down bins and boxes, placing them on the bed. I even checked inside the bread machine. Empty.

A canvas bin contained nothing but baseball hats and T-shirts — a crab shack on the Cape, 'NOLA Proud,' Mickey Mouse. Most of them were tiny, probably Buckley's souvenirs from before she talked like a sailor. I felt like I was watching Jack's life on fast-forward.

I reached the final container: a faded Cole Hahn shoe box. Two different kinds of packing tape hung loosely from the box top. Inside were old birthday cards, ticket stubs, a cardboard coaster from a Parisian café. I pulled out all the photographs mixed into the pile and began flipping through them. I paused three pictures in. Owen and Jack, windblown hair and tanned faces, their matching green eyes smiling at the camera, sun-sparkled ocean water in the background. It was Montauk. Junior year for me and Jack. First year on the job for Owen. Things were still good then, before the engagement. We were happy, and everything seemed easy. That, to me, was the first time I felt anything I was willing to call love. They surfed. I picked up lobster rolls to go from Cyril's Fish House. And I took this picture.

Owen and Jack, mirror images of each other. So alike in appearance, but reversed on closer inspection. A stranger looking at the picture would probably think Owen and I were the couple. He was edgier and more confident than his brother. As far as I could tell, Jack was like his mother, and Owen was like their father. From what I heard, their father was the patriarch who loved his wife and sons, but had a temper, often set off by having to make ends meet as a caretaker for a family as wealthy as Charlotte's. Their mother learned to tiptoe around her husband's pride. Like his mom, Jack learned not to make waves. He liked music and books. He was quiet. Owen, though not an angry person like their father, was determined not to be a doormat. Never a pushover, he stood enough ground for both himself and his little brother. He'd been a high school jock and student body president, and seemed perfectly comfortable wielding the authority that came with a badge.

Or maybe that was all a bunch of psychobabble because I had a tendency to trace people's baggage to their parents.

I forced myself to place the picture at the bottom of the stack and continued shuffling. The images were all old, pre-Buckley, pre-Molly. The newer Harris family photos were somewhere else. These were separate. These were of Charlotte, Owen, Jack's parents.

I tucked the photos back into the box and removed a white mailing envelope that had been torn open. More photos. I had seen only the first three — all of Jack and me — when the bedroom door opened.

I dropped the envelope into the box, but Buckley had already seen. 'Are those the infamous 'perfect Olivia' pictures? That was the worst fight my parents ever had.'

'People keep memories from college, Buckley. You'll see.'

'That's what Dad said. But it's not just that he had pictures. He had them all together, like a collection. And they were hidden, or at least that's how Mom saw it. I could hear everything. I think it's the only time I remember them really screaming. Mom found them when she was reorganizing the closets, then taped them all over the bedroom so Dad would find them when he got home. Kind of weird to know your mom can be cray-cray jealous, huh? '*You want a shrine to your perfect Olivia?*' Buckley imitated an outraged voice. ''*Here you go!*' Anyway, he promised to get rid of them. Guess he didn't. He must've hidden them better when Mom was alive.'

'I'm not sure what to say.'

'That woman he saw on the pier — he said she had long dark hair. He was talking about you. That's why he liked her.'

I looked down at my lap. 'Don't make too much of something so superficial. Everyone has old memories. It was the book that made him remember your mother. He told me how much they loved each other.'

She shrugged. 'So does it look like they took

123

anything from here?'

And just like that, we were back to work. I was beginning to envy teenage resilience. 'Your dad's nightstand's nearly empty. Is that normal?'

'I wouldn't know,' she said a little too quickly. 'I don't look in there.'

I didn't know much about kids, but I used to be one. 'Can you take a quick look and tell me what you think?'

She touched the drawer pull nervously and took a peek. 'That seems like what Dad would have,' she said. Yep, she was a normal, snooping kid after all. 'The main stuff they took from the office were his computer and his files.'

I looked at the police inventory: '17 file folders containing paper.'

'Can you tell which files?' I asked Buckley.

'About the lawsuit.'

As one of the plaintiffs suing Malcolm Neeley, Jack would likely receive all important filings — the complaint, motions, the dismissal order. Some clients barely paid attention to their own cases. Others kept meticulous copies of every single document. If Jack was thorough and kept each document in a different file folder, I suppose it could add up to seventeen files.

Buckley added, 'It would have been easier for them to just take the entire file cabinet.'

'You mean one file drawer, right?'

'No, like the whole cabinet. It was all his research on Neeley — newspaper articles, that kind of stuff.'

'What newspaper articles?'

'You know, about Neeley. Our research and

everything — all that stuff we saw on his laptop. The police left the cabinet, but took everything in it.'

I walked to Jack's office and saw a four-drawer metal file cabinet.

'That was *full?*' I asked.

'Oh yeah, crammed. I was telling him to buy another one, but there's no room.'

I had wandered into fuzzy ethical territory by leaving Jack's laptop at Charlotte's apartment the previous night. Now it turned out there was no point. The evidence of Jack's Web-surfing habits was already with the police. Jack — retro Jack, lover of traditional paper — had printed it out, organized it, and kept it in its own metal file cabinet. I knew precisely how it would look to the police.

'I need to get some stuff from my room to take back to Charlotte's,' Buckley said. 'You can go without me.'

'That's okay. I'll wait.' Charlotte had texted me ten minutes earlier, asking me to make sure that Buckley got back in the car with Barbie.

While Buckley packed a roller bag she pulled from her closet, I sat on the bed and looked around her room. The decor was tasteful compared to stereotypes about teenage girls. Not a pop of pink in sight. In a line above her headboard hung three framed album covers: Kanye West's *My Beautiful Dark Twisted Fantasy*, *Abbey Road*, and an album by someone called Childish Gambino. Among the books on her shelves were a few trophies and ribbons, soccer and softball from what I could gather. A giant poster of One Direction was the only surprise.

She must have seen me looking at it. 'My friend Jake gave it to me for my birthday. We say we hate them so much we sort of love them. So how long should I be packing for?'

I had no idea how to answer that question. For all I knew, she would never live here again. 'The bail hearing's this afternoon, but these kinds of things can take a few days to process. You can always come back if you need to.'

She pulled three more shirts from hangers, balled them together, and shoved them into the bag.

'Speaking of the bail hearing,' I said, 'we haven't talked about whether you should go, but — '

'I'm going. Of course I'm going.'

'Good.' The fact that Jack was a single parent was my best shot, however slim, at getting him released pending trial. And Buckley's presence was a reminder that Jack was also in some ways a victim of Malcolm Neeley. 'Wear something conservative but don't overdo it. Judges can tell when you're faking it.'

She held up a short-sleeved, navy blue cotton wrap dress. 'Is this okay? I wore it to my dad's editor's wedding.'

'Perfect. With flats, please. And Doc Martens don't count.'

'Channel my inner One Direction fan — got it. Any chance you can help me convince Charlotte to let me stay here by myself? I'd be perfectly fine. Doorman out front. Takeout every night. I promise not to stick my fingers in any electrical outlets.'

'I don't think Charlotte will go for that.'

'I know. And I already tried to convince her to stay here with me. She patted me on the head and said I was *adorable*. She thinks of anything south of Forty-Second Street as the ghetto.'

I was surprised when she sat next to me on the bed. 'So how reliable is that gunshot powder test you told me about?'

'You mean gunshot residues? Well, basically, when a gun is fired, gunpowder gets ignited by hot gas, which causes it to explode. The expanding gas is what forces the bullet out. That process emits what people call gunshot residues.'

'And the police found that on Dad's shirt?'

I nodded. 'But here's the thing. Have you ever used baby powder, and you keep finding it everywhere for days because it sticks to everything?' She was nodding. 'So gunshot residues are even finer than talcum powder. You can't even see them. They get transferred from surface to surface. So if a police officer fired a gun in training and then leaned against a wall in the police station — '

'And then my father leaned against the same wall — '

'Exactly.' I realized I should have explained all of that when I first told her about the GSR results.

'You're a really good lawyer, right?'

'Reportedly.'

'Like, you get people off even when they're guilty.'

127

'That's probably happened more than a few times.'

'Just do your best to help my dad, okay?'

'Of course, Buckley. I promise.'

I heard her sniffle as she gave me a quick hug before zipping her suitcase.

10

I barely recognized the bald, barrel-chested man in a custom-cut suit who welcomed me into his office at 1 Police Plaza. When I had known him twenty years earlier, Lieutenant Ross Connor was merely *Officer* Ross Connor, skinny, with big ears that stuck out from the backward baseball cap he always wore off duty. That skinny officer's partner had been Jack's brother, NYPD Officer Owen Harris.

When I'd asked Einer to track Ross down for me, I had expected him to be retired by now, living in Idaho or Florida or one of those other places where police officers moved to grow old. But with a Google search, Einer had told me that Ross was still with the NYPD, chosen to head the department's Intelligence Bureau. I couldn't think of a better person to support Jack's request for bail.

'It's not any defense lawyer I'd let into my office without an appointment. But when I heard your name, curiosity got the best of me. Now I'm just pissed. How do you look just the same when I look like an old guy who ate my younger self?'

We hugged awkwardly. 'From that suit and these digs, I'd say you're doing pretty well. I was shocked that you were still on the job. You've got to be coming up on your twenty-two years.' Ross had been the younger of the Ross-Owen pairing.

'A little bit past it. But if I stay on two more years, my pension will be based on what I'm earning here in the Intelligence Bureau. So, yeah, I'm doing all right. But you're not here to catch up on my retirement plans. This has to be about Jack.'

'His bail hearing's today. He could use your support.'

'I don't know what Jack told you, but I don't know the man anymore.'

'But you used to, so you know Jack couldn't have done this. Just having you there on his side would make a difference.'

'No offense, but I'm not in the habit of being used by defense lawyers.'

'Come on, Ross. You and Owen were like brothers.'

He shook his head. 'So that makes Jack my brother by extension? I don't think so.'

I knew that coming here would be a long shot; I was asking a member of law enforcement to stand up for a murder defendant. But I did not expect Ross to be this hostile. 'Where's this coming from?'

He paused before answering. 'At one time, you were right: I thought that bond between me and Owen sort of tied me to Jack, too. But when Owen died, Jack totally blew me off. I got that he was hurting, but so was I. Owen was about as close to a brother to me as I was ever going to get, and I needed Jack after he died. Like, *really* needed him. I had to extend my leave from the job. I was drinking too much. My wife was starting to lose her patience. And Jack couldn't even return my calls.'

I started to explain that Jack had gone through a difficult time, but Ross interrupted. 'The psych ward. I know. Not because he told me, mind you, but I found out all the same. Tried to visit him. Tried calling when he got out. He eventually got back to me, but was always too busy to get together — book deadlines, child care, some excuse. I only saw him twice over the next few years, and it felt forced both times. I finally stopped trying.'

'So he shut down, and shut everyone out. He probably just didn't want to be reminded about Owen's accident. But there's no way he did this. We have to help him.'

'Did he tell you I was the one who delivered the news about Penn Station?'

The fact took me by surprise. I shook my head.

'When you lose a partner — even if it's not on the job — it sticks with you in the department. Your fellow officers are respectful about it, you know? So when Molly was killed, one of the officers on the scene happened to be at the 44th with me and Owen back in the day and made the connection when she saw the name of Molly's next of kin. I got the call, asking whether I wanted to be the one to notify Jack. I hadn't seen him for fifteen years, but I thought he'd still rather hear it from me than a stranger, you know? When I showed up at his place, the whole situation was kind of weird — him pretending like he meant to call me, or that we'd only been sort of out of touch. He was just, I don't know

131

how to explain it — like I'd never known him. I was really starting to regret saying I'd deliver the news. Then when I did — I just pulled off the bandage, you know? *There's been a shooting, Molly was there, she's gone. Done.*'

'That can't have been easy.'

'No, it wasn't, but you learn how to do it when you're a cop. And I've seen a lot of responses over the years. Jack's was ice cold. I actually wondered for a second if he'd heard me.'

I pictured Jack repeating *I can't believe this is happening* over and over again after his father died. Who knew what coping skills he had learned during his hospitalization. 'Maybe that flat response was his way of handling the shock.'

'It wasn't just that one moment,' Ross said. 'I left my card and told him I was there for him if I could help in terms of providing information about the case or facilitating anything else with the department. It's not like I expected him to be my best buddy, but, man, he never even thanked me for coming. I called his house a few months later to see if he wanted to go out for beers. Left a message on his answering machine. But, just like before, he never called back.'

'He was grieving, Ross. Molly was the love of his life.' Or at least one of them, I thought. 'I understand that your feelings were hurt because he didn't return your attempts at friendship, but that doesn't make him a murderer. Can you really picture Jack executing someone in cold blood?'

His expression was almost a wince, followed by silence. When he finally spoke, his voice sounded distant.

132

'Look, there's one more thing. I wasn't going to mention it, but you're obviously not getting my point. When I broke the news, he dropped the book bag he was carrying — he hadn't even set it down yet. A couple of condoms came falling out.'

'Awkward.'

'Very, but it didn't need to be a big deal. If anything, it kind of provided some dark comedy. But Jack got all freaked out, stuffing them back into the bag, offering all kinds of reasons. I was like — hey, man, it's nothing. And then basically he couldn't get me out of the apartment fast enough.'

'You know Jack. He was probably just embarrassed.'

'That's what I told myself, too. But not long after that, he started giving interviews to the press. You remember?'

I did. Molly was the heroic teacher who tried to stop the shooting; the loving and devoted mother; the wife who worked full-time and supported him while he wrote his first book. Jack was the adoring husband — a successful novelist who volunteered his time teaching writing workshops for the kinds of students his wife was so devoted to.

The Jack and Molly love story.

Ross continued. 'So one of the guys at the house — who doesn't know my connection to Jack, obviously — says something snarky about Jack milking the press, to sell books or something.'

I made a disgusted sound, but Ross cut me off.

'Hey, you got to understand — we see it all the time. Some thug gets hit by a stray bullet in a drive-by. What picture do the papers run? Not the one where he's in colors, posing with a forty-ouncer and a Glock while throwing signs. No, they run the high school graduation shot, all shiny blue robes and proud smile.'

'Or maybe,' I said, 'all the gangsta bravado was a pose, and the real kid was the one in that graduation picture.'

'Spoken like a true defense lawyer,' Ross said.

'So what's your point about Jack's interviews?'

'I still had a bad taste in my mouth about how he treated me like a total stranger — after Owen died, when he got out of the hospital, and again after Molly. And I got to admit, I started thinking: Maybe this is all a little too good to be true. It's like to your face, he's all honest and thoughtful, with that 'just be happy' demeanor. It wouldn't be the first time that a family produced two sons — one a Boy Scout, the other a loose cannon. Despite all appearances, Jack's got a dark side there.'

'Jack, dark? You're forgetting how many years I spent with him.'

'And you're forgetting how long I've been a cop. I saw a glimpse that day in his apartment when his bag spilled open. I'd seen something he didn't want me to see. I had peeked behind the light, cheerful facade. And my guess is that his dark side is what landed him in a psych ward after Owen died. And now all these years later, with a man like Malcolm Neeley, who knows where the darkness took him?'

134

I should have realized it was a waste of time to come here. Ross was on the verge of retiring. There was no way he was going to rock the NYPD boat, even if that meant convincing himself that someone as decent as Jack might be guilty.

★ ★ ★

When I walked into Veselka, I spotted Gary Hannigan at the front counter. Even though I was five minutes early, he was already a third of his way through a Reuben sandwich. He wiped his right hand with a wad of tiny paper napkins from a stainless steel holder before a quick shake. 'I recognize you from around the courthouse.'

'Same.' Hannigan was the lawyer for the families of the victims killed at Penn Station. By reputation, he was an old school liberal who saw his multimillion-dollar lawsuits as a way to rage against the machine. When I'd called him on my way to police headquarters, he told me that he could give me thirty minutes over lunch — 'your treat, of course.'

'You know that's not a real Reuben, don't you?' Veselka used dry sausage instead of corned beef or even pastrami.

'Don't care. It's delicious.' He moved his briefcase from the seat next to him, and waved at the waitress while I got settled in. I ordered a plate of pierogies without looking at a menu.

'A fellow regular,' Hannigan remarked. I didn't tell him that my visits to this twenty-four-hour-a-day Ukrainian diner were typically at three in the morning. 'Not too many lawyers left who are still fearless about going to trial. I respect that about your partner, Don Ellison. Looks like he gave you the bug. Wouldn't in a million years have guessed that Jack Harris would ever need a criminal defense lawyer, though. The man's clean, you know. Squeaky, like Soft Scrub. And not in that creepy way, the way some people are so nice you think they gotta have some bodies in the basement. He's a good guy.'

There was that word 'clean' again. What Hannigan saw as authentic, Ross had seen as a cover. 'It was actually Buckley who called,' I said. 'I went to college with Jack.'

He smiled at the mention of Jack's daughter. 'That kid's tongue could cut through diamonds, but she's all talk. I hope to God the police are wrong about this.'

I noticed that Hannigan didn't say he was *sure* the police were wrong. I explained how Jack had first become a suspect, with a primary focus on motive, before asking his impression about just how much anger Jack shouldered against Neeley.

'It's probably bad karma to speak ill of the dead, but Malcolm Neeley really was one mean son of a bitch.' Hannigan licked a glob of Russian dressing from his thumb. 'He was a shitty husband, a cruel and distant father, and had absolutely no empathy for other human beings.'

'Tell me that he kicked puppies on weekends, and I think I'd like to call you to the stand.'

'Look, I'm in a tricky situation here — with

136

those pesky professional ethics and whatnot. We've got a mutual client in Jack, so I want to help. But I've got clients from a dozen other families, and if I had to guess, you'll get around to arguing that any one of them might've pulled the trigger instead of your guy. To be honest, I can't see any of them doing something like this, but at the same time, I guess I could see any one of them doing it, if that makes any sense. I mean, it's an off-the-rails, jacked-up loony thing to do, but people do crazy stuff over far less disgusting people.'

'Disgusting? Sounds like you took this case personally.' The waitress was back with a plate of steaming-hot pierogies.

'I take all my cases personally, Ms. Randall. Let me tell you one story about Malcolm Neeley — just one of many — that kind of sums it up. You know how Todd had an older brother in college when the shooting happened?'

I nodded, remembering a few articles obliquely juxtaposing the idea of two such different boys emerging from the same household.

'His name's Max. Works for the dad's hedge fund. Decent enough kid from what I can tell, given the bloodline. Anyway, this is the kind of person Malcolm Neeley was. When I had him in the deposition, he became unleashed and strayed from the talking points his lawyer had fed him. He starts yelling about what a dedicated father he was — how hard he worked to make sure his boys had *character*, as he called it. When the older son Max was sixteen years old, he wrecked

137

dad's Jaguar up in Connecticut and didn't take it seriously enough for Poppa — you know, *insurance will fix it, what's the big deal.* So Neeley throws Max in his car, drives him to their housekeeper's, and bangs on the door. She's probably wondering — what the hell, you know? And in struts Neeley with young Max in tow. He says, *See how other people live? Can you imagine living here? Clean up your act unless you want to end up like this.* That was the story he *chose* to tell about himself, mind you, as one of his better moments.'

'But you weren't suing him for being a bad person. You blamed him for his son's decision to commit mass murder.'

'I don't know you, Ms. Randall, but do you have good parents? Not, like, perfect-1950s-television-style parents, but basically decent parents who loved you and supported you?'

'Yes. Very much.'

The lie came effortlessly. Hannigan didn't need to know that Hank Randall was an alcoholic who told me that I was 'selfish' for going away to a 'fancy New York college' instead of staying in Oregon because my mother 'needed me.' Or that the reason my mother needed me was that, when my father wasn't hitting her, she made herself feel better by reminding me at every opportunity that I wasn't nearly as good as I thought I was.

'Good for you, because there is no greater misery than to know that your own parents are disappointed in you. Malcolm Neeley was the kind of person who was disappointed in every

138

single person who wasn't named Malcolm Neeley, but he was especially unforgiving of the people he was supposed to love and protect. Okay, one more story, this one from Max's ex-girlfriend. She came to me on her own, all too happy about the prospect of nailing the elder Neeley to the wall. I got the impression that Neeley basically controlled Max and it took its toll on their relationship. Anyway, the day Todd and Max's mom overdosed — Vicodin and vodka, if you're wondering — was two days after Max went back to Princeton for his senior year. Afterward, whenever Todd would act especially withdrawn — staring into space, rocking back and forth, totally out to lunch — their father would yell at Todd: *This is why your mother didn't want to be alone in the house with you.* It was a two-for-one mind fuck: Todd got the message that Mom killed herself because he was a head case, and Max got the message that it wouldn't have happened if he hadn't been away at school. I asked Neeley about it in his deposition. His response? He was trying to get Todd to *learn from his mistakes and act more like a man.*'

'Okay, kicking puppies is starting to sound like a step up for this guy.' I asked Hannigan if I could get a copy of the deposition transcript, and he tapped a quick note into his phone.

'I still think we had a good lawsuit,' he said. 'Neeley was the one who purchased the guns his son used at Penn Station. And he knew his son was seriously disturbed — arguably he even made him that way — and he actively blocked

139

the mental health system from providing much-needed care.'

'So why'd the case get dismissed?' The media had reported the fact of the lawsuit's dismissal, but not the reasoning behind it.

'I looked you up. *Columbia Law Review.* You can probably guess.'

'No proximate cause: Todd was responsible for his own actions. And if that's the case, you're suing Neeley for failing to stop his son, and there's no duty to protect strangers.'

'You nailed it. We tried to argue that he and his son in concert were the cause, because his son couldn't have acted without his father's assistance. The judge didn't buy it.'

I used his summary of the dismissal as a way to circle back to what I really wanted to know. 'And just how angry did Jack seem about that?'

He inspected the last piece of bread crust in his hand, dropped it to his plate, and began pulling fresh napkins from the stainless steel holder. 'People say things they don't mean, Ms. Randall. You're a criminal defense attorney. You know that.'

I pushed my final remaining pierogi away with my fork and braced myself for what was coming next. 'What exactly did Jack say that he didn't mean?'

'He said, 'If there's any justice in this world, Malcolm Neeley will find out exactly what it feels like to have some gun-happy madman ruin his life.''

I closed my eyes. 'Is that a direct quote?'

'Pretty close.'

'Why didn't you just lead with that?'

'Because I wanted you to have some sense of why I didn't read anything into it, and why I still don't. In context, it was an extremely natural emotion to express.'

'And please tell me you were the only one to hear him express it.' Communications between Jack and Hannigan were covered by attorney-client privilege.

'There was one other plaintiff there.'

'Who was it?'

'Nope, can't do that. But Jack will be able to tell you. And then I guess you'll find out sooner or later if the police know about it, but it won't come from me.'

★ ★ ★

'Don't take this the wrong way, Olivia, but you literally smell good enough to devour.'

The words could have been stomach churning if they hadn't come from Don, and if I wasn't acutely aware of the scent of smoked meat that accompanied me into the conference room. 'Gary Hannigan would only make time if it involved a Reuben from Veselka.'

'You're killing me. Any luck with the brother's former partner?'

'No, but I did bring back this.' I revealed the takeout bag I'd been holding behind my back.

'An angel,' he declared. 'A goddamn angel.'

As he dug the supersize sandwich from its Styrofoam container, I perused the documents spread out across the table. 'Any luck?'

'Possibly, at least enough for a few surprises.'

Today's hearing wasn't just about a bail determination. This was a high-profile case. Even worse, it fell into a prescripted narrative — from VICTIM TO VIGILANTE, as the *Post* proclaimed. The odds of getting Jack released were close to zero, but the bail hearing might be our only shot to reframe the conversation before the entire jury pool made up its mind.

'Don't suppose you came up with one clear theory that explains away all their evidence.'

'I'm good but I can't make GSR disappear,' Don said.

Our best hope in the long run would be to argue that Jack had not gone to the precinct with Detective Boyle consensually. If the police arrested him without probable cause, we could suppress any evidence gathered at the station, including the GSR testing. But that motion wouldn't be made for weeks, maybe months. More important, what we needed to do today was to raise real questions about whether the police had arrested an innocent man, not whether they had used the right procedures to catch a guilty one.

'It's not a total lost cause,' Don said, setting down his sandwich. 'We've got enough to make some waves.'

★   ★   ★

Don fed me talking points like a ringside trainer calling jabs and hooks. 'Stay on the theme of tunnel vision. The police admit they homed in

142

on Jack the second they saw him on the video; they had him at the precinct within the hour. Hammer away at that. What have they been doing since? Did they even bother looking at other possible suspects? No. They haven't had time. And then we start lining up all the other possible candidates.'

'The fifty-nine other named Penn Station plaintiffs,' I said, ticking off this first point on my thumb. I had to be careful about how I handled this point. I wanted the other families to support Jack publicly.

Don pushed one of several piles of paper toward me across the conference table. 'And it turns out that the Penn Station lawsuit was only one of many disputes against Neeley, or at least against the Sentry Group. Eight SEC complaints against his hedge fund, some settled confidentially, a couple still pending. And here's a real gift: a lawsuit filed by Red Pin Capital, demanding the return of its $72-million stake in the Sentry Group.'

'Sounds like something for the financial pages.' As a motive for murder, a corporate fight about money wouldn't resonate in the same visceral way as revenge for a wife's death. 'Rich people sue, they don't shoot.'

'Ah, but you're missing the best part. The creator of Red Pin Capital is another little Wall Street asshole named Frederick Gruber. In addition to his Harvard MBA and an oceanfront estate in East Hampton, Mr. Gruber also has a wife, Marnie Gruber. Guess who Malcolm Neeley was sleeping with?'

'How'd you get this so fast?'

'It's all there in black and white,' he said, tapping the table excitedly. 'Look at the complaint. The basis for the lawsuit is that Gruber invested in Sentry by relying on his wife, an experienced and respected financier in her own right. Gruber claims Neeley and his wife hoodwinked him by concealing their affair and overstating Sentry's performance when the fund was overextended and needed a fast cash influx.'

'This is amazing, Don. There's no way the prosecution will know about this, not yet.' This man's involvement in Neeley's murder was a theory that might easily be debunked once investigated. Marnie could have reconciled with her husband by now. Gruber could have an alibi. Seventy-two million dollars might be chump change in that kind of world. But for today's purposes, this was exactly the kind of evidence we needed. We'd catch the prosecution by surprise and show both the judge and the media how much the police still didn't know.

'You're welcome,' Don said, snagging another bite of his lunch. 'You should remember to point out that there are also two other victims, and that the prosecution is simply assuming that Neeley was the target.'

'What do we know about them?' The Jack versus Neeley angle had been so prominent in the press coverage that the other two victims were purely an afterthought. Clifton Hunter was described as an unemployed janitor, and Tracy Frankel as a part-time college student.

'Hunter's forty-one but looked sixty. Multiple

144

arrests and a few convictions, all for low-level stuff: public intoxication, shoplifting, a lot of criminal trespasses. Last known address was three years ago in Hoboken.'

'So he was homeless.' A homeless man wasn't a likely target for murder, but the only point I needed to make was that the police probably hadn't even bothered to check whether he was involved in something rough on the streets.

'That leaves Tracy Frankel,' Don said, 'and she's looking pretty interesting. Her only college experience was one class last semester at CUNY. Looks to me like it may have been for show. A few months before that, she got picked up trying to buy heroin from an undercover officer in Washington Square Park. She got diversion treatment for a first-time offense, and my guess is that enrolling in a college class helped. She dropped out once her case was dismissed.'

'Now how in the world did you find that out?' Education records were notoriously hard to access.

'I have a very grateful former client who works at the college.'

If this were a trial, I'd need admissible evidence. But at a bail hearing, I could argue anything as long as I had a good-faith basis for asserting it. This was good. Either Tracy or Clifton was just as likely to have been targeted as Malcolm Neeley.

'There's one more person we might want to add to the list,' I said. 'Max Neeley.'

'The son?'

'Todd's older brother. He works at Sentry. Just

the quick conversation I had with Hannigan made it sound like there were some major issues there. And if the hedge fund was having money problems — '

Don completed the thought. 'The son might be eager to take over whatever was left of the family fortune.'

'I know, it's a long shot.'

'We've had stranger theories pay off.'

Max Neeley had experienced his mother's suicide, his younger brother's mass murder and subsequent suicide, and now his father's murder. But we would take him and use him however we needed. 'Okay, so we'll dig a little more on Max.'

There was a knock on the door. Einer popped his head in the conference room. 'Hey, not to interrupt, but those plaintiffs are starting to show up. I've got them gathered in the lobby, but you're probably going to want this room, right?'

Don threw his Styrofoam container in the trash and began stacking documents to clear the way for another group of people for us to use as pawns in Jack's defense.

11

I barely recognized Buckley when she met me in front of the courthouse in the navy wrap dress and modest black flats, as promised. Her messy strawberry blond hair was secured in a tidy ponytail at the nape of her neck. At my request, she came unaccompanied. If Charlotte were there, the judge would start asking her questions about whether she was willing and able to continue caring for Buckley while Jack was incarcerated pending trial, and nothing good could come of that — not only because her answers to both would be yes, but because she was Charlotte, meaning she'd undoubtedly piss the judge off.

When we got to Judge William Amador's courtroom, Don was waiting on a bench in the hallway outside. 'Well done rallying the troops.'

'Thanks.' It had been my idea to gather a group of Jack's fellow plaintiffs at our firm as potential supporters. After our meeting, Don had escorted the willing participants to the court-house, while I stayed behind until the last minute, preparing for argument.

'Where's Dad?' Buckley asked as we walked into the courtroom, her wide eyes scanning the crowd.

'They'll bring him in when his case is called.' I was doing my own survey. I recognized at least three reporters and nearly a dozen of the Penn

Station plaintiffs. Don was right: it was a good turnout. 'We're not the only matter on the docket.'

After three other short hearings, the arraignment ADA, whom I recognized as Amy Chandler — probably six years in the office — called the matter, and an officer walked Jack into the courtroom in handcuffs and an orange jumpsuit. His eyes were downcast, and he walked with an arched back, almost shuffling. I had warned Buckley that her father would likely look bedraggled — I had actually used the word 'bedraggled' — but she grabbed my hand and squeezed it as Don and I stood.

'Your dad's stronger than you know,' I whispered, even though I'd never known Jack to be strong. She released her grip, but I gave it one last squeeze before leaving to take my place at counsel table.

Jack took the seat between Don and me. 'Are you okay?' I asked. He just shrugged.

Before there was time for further discussion, the state was asking that Jack be held without bail, as expected. I was glad to see Chandler handling the arguments. On the one hand, the fact that Scott Temple hadn't bothered to appear personally meant the state believed that a no-bail hold was guaranteed. But Temple was better than Chandler. I had a greater chance of reframing the issues with her on the other side of the aisle.

'This was an especially heinous and dangerous crime,' Chandler droned in a high-pitched monotone. There was a reason that Chandler

148

was assigned to arraignments instead of jury trials. 'The defendant not only premeditated the shooting of one victim, Malcolm Neeley, age fifty-seven, in cold blood, but also was willing to shoot two other people at random: Clifton Hunter, age forty-one, and Tracy Frankel, age twenty.'

I heard Jack suck in his breath at the mention of the final victim. He turned to look at Buckley, who was staring straight ahead. Tracy Frankel was only a few years older than Jack's own daughter. Don leaned over and told Jack not to show any reaction, but Jack was obviously shaken.

'Not only was the crime in this case especially cruel and calculating, Judge, but the People have a very strong case against the defendant. We have video of the defendant near the crime scene just before the shooting. The defendant had a long-standing vendetta against victim Malcolm Neeley — '

I half-rose in my seat — 'Objection to the word 'vendetta,' Your Honor.'

Judge Amador waved me back down. 'There's no jury here, Ms. Randall. But, she's correct, Ms. Chandler: Enough with the heinous and the calculating vendetta stuff. Facts pertaining to release, please.'

I'd made the objection only for the sake of the considerable number of reporters in the courtroom. I did not want to leave the impression that we were accepting the prevailing narrative about the reasons for this shooting.

'My point,' Chandler said, clearing her throat,

'was pertaining to *motive*.' She went on to describe the fact that Jack was a named plaintiff in a wrongful death suit against Malcolm Neeley that had been dismissed less than a month ago. Of course, she did not mention the basis for the lawsuit, which would have reminded Judge Amador that Jack had been a sympathetic figure until yesterday. 'We also have evidence showing the defendant's obsession — '

I objected again. 'Facts, please, ADA Chandler,' the judge snapped.

'The police seized an entire file cabinet of materials from the defendant's house, all pertaining to victim Neeley. It would be a strong coincidence indeed that the defendant just happened to be feet from Mr. Neeley's execution — I mean, fatal shooting. Physical evidence also links the defendant to the crime.' At this point, she was obviously reading from file notes, learning the facts for the first time herself. 'He was seen in close proximity to the shooting carrying a picnic basket — a basket that he was holding when he left his apartment, but no longer possessed when he returned home, according to footage from the elevator in his building. It is the People's theory that this basket was used to conceal the murder weapon. Most important, the shirt the defendant was wearing just shortly after the murder tested positive for gunshot residue.'

Next to me, Jack began quietly protesting in my ear. 'What? That's got to be wrong.' He was looking over his shoulder again. It had been a mistake to bring his daughter. He was worried more about what Buckley thought than his own freedom.

I wrote, LATER, on my legal pad, while Chandler continued. 'In short, this is a murder case involving multiple victims — first-degree murder — and a very strong case. The People request detention without bail.'

Chandler's cut-and-dry approach was exactly what I'd been hoping for. Now it was my turn.

'Your Honor, I objected to Ms. Chandler's rhetoric for a reason. She is trying to get you to stereotype this case — to make you, and most likely the public, think you already know what this case is about: yet another person with a long-harbored grudge who grabbed a gun to solve the problem. But she glossed over important details. What evidence did she actually present? That my client, Jack Harris, allegedly had a motive? She has told you nothing to suggest that Mr. Neeley was the intended target any more than the other two victims. Even after only one day, our independent investigation reveals that Mr. Hunter was transient and Ms. Frankel was involved in recent illegal drug activity. It's at least as likely that one of them was the intended victim, rather than Malcolm Neeley.'

I heard murmurs in the gallery. The reporters, like the police, had been chasing down the connection between Jack and Neeley, not bothering to check out the other two victims. I continued my argument. 'The ADA emphasizes the lawsuit against one of the three victims, but fails to mention that my client was one of nearly

151

sixty other plaintiffs who sued Malcolm Neeley for failing to supervise his minor son, who killed thirteen people in Penn Station three years ago.' I gestured toward the group of Penn Station families in the courtroom, several of whom either rose or waved. 'If you are interested in hearing from them, Your Honor, one of these plaintiffs, Mr. Jonathan Weilly, will testify that, like my client, he was also within close proximity to the shooting yesterday morning, hitting practice balls at the golf range at Chelsea Piers before work. Another, Ms. Lila Condon, was two blocks east at a yoga studio. I have been asking the district attorney's office for surveillance video from the morning of the shooting to establish that my client was blocks away from the football field at the time of the shooting, but they have failed to turn over any video footage.'

I have been asking was a bit of an exaggeration, given that I had made the request only once, informally of Scott Temple, on the phone last night. But Scott wasn't here to correct the impression.

'Save all that for trial, Ms. Randall, but I get your point. His mere presence at the waterfront does not overwhelm me, nor does this business about the picnic basket. Last time I checked, plenty of people find ways of carrying guns without using elaborate containers to disguise them. But what about the GSR evidence?'

This was where Chandler's choice to go for a barebones presentation of the People's evidence could pay off for Jack. 'Several police officers appeared at Mr. Harris's home, based solely on the fact that he was near the shooting location — just a few blocks from his apartment. I have seen no information about how many of those officers had recently fired their weapons, handled other weapons, or processed suspects who may have handled weapons. They also dragged him down to the precinct, where any number of people and items could have been sources of contamination. As you know, Your Honor, gunshot residue is just a matter of transfer. *If* my client's shirt tested positive for GSR — and I'm simply taking ADA Chandler at her word on that point — that is not proof he fired a gun. His shirt likely came in contact with residues from one of the many police officers who descended on his apartment without probable cause, or while he was in police custody. Importantly, no trace of residue was found on his hands.'

If this were a real trial, the state would be prepared to call each and every officer to exclude as a potential source of transfer. But, for now, I was confident that Chandler would have nothing to rebut my basic point that GSR evidence had its limitations.

'We have also learned,' I continued, 'that Mr. Neeley was involved in far more combative litigation than the case my client shared with his fellow plaintiffs.' I heard more whispers as I launched into the fraud allegations against the Sentry Group based on Neeley's affair with the wife of one of his principal investors. 'And that wasn't the only dispute about money. We are still investigating, but Mr. Neeley also had some contentious financial disagreements with

153

members of his family that we are exploring. In sum, the People have no evidence. Moreover, ADA Chandler did not even discuss the most important factor for your consideration, Your Honor: whether my client is a flight risk. He is absolutely not. He is a widower. He is the sole parent to a sixteen-year-old daughter, Buckley Harris, whose mother was murdered in Penn Station. Neither he nor his daughter has ever lived outside New York. Mr. Harris writes for a living. His only money comes from book royalties, which he can only earn if his publisher knows where he is. He is in no position to go on the lam.'

Chandler sprang from her chair. 'Your Honor, I object to this elitist argument. You mean an award-winning author should be shown favor over a regular workingman?'

'Ms. Chandler can throw around as much hyperbole as she wants, but she's right about only one thing — this was a heinous crime, a triple homicide, committed only yesterday. If the People get a no-bail hold, they'll be under the clock of New York law to seek an indictment. They'll rush the investigation, as they've already done, and as we've seen them do in other high-profile cases.'

'Your Honor,' Chandler said, 'discussion of other cases is highly inappropriate.'

Perhaps, but Judge Amador had to remember that, just last year, the district attorney persuaded him to hold a defendant without bail based on preliminary information. Only after the man was brutally assaulted in jail did

154

prosecutors discover evidence proving his innocence.

'What's inappropriate is taking away a man's liberty based on nothing but inflammatory rhetoric. And if that happens, Your Honor, my client will have to wait and wait and wait for his day in court, while he endures the hardship of custody, while he's separated from his daughter, and while his daughter is forced to live without the only parent she has left.'

I wanted the reporters to remember that Jack was a real person — a widower and a father. 'The sole consideration today is whether there is *some* set of circumstances to assure you my client will appear for trial. We know the charges are as serious as they come, but they can't come in here with no concrete evidence and pull this two-person family apart. My client will do whatever is necessary to assuage any concerns you have: a gag order, turning over his passport, home confinement — '

'Electronic monitoring?' the judge asked.

I answered immediately, while we had momentum. 'Absolutely.'

Chandler was up again. 'Your Honor, this is ridiculous. It's a triple homicide. This is a classic no-bail case.'

'And that's the problem, Ms. Chandler. Someone sent you here thinking your job would be that easy. Do you have any other evidence to show that Mr. Harris is a flight risk, if he's on twenty-four-hour home arrest with monitoring?'

Chandler was flipping through file pages to no avail.

'That's what I thought. Mr. Harris, I have no idea whether you're guilty or not, but the last time I checked, we have a presumption of innocence in this country, and I don't appreciate the way the prosecution tried to ignore that fact today. I am troubled that your lawyers seem to know more about the relevant evidence in this case than the prosecution.'

As the judge read a long list of the release conditions, even I could not believe what I was hearing. 'Bail is set at one million dollars.' Charged with three counts of first-degree murder, Jack was going home.

★　★　★

Don was giving me verbal pats on the back as we stepped into the courthouse elevator. The doors were stopped by a last-minute hand, and a young man stepped forward to hold them open. He looked familiar, but I did not immediately place him.

'Is that how you plan to defend my father's killer?' The spittle that flew from his lips with the 'f' in father landed on my face, and I wiped it with the back of my sleeve. Now I recognized him. Max Neeley's sandy blond hair was swept back the way he'd worn it for his photo on the Sentry Group website. 'You can't just drag a dead man through the mud that way. I'll sue you for slander. Leave the fund out of this. That's his legacy, don't you get it? Sentry Group is all I have left.'

I was pushing the Door Close button, and the

elevator alarm began to sound.

'This isn't the place, son — ' Don placed a gentle hand on one of Max's shoulders, but Max immediately pulled away.

'Don't touch me. And don't you dare call me son. How the hell can you people sleep at night?'

He stepped backward, leaving us alone in silence. Buckley was pressed into the corner. When I asked if she was okay, she nodded, but she was obviously rattled.

As we stepped from the elevator, Don whispered to me, 'So which was it? Protecting his father's legacy or all that money?'

I had walked into the courtroom with so many alternative suspects that I'd had a hard time keeping all the theories straight. Max Neeley had just made himself a lot more interesting.

My call to Gary Hannigan went to voice mail. 'I'm hoping that lunch at Veselka entitles me to one more favor. You mentioned that Max Neeley had an ex-girlfriend who wasn't too fond of her would-be father-in-law. Do you happen to have a name and number for her?'

★   ★   ★

Two days later, I arrived ten minutes before my scheduled appointment, my umbrella still dripping from the summer rain. But when I walked through the front doors, Einer immediately glanced toward a woman sitting in the waiting room. She was early.

I had Googled Amanda Turner after getting her name from Gary Hannigan, so I had seen a

157

few photographs of her — one on her LinkedIn profile, a few on her otherwise private Facebook page, a charity fund-raiser in East Hampton. But in person, she was stunningly beautiful, the kind of pretty you don't expect outside the airbrushed, Photoshopped pages of a magazine. She was wearing jeans, but they were fancy skinny jeans, paired with high-heeled sandals and a bright pink silk blouse. Even though it was humid and sticky outside, her long caramel-colored hair looked freshly blown. I knew from last spring's 'must have' list in the Bloomingdale's catalog that the handbag on her lap had a four-digit price tag.

She must have recognized me, too, because she bounded from her chair when she saw me, thanking me for taking the time to talk with her, even though I had been the one to request the meeting.

According to Gary Hannigan, Amanda had been all too eager to dish the dirt on Malcolm Neeley. My hope was that she had new tales for me as well, perhaps some involving Max's animosity toward his father. I greeted her with my warmest smile. 'I love that bag. Tod's? So cute.'

Amanda had the looks of a kept woman whose only jobs were shopping and staying pretty, but her demeanor reflected the education and experience listed in her LinkedIn profile: an art history degree from Sarah Lawrence and three years' marketing experience with a major cosmetics manufacturer. Across from me at the circular table in the corner of my office, she sat upright in her chair with crossed legs and the kind of open body language taught in public-speaking classes to convey honesty and confidence to an audience.

'I understand you were in a relationship with Max Neeley.'

'On and off, yes. Serious for a couple of years, in fact.'

'Does Max know you're here?'

'Definitely not, and I hope you won't have reason to mention it to him. I'd like to help you, though.'

'I can't imagine why. Max has made it clear he's not very happy with the arguments we raised at the bail hearing.'

'You barely scratched the surface. Malcolm was not a good person. He was cruel and controlling.'

'Unfortunately for my client, the victim-was-an-asshole isn't a defense.'

'Maybe not officially, but when juries like the so-called bad guy more than the victim, they don't put anyone in jail. You see it all the time on the news. From that chick who cut her man's pecker off to the racists who get away with killing kids in hoodies. It's a popularity contest.'

She was right. If Malcolm Neeley had been the only one to die at the waterfront, I'd fillet him so thoroughly that no jury would care about his death. 'Sounds like you should be a lawyer.'

'Not enough money in it anymore, but thank you.' My office suddenly felt small, and I noticed smudges on the glass of the table. 'I know enough to guess that you'll be pointing to alternative suspects. I'm hoping, for Max's sake, you can refrain from highlighting the dispute between the Sentry Group and the Grubers.'

Frederick Gruber was the investor who had sued Neeley's hedge fund, arguing that his wife and Neeley were lovers who duped him into investing. Gruber had looked like a prime alternative suspect, but unfortunately, we'd already debunked the theory. Gruber was worth billions, so his investment in the Sentry Group was a pittance compared to his overall wealth. Perhaps more important was the evidence the Sentry's lawyers had filed to show the Grubers had an open marriage, meaning jealousy wasn't a likely factor.

I saw no reason to share any of this with Amanda. 'Max isn't my client, so his well-being is really not my concern.'

'But that's why I'm offering to tell you whatever you want to know about Malcolm. He had other girlfriends, and I'm sure some of them were married, too. And there was a reason Frederick Gruber wanted to pull his money. Malcolm was overstating the fund's assets. He wasn't as rich as he let on. That's why Max wanted to go out on his own — to start his own hedge fund. But Malcolm was such an asshole, he wouldn't give Max any seed money. And he didn't even pay him what he was worth as a salary. He used his money to control Max.'

'I get the impression this is personal for you.'

She looked out my office window for a few seconds before focusing on me again. 'Max loves me, but we broke up because his father told him

160

he should marry rich. He said he married Max and Todd's mother for love, and look what happened. He told Max his best bet at seed money for his own fund was to find a sugar momma and a generous father-in-law.'

'And here you are, fighting for a man who actually listened to that garbage.'

'Part of why I love Max is that I think I understand him. It's like his whole family was afraid of love. Malcolm was a bad person, but I do believe he was crushed when his wife killed herself. And the news never really reported this, but a broken heart was the reason Todd was so distraught before — you know, Penn Station. He was head over heels for some girl at school who wouldn't give him the time of day. He said she was all wrapped up with some older guy. He'd talk about all these plans to break them up, like awkward, scrawny Todd could save Rapunzel or something. And in Malcolm and Max's eyes, look what that love did to him? It turned him into a madman.'

I found myself looking away. Amanda made it sound like a fear of love was the saddest thing in the world.

'And what about Max?' I asked.

'Now that Malcolm's gone, he has a shot. He can run the Sentry Group better than his father ever did. And he'll get Gruber to drop that lawsuit and keep his money with Max. But if you start dropping Gruber's name in a murder trial, he'll run as far as he can from the Sentry Group. But if things work out for Max at work — '

'He can be with the woman he actually loves.'

161

She smiled. 'And that's why I'll tell you whatever you want to know about Malcolm Neeley. Do we have a deal?'

I made up some wishy-washy ethical reason for why I couldn't make any guarantees, but promised to consider her wishes. 'You know, you've said Malcolm was a bad person and a horrible father, but you haven't mentioned how Max felt about him. Did the two of them get along?'

A worried look crossed her face. 'You asked that because of what happened at Princeton.'

'I was only asking for your opinion.' She could construe my response however she liked.

'He was drunk and pissed off. It got totally blown out of proportion. Max loved his father, even though Malcolm didn't deserve it.'

As soon as she left my office, I hit the Speaker button on my phone. Don answered immediately. 'Turns out Max and his father had serious issues over money. We need to find out how much Max inherits now that his dad's out of the way.' An alarm on my phone reminded me that it was time to go. 'And can you ask Einer to see what he can find out about Max's time at Princeton? It sounds like there was some kind of episode.'

I wouldn't have time to look into it myself. Jack was coming home today.

12

It had taken two days for the police to schedule a time to inspect Jack's apartment to approve the conditions of his release. I wanted to be here to make sure everything went smoothly. Of course, Charlotte insisted on being with Buckley to 'oversee the process' and had hired cleaners to make the apartment pristine after the police search.

While two men installed the boxes that would monitor the signal from Jack's electronic monitoring anklet, Charlotte was monitoring the blogosphere's coverage of Jack's case on her iPad. Since Jack's arrest, she and I had fallen into a comfortable rhythm, but we still had never spoken without Buckley in the room, which limited the scope of our conversations. 'I got to hand it to you, Randall,' she said, 'every paper's got a quote from at least one person wondering if the cops rushed to judgment. The *Daily News* even mentioned the female victim's drug arrest, like maybe she was the intended target or something. They got a little picture and everything.' She turned her tablet screen toward me. 'She looks a bit like a young you, don't you think? More strung out, mind you, but the resemblance is there.'

Buckley popped up from the sofa and grabbed for the iPad. 'I want to see.'

We were both looking at what was apparently

163

a booking photo of Tracy Frankel. Dark hair. Wide-set eyes. Heart-shaped face. But that was as far as the similarities went. 'You're crazy,' I said.

'And you're blind,' Charlotte said, letting Buckley wander back to the sofa with her. 'But you know what? You're also a fucking miracle worker. Malcolm's son is trying to make him sound like a saint, but you totally turned the story around, and now Jack is coming home.'

I wanted to remind her not to get her hopes up, but for Buckley's sake, let the optimism fill the air.

'Ma'am,' one of the deputies said, 'to be clear, you're taking that tablet with you when you leave? We'll have to make sure of that.'

'Yes sirree.'

As a condition of his release, Jack could have no visitors to the apartment other than his daughter and lawyers. The court had also added a no-Internet provision, which was usually reserved for sex offenders or other people whose crimes could be facilitated on the Web, but I had decided to quit while we were ahead. The *New York Observer* had already asked if there was any chance of a black man being released pending trial on murder charges, and I had to admit there was not.

'And the girl here knows the condition applies to her, too, right? No iPhones, Google phones, Samsungs, blueberries, strawberries — nothing.' You could tell it was a joke the officer had used hundreds of times.

Buckley waved the brand-new basic flip phone

164

Charlotte had purchased two hours ago. 'The *girl* here has her vintage 1990 mo-bile ready to go.' She pronounced 'mobile' as if it rhymed with 'mile.'

The fact that Verizon wanted a full-day window three weeks from now to install a landline probably explained why I, like the Harris home, no longer had one.

'Stop staring at a picture of a dead girl,' Charlotte said, snatching her iPad back from Buckley. 'It's not healthy.'

'Sorry. It's just — she's so *young* there. Like, not much older than me.' She seemed shaken by the thought of someone her own age being killed. 'Hey, by the way, how do they even know if we're following all these rules?'

I looked around to make sure the officers were out of earshot. 'Because they're installing a camera at the door and have the right to conduct random inspections, so don't even think about it. You can live without a smart-phone for a while.'

Buckley jumped from the sofa at the sound of the doorbell and ran to the front hall.

Jack was wearing the clothes Einer had dropped off yesterday at the jail for him — khakis and a white polo shirt. They both seemed baggy. The officers had draped a jacket over his handcuffs. Buckley threw her arms around her father. When the officer looked at me and cleared his throat, I tapped her shoulder gently and explained that they needed to get Jack situated before she and her father could have a real reunion.

'You took the freight elevator?' I asked the

165

oldest of the three officers, whom I assumed to be in charge.

'As directed,' he confirmed.

Jack's building had a keyed exit for residents in back, next to the freight elevator, with no cameras. I didn't want footage of him disheveled and in handcuffs getting leaked to the media.

They attached his ankle bracelet and checked the signal while he walked through every inch of the apartment and then out into the hallway to make sure that the monitor alerted before he made it to the elevator or staircase.

During the entire process, Jack moved like a scared cat, hunched, like someone might grab the scruff of his neck at any second and throw him back into a box of other animals. When the officers finally left, they made Charlotte leave with them, and she gave Jack a final kiss on the cheek before departing. When I locked the door behind them, Jack seemed to grow two inches taller.

I looked out the window, watching a woman on the sidewalk wrangle a dozen dogs ranging from a mastiff to a rat terrier, while Buckley and Jack hugged and cried. The emotions that come with pretrial release are complicated. There's the obvious relief of being home. There's the temptation to think that a favorable bail decision bodes well for the future. But there's also intense sadness at the thought that these days may be numbered. The days pending trial can become a kind of prison sentence in and of themselves.

Jack let out a small whoop of relief. 'Is it terrible that all I want to do is take a shower and

166

sit on the sofa with you and eat pizza and watch movies?'

Buckley ran to the coffee table and held up two DVDs that she had already set aside: *Working Girl* and *Ghostbusters*. 'Great minds think alike. I've got your favorites ready to go.'

'Excellent. Just let me talk to Olivia about some legal matters before she goes.'

★   ★   ★

Jack gave me a quick hug once we were alone. I was surprised by how natural it felt. 'I still can't believe it. I thought I'd never get out of there. I don't know what I would have done without you.'

The look in his eyes took me to a night at Arlene's Grocery, back when it was first converted from a bodega-slash-butcher shop into a bar with live music. Jack and I were dancing near the front of the stage. The band was one of our favorites — the Spoiled Puppies. That night, the band broke out into a cover of 'Anything, Anything' by Dramarama.

We danced so hard while the singer promised candy, diamonds, and pills that Jack's arms were slick with sweat when he wrapped them around me as we jumped to the beat. And when the final chorus came, the band added one more repeat of the line, 'Just marry me, marry me, marry meeeee.'

The lights came up, the band fell silent, and Jack dropped to one knee. I couldn't even hear what he had to say over the sound of applause and wolf whistles from the back of the bar — Charlotte, Owen, some college friends who I thought had all come to celebrate our graduation. But I saw the ring. And I saw the look in Jack's eyes — longing, pleading, vulnerable. He needed me so badly, and, in that moment, I believed we'd be one of those couples who brought out the best in each other for the rest of our lives. I made him stronger. He made me softer.

I shook myself out of the memory. Jack needed me now, but for a very specific purpose, and I had done my part so far by getting him home.

I acted like my performance at the bail hearing was no big deal.

Jack settled into his sofa like it was the most comfortable place in the world. 'I had no idea about the gunshot residue until the ADA mentioned it. Is that why they suddenly booked me?'

I nodded.

'The detective wouldn't tell me. That test has to be wrong. Or the police faked the results or something. Do they really do that?'

I wasn't above arguing that police would intentionally doctor the evidence — it was an argument I'd made more than could possibly be true — but did I really believe it? No. And, sure, accidental transfers happened, but it was yet another unlucky coincidence, and too many of those could add up to proof beyond a reasonable doubt. 'Jack, can you think of any way you would have that residue on your shirt? Were you ever around a gun, or someone else who fired a gun?'

168

I was shocked when he answered yes. Long before Molly was killed, Jack already hated guns. I was there the first time he ever held one. My father took us to the range. Jack was terrified, positive that he was going to be the first victim of an accidental shooting in the history of the Roseburg Shooting Club.

'It's research for a book,' he said. 'I've been going to a shooting range, trying to understand the gun culture.'

'A book about Penn Station?'

'Not directly. Fictionalized.'

From what I gathered, Jack's previous novels were all fictionalized versions of his real life. His debut novel — the one he'd written while Molly supported him — was about a young couple whose female half was a pathological liar and a serial cheater. The second was about a man who became a father after struggling with mental health issues. The third was about a male writer whose only meaningful relationships were with his wife, daughter, and lesbian best friend. You get the drift.

'That's great, Jack. If we can explain that GSR, all they have is speculation. Why didn't you tell me this at the bail hearing?'

'I don't know. I guess I was still in shock. And I didn't think that was possible. I mean, it would have been probably a month ago. And I don't even know if I wore that shirt.'

'But you could have.'

'I honestly don't remember. How long can that stuff stick around?'

'Let me worry about the details.' I had him

169

write down the name of the shooting range.

'And your book will make clear that you were doing this research?'

'The one I'm working on now is almost finished. The gun research was for the next one.'

'But do you have notes or something?'

'No, I don't work like that. It lives in my head until I find the story. But I told the guys there that I was a writer and wanted to learn about guns. I'm sure they'll remember.'

He still didn't seem to understand that the prosecution wasn't going to accept everything he said at face value.

As he handed the notepad back to me, he asked if I had gotten in touch with Madeline yet. 'Once she tells the police that she was the one who picked our meeting place and time, that knocks out the coincidence of me being at the field that morning.'

I had sent an e-mail to her from Jack's account after he was arrested, but, with everything that had been going on, I hadn't even logged into Jack's e-mail accounts for the last couple of days. 'I wanted to talk to you about that, Jack. Maybe it's not just a coincidence. Other people had a motive to go after Neeley. If someone else wanted Neeley dead, you were sort of the perfect fall guy.'

'You think Madeline set me up?'

I explained the possibility that someone had read his e-mail exchange with Madeline and then took advantage of knowing exactly where he would be. When Buckley had first raised the possibility the night of Jack's arrest, it had sounded fairly simple. Now that I was explaining the theory aloud, I saw the flaws in the hypothesis. Einer had already contacted Gmail with a privacy release from Jack. The only log-ins to Jack's account since he first told Charlotte about seeing the girl in the grass were from the IP address at Jack's apartment, so there was no way anyone had hacked into his account unless they did it from his own wireless network. Most important, even if someone had known where Jack would be that morning, they'd also have to know that Neeley would be there. The whole setup sounded too complicated.

When I was done thinking aloud, Jack stared at me in silence. It dawned on me that this was the first chance he'd had to focus on me since his arrest. At both the precinct and the bail hearing, he'd been panic-stricken, threatened with imminent incarceration. He was no longer looking at me like his savior. He looked hurt.

'Is this a cross-examination?' he asked.

'What? No. Jack, I'm just going through every possible explanation.'

'Except you pretty much trashed that one all on your own. You don't think I did this, do you?'

'Of course not, but I'm seeing the problems now with the e-mail hack theory. And I have to think about how all this is going to look to the prosecution. They seized an entire file cabinet of material about Malcolm Neeley from your office, Jack. And I saw your Internet history — you did an awful lot of fishing around about Neeley.' I had been very careful not to ask Charlotte and Buckley what had become of Jack's laptop. 'You

171

told the police that you were only going along with the other families in the civil suit, but the DA will make it look like you were obsessed. I mean, the value of Neeley's real estate?'

'It's a civil suit. How much the man's worth is relevant. You know, maybe you should go work for the other side, because you're twisting everything around.'

'No, you are.' I actually said the words, *No, you are*. I forced myself to take a deep breath. I knew my tone had sounded harsh, but this conversation was reminding me of how sensitive he had always been, so quick to feel rejected. When the first literary agent he approached turned down his work, he had torn the rejection letter to shreds and refused to write another word for two months. To Jack, what every writer expected as part of the journey was utter humiliation.

We heard footsteps in the hall. Buckley was standing in the doorway, looking at me suspiciously. 'Is everything okay?'

'It's fine,' Jack said. 'I'll come get you when we're done.'

When we were alone again, I reassured Jack that I wasn't accusing him of anything. 'My job is to get your side of the story, which means asking hard questions.'

'Then just listen, okay?' His voice was calmer now. 'Most of the stuff in the files was just paper sent to all the plaintiffs by our lawyer. As for the rest, the research on Neeley was something we did together — Buckley and me. It's something her therapist suggested. I know, it sounds weird, but I've been encouraged to stop sheltering her from information about the shooting. They tell me to be open about everything — *absolute truth*. Molly's death was hard on Buckley — '

'Obviously — '

'No, more than the obvious. The morning of the shooting, it was snowing. Molly was substituting at a school in Port Washington, so she was reverse-commuting for that. She and Buckley had both been hoping for a snow day, and it didn't happen. But Buckley wouldn't wake up, and then she tried playing sick. It's just a stupid thing kids do in the winter. But Molly spent so much time dragging Buckley out of bed that she missed the early train. She waited twenty minutes to catch the next one. I still remember her joking that she might not get her lessons planned, but at least she had time for oatmeal.' For a second, he was back in that memory, but he quickly pulled himself out of it. 'Anyway, the first thing Buckley said when I told her about the shooting was, *I should have gotten up.*'

I started to say that a child couldn't possibly take the blame for something like that, then remembered Don telling me the same thing about the car accident that killed Owen. Buckley's reaction to my reprimand for running late the morning of the bail hearing made more sense now. All I said was, 'I'm sorry, Jack.'

'So, anyway, that's why we've got all those files. I suppose if it comes to it, you could get Buckley's therapist to explain — '

'Okay, that's good. If it comes to that. I know

173

it feels like I'm hammering you with negative information, but I have to ask you one more thing.' I told him that I had met with his civil lawyer, Gary Hannigan. 'He says you made some remark when you found out about the dismissal? Something like karma needing to catch up with Neeley?'

'Did I? Maybe. Come on — they can't possibly be saying that was some kind of a threat.'

'No one's saying anything yet. But apparently one of the other plaintiffs was there, and that person's not bound by attorney-client privilege. He or she could go to the police, or the prosecution could try to compel the testimony if they think to start questioning your co-plaintiffs.'

'When we found out about the dismissal, I was in Gary's office with Jon Weilly. He was there at the bail hearing.'

Weilly told me he couldn't recall Jack saying anything threatening about Neeley. I hadn't pressed further, and hoped the police wouldn't, either.

'Just please find Madeline,' he said. 'If she backs me up about why I was there at the football field, maybe this can all go away.'

As I promised I would keep trying to find her, I couldn't look him in the eye. There was no chance this would *all go away*.

13

The following afternoon, I was adding three witness names to the file, employees at the West Side Range who would testify that Jack had come to their establishment the previous month to research gun aficionados. During my visit to the range, I'd made sure there was no camera footage of Jack wearing something other than the shirt the police had tested for GSR.

Anything that couldn't be disproved was good enough for reasonable doubt, in my book.

Not to mention, before my trip to the gun range, I'd made yet another phone call to the clerk at the surrogate court, who finally had some news. Max Neeley was about to get the family money without conditions. Only fifty hours after his father's death, Max had a lawyer commence the probate process for Malcolm's will. Malcolm had left two hundred thousand dollars to Princeton University, fifty thousand to the Stinson Academy, and the remainder of his estate to Max.

I had just finished writing my interview notes when Einer knocked on my office door and handed me a sheet of paper. 'I found out what happened at Princeton.'

* * *

The short newspaper article, printed from the

Daily Princetonian website, was dated May 2, 2010:

> The Faculty-Student Committee on Discipline has decided not to discipline a senior whose roommate alleged that the student had made threatening comments that made him feel unsafe. According to the complaint, the offending student was screaming repeatedly one night about plans to kill his father while he was sleeping.
>
> After hearing testimony from both students at an open hearing, the Committee announced that, while there was clear and persuasive evidence that the student's conduct violated University housing regulations, discipline was unwarranted. Among the mitigating factors mentioned in the Committee's decision were the student's intoxicated state, the suicide of the student's mother last fall, and the isolated nature of the incident. The complaining student told the Princetonian that he has no plans to pursue the matter further and only reported the incident 'just in case something happened.'

Though the article didn't use names, Einer had managed to convince someone in the office of student housing to 'unofficially confirm' that the senior in question was Max Neeley. I pictured him standing over his father's bed, a gun in his hand. Had he come up with a better plan in the years that had passed?

My direct line rang. I recognized the number

as the outgoing one for the district attorney's office.

Scott Temple didn't bother stating his name. 'I knew I should have handled the bail hearing myself.'

It was the first time we'd spoken since the surprise ruling by Judge Amador. 'I'd like to take credit, but I think Amador was just rebelling against the shrillness of Amy Chandler's voice. She needs to bring it down an octave.'

'I had a meeting with a domestic violence task force, or I would have been there personally. You're making me regret helping battered women, Olivia. I think that officially makes you a bad person.'

'You're a funny man, Scott Temple. And, frankly, I'm surprised you're not more upset. Did Chandler tell you what the judge said at the end of the hearing? He basically told the press you guys overplayed your hand.'

'So you got one round of the media cycle on your side. You know how fickle the news is. Tomorrow, the wind will blow in the other direction. And don't ever quote me on this, but a guy like Harris on house arrest isn't going to make me lose sleep.'

'You're accusing him of triple murder.'

'I am, but the one person he wanted dead is gone. If he hadn't taken out two others as collateral damage, I might be worried about jury nullification. With Neeley gone, he's not going to hurt anyone pending trial, and the bracelet is a pretty good guarantee he'll show up when the time comes. Nice job, by the way, planting the idea for the gag order.'

I found myself smiling. I literally got in the last word at the bail hearing, right before Judge Amador issued the gag order. Now Temple wasn't allowed to say anything in response.

'You got my discovery demand?'

'That's why I'm calling. What's up with all this surveillance video? The entire waterfront between Battery Park and Chelsea Piers for the day of the shooting and one month prior?'

'Correct.'

One of the great myths about criminal cases is that prosecutors have to give defense attorneys access to all their evidence. Don called it the nonexistent 'law of Cousin Vinnie.' In reality, prosecutors were generally allowed to keep the defense in the dark until we got closer to trial, but had to turn over 'material, exculpatory evidence' — called Brady evidence. They could keep the stuff that hurt us as long as they turned over the big stuff that might help us.

Scott was clearly skeptical. 'An entire month of video is Brady evidence?'

'Are you willing to bet it *isn't* without seeing it?' Evidence that might look unremarkable to a prosecutor could be a gold mine to a defense attorney.

'I'll see what I can do,' he said. 'And by the way, Chandler told me you made it sound like we were stonewalling you on this.'

'You've got your job, I've got mine. Judge Amador won't be happy if I don't get my videos.'

'You're wasting your time.'

Against my better instincts, I tried again to

shoot straight with him. 'I know the GSR evidence looks bad, but it was only on his shirt. If he was smart enough to wash his hands, he could have changed clothes. If we sit down and talk — '

'I only called because I respect you, Olivia. You're backing the wrong horse on this one. The case is tight. I asked around, by the way, after you called me down to the precinct. I talked to Jacqueline Meyers from the drug unit.' I recognized the name from my law school class. 'She told me that you and Harris were engaged.'

I saw no reason to hide the truth. 'In case you're wondering, I already checked whether there was an ethical conflict. If you're even thinking about moving to remove me as counsel — '

'Whoa, stand down, Olivia. I wasn't going there. My whole point was, maybe you should ask yourself why you're so sure this guy's innocent.'

'I know him, Scott. He didn't do this.'

'No, you knew him twenty years ago.' I let the line be silent. 'Just take a fair look at the evidence as it comes in, okay? I have a feeling we'll be talking about a plea at some point.'

When I hung up, I closed my eyes again and ran through everything I knew about the case against Jack. That damn GSR. I had witnesses who could testify that Jack was at the gun range, but it was a full month before the shooting, and I had no proof it was for research instead of target practice. And I had seen Jack's closet; he

179

owned a lot of shirts. At least when I knew him, Jack never re-wore a shirt without washing it.

I had called Scott after Jack's arrest for a reason. I trusted him.

I wiggled my computer's mouse and pulled up the Paperfree website's log-in page. I checked my notes for Madeline's e-mail address: mlh87@paperfree.com

I had Jack's standard password committed to memory: jack<3smollybuckley

The account and/or password information is incorrect.

What had I been expecting?

Still, the fact that I had bothered to check whether Jack's habitual password might open 'Madeline's' e-mail account meant that Scott's words had gotten to me. So had Ross Connor's: *It's like to your face, he's all honest and thoughtful . . . But there's a dark side there.*

Which brought me to the simplest explanation of all: maybe Jack tested positive for GSR because he shot three people hours before his arrest.

The padded envelope waiting on my desk was two inches thick, delivered by messenger. I could see from the label that it was from Gary Hannigan, the civil attorney in the Penn Station lawsuit.

Inside was a spiral-bound copy of the transcript of Hannigan's deposition of Malcolm Neeley. The case had not proceeded far enough for Neeley's lawyers to have deposed the plaintiffs, so I didn't need to worry about a written record of anything Jack may have said.

But I wanted to make sure there was nothing in Neeley's deposition that indicated any kind of personal confrontation with Jack.

Twenty pages into the transcript, I could see that Hannigan believed in the 'what did you eat for breakfast' approach to depositions. Some lawyers — Hannigan clearly included — believed that asking witnesses left-field questions could lead to areas of inquiry the lawyer would otherwise have never pursued. As a criminal litigator, I didn't have the luxury of that kind of meandering. I could only question witnesses in front of the jury, where every answer needed to be one I could predict in advance.

Some topics of the deposition were obvious: Neeley's knowledge of his son's increasingly erratic behavior and social isolation, his failures to follow up on numerous suggestions that the boy get mental health treatment, his decision to buy Todd guns and encourage shooting as a hobby. But Hannigan also asked Neeley open-ended questions about his work, occasionally interrupting to ask how he was able to act as a father to Todd and his brother Max while building a successful hedge fund. Though the questions seemed general and conversational, the strategy was remarkably effective. While Neeley's attorneys had prepared him to give rehearsed and controlled responses to the obvious questions, when he was allowed to go off script and talk about himself as a financier and a father, the results were damning. He was a selfish, crappy parent.

I skimmed over the part Hannigan had

recorded where Neeley talked about showing up to the help's house unannounced, young Max in tow, to teach him to appreciate the wealth he'd been born into. Neeley must have gotten a warning look from his lawyer that made him realize that other people didn't think much of his great parenting story. When he finished telling it, he immediately began listing more traditional efforts he had made to be close to his sons. I flipped pages as Neeley made himself sound like a regular Ward Cleaver: fishing at a camp in Pennsylvania, golf lessons at the country club in Connecticut, coin collecting, teaching the boys how to spiral the pigskin, spring breaks scubadiving in the Caribbean. I stopped and flipped back a page, hoping I hadn't actually seen what I thought I'd just read.

No. No, no, no.

I pulled up Buckley's cell phone number and she answered immediately. 'Olivia, hi. Do you want me to get Dad — '

'No, just a quick question for you. The files that your father had about the civil case — would he have had a copy of Neeley's deposition transcript?'

'Deposition?'

'When the families' lawyer, Gary Hannigan, got to ask Neeley questions under oath.'

'Oh, yeah, sure. The lawyer sent us everything he thought was important. He calls it — what did he say? A *client-focused* approach to lawyering or something. Anyway, we kept it all in the file cabinet.'

Right, the file cabinet filled with documents

that Jack said he never really paid much attention to.

When I hung up, I looked again at the transcript open on my desk.

A. I met Todd every single Wednesday morning at the park by my office to work on passes. Seven AM, like clockwork. No matter how busy I was, we always did it.

Q. You don't think that was a little rigid that you kept your hobbies with Todd on a timed schedule without exception?

A. Routine was good for Todd. And football was the only sport he ever showed any interest in.

Q. Other than shooting, you mean.

A. I mean physical sport. Todd said he wanted to be able to play football in high school, the way I did, and the way his brother did. I knew Todd wasn't good enough or strong enough or fast enough to play on any kind of team, but he liked it. And I liked teaching him. Those were probably the best times we ever had. Even now, I still take my coffee to the football field on Wednesday mornings, just to keep the schedule. To take a few minutes and remember the best of my son. I was a victim that day, too. I know your clients will never accept that, but I lost my boy, just like they lost their families —

Q. Let's talk next about your son's move from

the Dutton School to the Stinson Academy.

It was the fifth school Todd would attend in seven years, but that's not what interested me. I wheeled my office chair over to the smaller desk where my computer lived, and then wiggled the mouse to wake up the screen. I typed 'Sentry Group' into the search window of the browser, hit Enter, and then clicked on the Map function.

Malcolm Neeley was shot at approximately 7:09 in the morning on a Wednesday, at a football field only seven blocks from the building where his hedge fund occupied the nineteenth and twentieth floors. And somewhere among the four file cabinets of material seized by the police from Jack's apartment was a piece of paper that proved Jack knew exactly where the man he blamed for the death of his wife would be at precisely that time.

I slapped a Post-it on the side of the page where I had stopped reading, closed the transcript, and threw it across the room.

★ ★ ★

Jack answered the door wearing a loose Columbia University T-shirt and cargo shorts. His hair was damp, and his face was unshaven. He looked good — relaxed and healthy, a completely different person from the one I'd seen the previous afternoon. He even smelled good. I remembered how much I used to love tucking myself into the crook of his arm at night. I fit there perfectly, and he always seemed to smell like soap and cedar.

'Hey, if I'd known you were coming, I would have changed. And straightened up the apartment.'

His version of messy was clean for me. 'No problem,' I said with a smile. 'I'm the one coming by unannounced.'

'Guess you knew I'd be here,' he said, gesturing toward his ankle monitor. 'Is everything okay? The judge didn't change his mind, did he?'

'No, of course not.' It was all the reassurance I could offer.

Once we were seated in the living room, I asked if Buckley was home. She was at a movie with her friends.

'Are you sure everything's okay? You're kind of freaking me out, Olivia.'

'Sorry, it's all fine. I just need to talk to you about a couple of things you'd probably like to leave in the past. We've never talked about it because — well, we never talked. But I know about the year you spent getting counseling.' I was trying hard to avoid any mention of our breakup, Owen's death, or the 'hospitalization' word. I started to reach a hand toward his knee, but stopped. 'Charlotte finally told me after I called her nonstop for a month.'

'I don't talk about that with anyone, Olivia. It's over. I went through — it was a bad time.'

We went from being engaged to never speaking again, but all he wanted me to know was that it was a *bad time*. 'Well, you need to talk about it with me. The prosecution will

185

probably find out, if they haven't already.'

He was staring at his hands, folded in his lap. 'I don't want to talk about that night. If I'd wanted you to be the person who helped me through all that, I would have come back home.'

He'd been so relieved to see me when I got to the precinct. Now we were having a version of the conversation we might have had if I'd ever bumped into him at a coffee shop over the years. 'But we both know you did more than *not come home*. That's the part I need to know about. Where were you?'

When he looked up, I saw a flash of resentment.

'The hospital, Jack. I need the name.'

He finally gave in, telling me he spent a year at the Silver Oaks Psychiatric Center in Connecticut. I wrote the name down on my notepad. 'I had what they call a psychotic break. It's temporary psychosis — '

'I know what it is.' I had used it as the basis for an insanity claim in an aggravated assault case two years earlier. An acute onset of temporary psychosis could be triggered by extreme stress, like the death of a sibling. Or perhaps, the dismissal of a lawsuit against the man responsible for the murder of a spouse.

A psychotic break could be marked by behavior ranging from severe depression to violent outbursts, or swings between the two. I asked Jack what version his was.

'I was a basket case. I was nearly catatonic for the first month. I wouldn't move or speak or eat or drink.'

'Violence?' I pictured Jack tearing up that agent's rejection letter in the lobby of our apartment building.

He shook his head. 'I basically ceased to exist for a year. Charlotte was the only one who knew where I was. I'm surprised she broke down and told you. Everyone else thought I was at a writer's retreat in Wyoming, trying to get going on that novel I was always fiddling with. When I got out of the hospital, I basically started over again. Meeting Molly helped, and then Buckley changed everything.'

'Jack, I've never had the chance to tell you this, but I'm so sorry about . . . everything. I was being a coward. And being cruel. And that was bad enough. But Owen — ' I let the sentence drop, because I wasn't sure how to finish it.

'I never blamed you, Olivia. God, you were always convincing yourself that you were such a bad person, and that I was a saint. It took me a long time to realize it, but I get it now: I smothered you. I kept trying to make you be someone you weren't ready to be. I made it impossible for you to leave me.'

'It doesn't excuse what I did — '

'You want to know who I blame for Owen's crash? Me. Saint Jack, as you used to say. I'm the one who called Owen after I . . . well, after everything in the apartment.'

We were both being so damn careful about calling it what it was. I had cheated, and I had lied. I took something that was sweet and good and made it ugly. I was the bad one. I always had been. It's okay. Go ahead and hate me.

But instead, Jack was taking the blame. 'I'm the one who kept buying round after round. If it's anyone's fault, it's mine.'

He was falling into the same old pattern: I had done something destructive, and Jack was trying to look past it. This time I did reach for him, but Jack pulled away.

'I really don't like talking about this. You said this was about the hospital, for my case.'

I placed my pen against my notepad perfunctorily. Back to business. 'So you spent a year at the hospital. Who was your doctor?'

'There were a bunch.'

'The one who knew you best.'

'The primary one was Dr. Scheppard. Robin Scheppard.'

'Is he still there?'

'She. I have no idea, but if I had to guess, she wasn't even forty at the time. I don't know if she'd still be at Silver Oaks, but she's probably still in practice at least.'

'Good, that's helpful. I mean, if we need her — I doubt we will. Any continuing treatment?'

'Twice a week therapy at first, then once a week, but only for the next year and a half or so.'

'No psych treatment at all since then?' I asked.

'I went back to therapy for about six months after Molly first died, but it wasn't like before. I didn't shut down or anything like that. I think the coping skills I learned at Silver Oaks probably helped me get through it. Plus I had to take care of Buckley. The only time I've seen a shrink in the past two years was to go with

188

Buckley when her counselor thought a family session was in order. Is the prosecution really allowed to use this against me?'

I told Jack I wouldn't put it past them, but the threat of the government discovering his hospitalization wasn't actually why I was here. If anyone was going to use this evidence in court, it would be me, to try to make out an insanity defense. But for now, I wasn't thinking about the trial. 'I need you to sign these forms so I can access your treatment records.'

'That's not necessary — '

My response was firm. 'It would be malpractice for me not to pursue this. We can't be caught off guard.'

'I don't know if that's a good idea, Olivia. It was so long ago, right after we broke up. I said some things — '

'This isn't about us. I've got a million things to do for your defense other than scour twenty-year-old medical records for your comments about our relationship.'

I handed him my pen, but he didn't take it.

'Jack, it's no big deal. I just need to have this stuff ready to go if the prosecution happens to brings it up.'

He took the pen and signed the most expansive medical release I keep on file. I could get whatever information I wanted. I could find out exactly how sweet, sensitive, fragile Jack responded when things went really bad.

★ ★ ★

I made it to Lissa's in time for the post-lunch, predinner lull. An older couple read the *New York Times* together at a corner table. The only other customers were both regulars, perched at opposite ends of the bar. 'Where's the boss?' I asked.

'Ran downstairs,' one explained. 'I'm minding the store, so feel free to whip up your own drink; I'll add it to your tab.'

I was tempted, but Melissa's martinis were better than mine despite years of attempted replication.

Melissa appeared hugging three bottles of Hendrick's to her chest. Once the bottles were safe on the counter, she leaned over the bar for a quick kiss on the cheek. 'Must be some kind of psychic connection that made me grab all that gin.'

'Just set aside one of those bottles and write my name on it. I'm about to get drunk.'

I gulped down half of a martini in three sips while she topped off the wineglasses of the two regulars. When she came back to me, she was carrying yesterday's edition of the *Daily News*. 'You probably already saw this, but I saved it for you. Maybe I should hire you as my marketing person.'

The *News* front page was the first since the shooting that had used one of Jack's publicity head shots instead of his booking photo. With his green eyes staring straight into the camera and a half smile, he looked impossibly harmless, HARRIS CRIES FOUL, COMES OUT SWINGING. Although I had already skimmed all the local coverage of the case since the bail hearing, I opened to the full article to take another quick read while Melissa summarized. 'The reporter even interviewed a John Jay professor who says the state's in trouble if all they have is the gunshot residue.' Melissa tapped her finger on the third paragraph. 'He says it won't be hard for — quote — a legal team as sophisticated as Ellison and Randall — unquote — to create reasonable doubt. We'll see just how sophisticated you are by the time I'm done with you,' she said, starting to shake another drink for me. 'So does the fact that you're here getting drunk mean that Jack got settled into his apartment okay?'

She knew I'd been nervous about something going wrong with his release at the last minute. 'No problem.' Except he might actually be guilty and I just tricked him into waiving his privacy rights so I could get a look at the side of him he never wanted me to know.

'And his kid?' Melissa asked.

'Buckley? She's fine. I thought she was sort of bratty when I first met her, but she's basically a daddy's girl.'

'That's good. Didn't seem like Jack to raise a brat.'

I thought about Ryan texting me the other night, saying it 'wasn't like me' to go to bed early. It was just a saying, but he didn't know what I was like, and Melissa and I didn't know what Jack was like. Not anymore.

I took a big sip from my second glass and finally got to the subject that had me drinking so eagerly. 'He had pictures of me in his closet, Melissa. In an old box.'

'Well, is it really that surprising? You were engaged. He's not going to throw away all evidence that you ever existed.'

'Then how come he never called?'

'Maybe he just didn't see the point. It was too painful or something. And then he met Molly, so was he going to mess that up by suddenly healing old wounds with his ex-fiancée? He just moved on. It's what people do.'

It's what most people did. Not me, at least not romantically. Short version: I started out okay with Kevin, the Roseburg High quarterback who deflowered me in the back of his pickup my junior year in high school after a year of patient but heavy petting. He cried when I left for college, where I got by on late-night hookups before settling in with Jack the end of sophomore year.

Since Jack, there were a lot of variations on my current situation with Ryan, meaning nothing serious and more than a little dysfunctional. I did manage one other long-term relationship: four years with Jared (in-house counsel at an insurance company), who even floated the idea of marriage, but only on the condition that I set aside what he called my 'all-consuming ambition.' Instead of leaving, I turned our relationship into a professional rivalry. Rather than accept my ring and commence with cake tasting, I hardened my efforts to kick ass at work, no matter the personal consequences, so I could make partner in big law, the way Jared never had.

But then that hadn't worked out, either. I lost the job and eventually Jared.

I only really tried one more time after that. Chuck was a good guy, much kinder than Jared. But I met him when I was just starting to work for Don. The learning curve was excruciating, and Melissa had personally vouched for me with her uncle. I was terrified of losing my job, so I kept choosing Don and our clients over me and Chuck. After too many canceled vacations and no-shows for dinner, Chuck made the mistake of saying he was tired of feeling 'like the woman' in our relationship. In a wine-fueled rage, I decided to show him what emasculation by me actually felt like. I said things that couldn't be taken back.

Maybe other people move on, but I hadn't. I moved more in circles. Sometimes when I thought about the connections from one man to the next, I thought that being alone was predestined.

I've never been able to explain why I did what I did to Jack. The best I can do is to say it was because he was *too* nice — at least for me. Just like Jack said, his kindness made it impossible for me to leave him.

What did my mother say after Jack's first trip to Oregon? 'I don't know how you got someone so nice to fall in love with you.'

★ ★ ★

'But he must not have moved on completely,' I said now to Melissa. 'Not if he had those pictures. Buckley even said something about Molly finding them once and flipping out. And he still kept them.'

'Olivia, I swear, if you of all people start crying, I'm cutting you off. And not to be rude, but ever since he got arrested, we haven't had a single conversation that would pass the Bechdel test.'

We'd learned about the test in college, probably from Charlotte. A woman in a cartoon by Alison Bechdel said she'd only see a movie if it had two women in it who talked to each other about something besides a man. If either Melissa or I droned on too long about a guy, the other would invoke the rule and change the subject.

'I'm not talking about some man. I'm talking about *Jack*. Not even, but about my instincts about Jack.'

'What's going on here? You can't possibly be thinking about you two starting — '

'Oh, of course not. I'm actually wondering if he might have kept the pictures for a different reason. What if — what if I really *broke* him? He was always so fragile.' Jack saw rejection and humiliation in even the smallest slights. But on the night we broke up, the hardship wasn't imagined. Me. Owen's crash. The psych ward. His first book, written three years later, basically about what a bitch I am.

'How many times have we had this conversation? He had a breakdown. His brother died. But everything worked out — '

'You're not hearing me. What if it didn't all work out? What if Jack never got put back

194

together again? I'm rethinking everything I thought I knew about him. Like that mix tape. It seemed sweet at the time, and now it seems a little obsessive. Maybe this side of him was always there, and I pushed him over the edge.'

'Okay, now that's just stupid. Take anything that's sweet for a twenty-year-old guy, and it's like serial killer shit on a forty-year-old. Dungeons and Dragons. Pet lizards. The Doors. Making those stupid Monty Python voices. Collecting . . . anything. Need I go on?'

'Stop it, I'm serious.'

'Come on, that was funny.' I wasn't budging. 'Where's this coming from, Olivia?'

I wanted to answer the question. I wanted to tell her that it was possible for GSR to linger on clothing for a month, but extremely rare. That Jack probably knew Malcolm Neeley would be at the football field that morning. That good people like Ross Connor and Scott Temple were telling me that maybe I didn't know Jack as well as I thought I did.

But I couldn't. I downed the rest of my drink and signaled for another. We stopped talking about Jack after that, but in my head, I continued an internal debate.

On one side were my suspicions. I had been so convinced from the second Buckley called me that Jack had to be innocent. But what grounds did I have for my assumptions? On the other side was my guilt. This was Jack — good, honest, and decent. Who was I to suspect him of something so heinous?

And then there was a voice trying to reconcile

the two sides. Maybe he was guilty. Maybe he was an angry, vengeful psychopath. But if he was, who had made him that way?

Me. I did that.

14

I finally dragged myself home after Melissa insisted on feeding me a plate of beef Stroganoff to help absorb some of the gallon of alcohol in my system.

Despite my promise to Melissa that I would take three aspirin with two glasses of water, I opened a bottle of Cabernet and carried it with an empty wineglass into my bedroom. Once I had changed into a T-shirt, I poured myself a big glass, climbed into bed, and flipped open my laptop.

The *New York Post* website had gone live with an article that would be in tomorrow's pages: an interview with Malcolm Neeley's son Max. 'I was appalled at the way the lawyers for my father's killer tried to blame the victims at the bail hearing. And I'm astonished that a sitting judge fell for it. My father wasn't perfect, and I know a lot of people blame him for the horrifying atrocity that my younger brother committed. But Todd was mentally ill, and my father loved us both as much as he knew how. I will not allow these lawyers to deprive him of his humanity.'

Scott Temple had mentioned that the media winds could change tomorrow. Now I was wondering whether Temple had encouraged Max to go to the press. Temple and I were bound by the court's gag order, but the victims' families were not.

I closed the *Post* article, pulled up Jack's e-mail account, and typed in the log-in information.

jack<3smollybuckley

I was in.

Scrolling through the messages felt like a more intimate version of the late-night drunken cyberstalking I'd engaged in occasionally over the years. Instead of author Q and As and book reviews posted to his Facebook page, I was reading his actual e-mail. About half was the same kind of garbage that filled my in-box: coupon codes for free grocery delivery, a reminder that his gym membership would lapse in two months, a nastygram from an online reservation system for no-showing at Gramercy Park Tavern the previous night. Most of the other half of the messages were from friends and acquaintances in response to the news of his arrest: 'Jack, I doubt you can check e-mail but didn't know what else to do. What is going on?' Lots of vague offers to help: 'Let us know if we can help?' 'Does Buckley need anything?' Only a few of these people had actually bothered to call Charlotte.

I clicked his Sent folder and scrolled down to the message he sent Charlotte after he first spotted the woman in the grass: 'She was carefree, sitting on the grass and reading a book, which reminded me of Molly. And she had long dark hair and was drinking champagne right out of the bottle, which reminded me of — well, you know who, but don't like it when I mention her name.'

When I'd seen this message the first time, I'd been in Charlotte's kitchen. I hadn't had time to parse Jack's words. Obviously he was talking about me, and not for the first time. If I had broken him, wouldn't he hate me? Would he still mention me like this — like he missed me?

I flipped through the messages between him and Madeline. After she responded to Charlotte's missed-moment post on the Room site, Jack sent her a quick note saying he had been mortified when his friend did something so rash, but thought the least he could do was follow up. 'I hope I wasn't staring at you like a weirdo. I really was curious about what you were reading, and why you were doing it in a gown with a picnic basket. As for my attire, the T-shirt was a gift from my sixteen-year-old daughter.'

Madeline's response: She was the maid of honor at her sister's wedding. The post-reception celebration continued in the bridal suite at the Gansevoort. When the newlyweds kicked everyone out, she saw the opportunity to watch the sun rise, snagged a bottle of champagne from their VIP bar and a book from her room, and walked over to the pier. 'P.S. The book was *Eight Days to Die.*'

That was when Jack responded with his schmaltzy e-mail about why the book was one of his favorites.

No response for two days, then Madeline explained that she'd been traveling for work. She said she'd started law school then became a social worker.

So she's like me, I thought, but also a do-gooder like Molly.

I closed the computer, took a few more sips of wine, and scooted down under my covers. As I felt the bed spin beneath me, I thought about all the conflicting thoughts I'd been having about Jack's case.

I couldn't just rely on my gut as if it were a Magic 8 Ball. Did Jack hate Malcolm Neeley? *Outlook good.* Did Jack really see the woman in the grass? *You may rely on it.* Did Jack murder three people in cold blood? *My sources say no.* Did someone find out where Jack would be that morning and set him up? *Better not tell you now.*

No, the only right answer here was the most frustrating of all, *Concentrate and ask again.* And this time I concentrated not on my instincts, but on the facts. Jack hated Malcolm Neeley. He made a threatening comment about Neeley when the lawsuit was dismissed. He had e-mails from this Madeline person, but there'd been no wedding party at the Gansevoort the night before he supposedly noticed her at the pier. There was, however, ironclad proof — both video and Jack's admission — that he was near the site of the shooting at the time bullets were fired, and had a way of knowing where Neeley would be at that very moment. Jack's explanation for being at that location and at that time was borderline fantastical. He left his building with a picnic basket and came back without it

— video again, this time courtesy of his apartment building. His shirt tested positive for gunshot residue just a few hours afterward. And Scott Temple, whom I trusted about as much as I'm willing to trust any prosecutor, told me the case was solid.

Things weren't looking good.

But then I remembered a client I'd had three years earlier who had refused to take what I was pushing as a no-brainer plea deal: two years for involuntary manslaughter in exchange for dismissing a murder charge. I spent half an hour, barely pausing for breath, running through all the evidence against him so he'd see the risks he was facing of a conviction at trial. When I was finished he said, 'But I know something no one else knows: I didn't do it. So please, for one second — just one — imagine that I really am innocent, and then maybe everything you just said will sound different to you.'

We kept digging, and three days later, Einer found a casino security guard who could testify that the state's principal witness was in Atlantic City when he supposedly saw my client shoot a liquor store clerk in the Bronx.

As much as I had been telling myself and anyone who would listen that Jack couldn't have done this, I had spent the day entertaining doubts. So, for one second, I imagined that he really was innocent. Yes, Jack hated Neeley, but he wasn't alone in that sentiment, and the comment he'd made about justice needing to find Neeley was by some standards a remarkably restrained reaction to news that the lawsuit was dismissed. As for Temple's representation that there was more evidence to come, he hadn't actually offered up the goods, and prosecutors engaged in early pretrial bluster all the time. If Jack wore that checkered shirt to a firing range and then hung it in his closet until he pulled it out to meet Madeline, it would explain the GSR. Gunshot residues were unpredictable. They could last days, weeks, even longer. They could even remain present on clothing after a washing.

That left the bizarre explanation for being at the waterfront at the same exact time Neeley was shot.

I sat up and opened my laptop again. I copied Madeline's e-mail address and composed a new message, this one from my law firm account.

To: mlh87@paperfree.com

In the subject box, I wrote, *Very important legal matter*, then realized I may as well have typed 'send me to your spam folder.' *From Olivia Randall, Esq.* That was better. *To the holder of this e-mail address, this e-mail account appeared in the course of investigating a legal matter for a current client. I would very much appreciate the opportunity to discuss the matter with you as soon as possible. Any communications we have would be considered attorney-work-product and would therefore be confidential. I would be happy to compensate you for your time* — I deleted that last sentence. I could always offer money later if she did not respond, but didn't want to open us up unnecessarily to the argument that we were paying this woman for her testimony. *It would* be better *if you reached out to me privately. If I do not hear from you, my client will have no choice but to share the information we have with the police.* I provided all of my contact information and then reread the e-mail three times, trying to will my brain into sobriety.

I hit the Send key. Or, at least I thought I did. I'd have to check the next morning when my head was clearer.

★ ★ ★

I'm reviewing my notes one final time at counsel table. When I reach the end, I smile to myself because I know every line of my opening statement cold. I even hear the intended inflections in my head — it's the '*government's* burden,' not the 'government's *burden*.' When Judge Amador enters the courtroom, we all rise, and I straighten the jacket of my best suit — the black Escada crepe with the zippered front. Everything is perfect.

ADA Scott Temple's opening seems to flash by in an instant, as if it never even happened, and then it's my turn. *Good morning. My name is Olivia Randall, and I represent Jack Harris. The ADA makes this sound simple — black and white, cut and dry — because that's his job.* One of the jurors coughs, and then I hear another one talking to his neighbor before a few others join in. *If I could have your attention.* But they continue talking. I look to Judge Amador for assistance, but he shrugs. Temple smirks at me from the prosecutor's table.

Again, ladies and gentlemen. They are speaking so loudly now that I can't hear my own voice. *My client has a right to be heard.* I am screaming but the din of the courtroom grows louder. I start pounding on the railing before the jury, and the man closest to me — juror number six, I'm certain he's a product manager for a soap company, but can't remember how I know that — begins to laugh. I knock on the wood so hard that my fist aches. 'I think I broke my finger, Your Honor.'

Somehow that one sentence is heard, and the judge tells me to exit through a door at the side of the courtroom so a nurse can check my hand. When I walk through the door, I'm in my old apartment — the one on Mercer. The one I shared with Jack. I walk through the living room into the kitchen, then back through again to the bedroom.

Jack's brother, Owen, is lying in the bed, his bare chest tan and lean against the crisp white sheets. He rolls over, turning his back to me. I see blood on the pillow.

I open the closet door, and find a room I never knew existed. It is larger than the entire apartment combined, but is filled with taped boxes and cotton-draped furniture. Jack is standing in the corner. He looks young, like when we were in college.

'Olivia, everything's fine. I hear you. Can you hear me?'

I know these are the words he is saying, but I can't actually hear him. 'No, I can't. But I know, Jack. I know.'

His lips keep moving, but I can no longer make out the words. I tell Jack that something is wrong. The room is silent.

Suddenly he's the one standing in the jury box, pounding on the wooden railing. The knock is quiet at first, then becomes louder and louder. I can tell he's yelling, but no sound comes from his mouth. I can only hear the pounding.

'Olivia!'

I reach for him and feel something cool and hard against the palm of my hand, and then it's gone.

The wine. Somehow I know it's the wine.

When I opened my eyes, I realized the pounding was real, and it was coming from my front door. A half bottle of Cabernet was seeping into the carpet next to my bed. I grabbed what was left and balanced it on the nightstand, then pulled off my T-shirt and used it as a towel to try to sop up the wine.

The knocking continued, and I heard my name again. Wrapping myself in the robe from my bathroom, I made my way to the front door. Thanks to the distortion of my peephole, Einer's nose looked inflated, like one of those dog-shaped balloons.

'What the hell — ,' I said, opening the door. I saw my building super, Vladimir whose-last-name-I-could-never-remember, standing behind him.

'This man who looks like clown said it was emergency. You need 911 or something?'

'No, Vlad. I'm fine. Thanks. This idiot works for me.'

I could tell Vlad was amused as he walked toward the elevator.

Einer was also amused as I stepped aside to let him in. 'You know what doesn't go with that outfit? A boyfriend.'

'Einer, what are you doing here?'

'You didn't answer your cell. I must've called ten times in a row. And you're like the only forty-year-old I know who doesn't have a landline.'

Einer had a way of saying 'forty' like it was a hundred and two. I blinked a few times, hard, trying to clear the clouds from my throbbing head.

'I just overslept.'

'Well, I can see that now. Don got all worried, saying you always answer your cell. And then I started thinking about that lady in Queens who had a stroke and spent seven hours immobile on her kitchen floor until someone came to check on her. I mean, you don't even have a cat or anything.'

'Nice to know you care, Einer.'

I looked around and saw my cell phone on the kitchen counter. Rookie fucking move.

Sixteen missed calls. And it was nearly noon. 'I must be coming down with something.'

'I call it the tequila nod.'

'Not funny, Einer. And don't repeat that to Don.'

'Fine, none of my business. Jack Harris has been calling the office, saying it's important. Something about the woman who sent those e-mails.'

Right. Madeline. I e-mailed her last night. At least, I thought I had.

My cell phone was ringing again.

'You want me to answer that?' Einer asked.

I checked the screen. It was Jack. I shook my head as I opened my laptop. I knew Jack was convinced that Madeline could make his entire case go away.

I was relieved to see that not only had I sent the e-mail to Madeline, but that it was appropriately firm, edging on intimidating.

I clicked over to my in-box and was excited to see a new message with my own name in the subject line: *From Olivia Randall, Esq.* Ugh, I had actually referred to myself as Esquire.

I clicked on the message. *Your message to the following e-mail address was rejected. The e-mail address wasn't found at the destination domain. It might be misspelled or it might not exist any longer. Try retyping the address and resending the message.*

I nudged the screen in Einer's direction. 'I sent a message last night to Jack's missed-moment woman, and got this in response.'

'You're sure you got the address right?'

I was fairly certain I had copied the address directly from one of Jack's e-mails, but double-checked. 'Yes. We didn't get that message before when we tried contacting her, right? What does that mean?'

'I'm no lawyer, but I'd say someone's going out of her way to make sure you don't find her. Maybe that's why Jack was calling.'

And just then, my phone rang once again.

I shepherded Einer to the front door as I answered Jack's call. As I offered a vague apology for not picking up earlier, Einer mouthed the words 'morning breath' at me before leaving me in peace.

'I was calling about Madeline,' Jack said.

No surprise. How could a person be smart enough to recite entire pages of William Faulkner from memory, casually mention the influence of *The Canterbury Tales* on everything from mystery novels to rap music, and publish three acclaimed best-selling books, but not realize that the DA wasn't going to dismiss first-degree murder charges all on the say-so of some woman from an online flirtation?

'Look, I know you think that she can back you up by saying she's the one who invited you to the football field, but your case is not getting dismissed. There's still motive. And the gunshot residue. And the deposition.'

'What deposition?'

I shut my eyes and forced myself to concentrate. Right, I hadn't asked him yesterday about the deposition because I wanted to make sure he signed the psych release. What deposition? he wanted to know. The one where Malcolm Neeley testified that he could be found at the football field every Wednesday morning like clockwork. The one Jack had kept a copy of in his file cabinet. I spelled it out for him now.

'I don't know what you're talking about. I told you, I never even looked at that stuff. I was as shocked as anyone when the police told me that Neeley was at the football field that morning.'

There was silence on the line. 'Oh my God, you think I did this. I heard it in your voice when I first got home. I told myself afterward I was being paranoid. Being in jail for three days can do that, I guess. But I was right. Do you seriously think I'm capable of something like this?'

'I'm just working through all the evidence, Jack. That's my job.'

'I swear on my life, Olivia, I did not read that deposition. Call Buckley's therapist if you don't believe me. You can make her sign a medical release, too, I guess.'

'Just stop, Jack, I believe you.' Did I believe him? Maybe. Why did Madeline dump her e-mail address? If I were a prosecutor, I'd be able to get information from her e-mail provider about the defunct account in a matter of days, but as a defense attorney, the same task would take me months, if the company bothered to respond at all. 'You called about Madeline.'

'Not just Madeline,' Jack said. 'The basket. The prosecutor at the bail hearing knew about the picnic basket I took to meet up with Madeline. They said they have footage of me carrying it.'

'They do, both from the waterfront and your building elevator.'

'Right, but they don't believe that it was all part of this stupid blind date. At the time, I just assumed that Madeline chickened out or something. But here's the thing: the prosecutor at the bail hearing accused me of using the basket to carry a gun, like I couldn't just stick it in my waistband.'

209

'They skew everything to fit their theory of the case.'

'That's not my point, Olivia. Was the basket reported on the news? Because if so, if you were Madeline — you'd put two and two together and figure out that the police arrested the person you stood up. If you were the one who said *you bring the basket* — '

I immediately saw where Jack was going. She'd call the police. Or me. She'd come forward to say that the guy on the news didn't do this, that the basket wasn't to hide a gun. But no one had come forward.

'Hold on a second. I need to think.' I pulled a bottle of Tylenol from my kitchen drawer and swallowed three without water.

I was trying to figure out how Madeline fit into all the possible scenarios, but Jack's fretting on the other end of the line was keeping me from thinking straight. 'I'll call you right back.'

★ ★ ★

The whole case started because the police were able to place Jack near the football field right before the time of the shooting. That was where I needed to start, too.

I forced myself to concentrate and started a list in my notepad:

Three explanations.
1. Coincidence.

The 'coincidence' theory had never sat right

210

with me, and the police clearly never bought it. And Jack was right: if it were pure coincidence that Madeline happened to send Jack to the site of the shooting, with some innocent explanation for not showing up, she would have made the connection between the shooter's picnic basket and her missed moment. She would have come forward. But instead, she closed her e-mail account. I was not liking this theory.

My cell phone was buzzing across the table. I turned it off and picked up my pen again.

2. E-mail hack/fall guy.

This had been Buckley's theory when she overheard Charlotte and me after her father was arrested: Someone who wanted Neeley dead went looking for a fall guy, identified Jack and perhaps others, and began spying on their e-mails in search of an opportunity. Jack's e-mail to Charlotte about the woman in the grass, followed by Charlotte's missed-moment post, provided that opportunity. The bad guy then responded to the ad as 'Madeline.'

The problem with the e-mail hack theory was that, according to Gmail, the only log-ins to Jack's account in the days before his arrest had come from Jack's own IP address. The hacker would have had to enter Jack's building to be able to piggyback off his wireless signal, a completely unnecessary risk.

I didn't like this theory, either.

3. Jack did it.

Jack hated Neeley, even more so when the civil suit got dismissed. He knew where to find Neeley because of his deposition testimony. He had been hanging around a shooting range recently, a fact he neglected to mention until I pressed him for an explanation about the gunshot residue on his shirt. He wrote the Madeline e-mails himself to provide an excuse for being near the football field in case someone saw him.

No muss, no fuss. I circled the period at the end of the sentence until it was a solid black circle.

I started to put my pen down. This was the only theory that worked.

Except it didn't. Not exactly. Not the way it seemed to yesterday.

The problem: I had e-mailed Madeline the night of Jack's arrest, and did not receive a 'closed account' message in response. So sometime between then and last night, 'Madeline' had closed her account. And Jack no longer had access to the Internet.

Maybe he called someone else to do it — Charlotte, perhaps, or a hired stranger. But why take that kind of risk when he could have left the account dormant?

Was there *any other possibility*? My pen began to move again.

4. Catfish

This was Charlotte's theory from the very beginning. It was like Buckley's theory, but more

212

complicated. Bad guy identifies Jack as the perfect fall guy, then mines the Web for information to plant the perfect woman on his running route.

Maybe they expected Jack to make the moves in person, and then planned to use the woman to frame him. Jack (being Jack) didn't take the bait, but then Charlotte's missed-moment ad gave them another chance. Along came 'Madeline.'

It was possible.

I started at the top of my notes and reconsidered every option. As screwed up as this catfish theory sounded, it had better be right.

Because, otherwise, Jack was guilty. I turned my phone back on and called him.

'I believe you: Madeline's the key to everything. I'll find her. I promise.'

I had no idea how.

★ ★ ★

It took me twenty minutes to get through the other messages I had missed this morning.

A bunch of voice and e-mails that could wait. Only two texts. The first was from Ryan, sent at two in the morning. *Are we good? Not sure what I did*.

One from Melissa. It was her day off, and she wanted to know if I could meet for lunch. How was it time for lunch already?

I was trying to think of somewhere to meet when my phone rang again. I recognized the digits on the screen as the district attorney's general number. 'Olivia Randall.'

'It's Temple.'

'Let me guess: you want to remind me that my client's guilty.'

'I said my piece yesterday.'

'You're calling to confess that you're the one who put Max Neeley up to that interview with the *Post* yesterday?' A grieving son, the last surviving member of the Neeley family, might actually be able to put a sympathetic face on his father. If he kept this up, I might have to leak his little episode at Princeton to some dogged young journalist.

'Not that, either. And I swear I didn't know he was going on the *Today* show this morning.' Another thing I had slept through. 'You got a pen?'

Temple gave me a name — Carl Wilson — and phone number, which I scribbled on my notepad. 'He can get you whatever video you need from the parkway. He's expecting your call and knows he should give you as much time and access as you need.'

'If only your office always rolled out the red carpet this way.'

'It's a lot easier to give defense attorneys what they want when we know it's a dead end. Have fun wasting your time.'

I never actually thought Temple would produce as much video as I requested. Now that I had access to it, I wasn't sure I wanted it. What if I found footage of Jack on his morning run, past an empty Christopher Street Pier — no woman in the grass, no picnic basket, no champagne? What if the missed moment had never happened? This video could confirm my worst suspicions.

I'd be scouring hours of grainy video searching for a woman who might not even exist. I could almost feel my eyes cross at the thought of it.

But if Jack was telling the truth, this video was our best hope of finding whatever woman had sent him to be framed for a triple homicide.

I sent a reply to Melissa: *No time for lunch, but do you have time to help me with something?*

Four crossed eyes were better than two.

★ ★ ★

Carl Wilson met us at police headquarters with a big smile, an enormous beer belly, and a strong handshake. 'Call me politically incorrect, but when the DA told me some criminal defense attorney would be fishing through video, I didn't expect the company of two beautiful women.' His words were directed at both of us, but his eyes were clearly focused on Melissa. 'You're both lawyers?'

In my gray sheath dress and matching blazer, I looked the part. Melissa, in her skinny jeans, black tank top, and biker boots, not so much.

'Watch your mouth,' Melissa said. 'I'm just helping my friend here. I own a bar.'

'Dear lord, woman. You're breaking my heart.' He led the way to a long, narrow desk lined with computer screens. 'When I talked to the DA, he didn't sound real sure on what exactly you were

215

looking for. Let me just say up front: don't get your hopes up.'

Carl continued to ramble, as Melissa and I got seated at the desk with him. 'People call us up saying, hey, I think my husband's cheating. Can you check whether his secretary comes to our apartment? If you ask me, the media's got people so scared of wiretaps and drones and Big Brother that the average American thinks there's a giant eye in the sky that hears and sees everything, and it's all uploaded to some magical cloud. Like, take your case, okay? The DA told me this is about the waterfront shooting, right?'

I nodded.

'Okay, so here's the thing: I can tell you right now that the actual shooting's not on film. No eyes on the football field.'

Scott Temple had already told me as much. I told Carl I was interested in all footage that might capture anyone heading to or from the field.

'Well, in theory, that could be a camera forty blocks north in Times Square an hour earlier. You gotta be reasonable. We're talking about the greenway, presumably, right? In which case, I can tell you what we've got. South to north: Battery Park, a whole lot around the World Trade Center site and the Holland Tunnel, then the Pier 40 parking garage, Christopher Street Pier, then Chelsea Piers, followed by of course a ton of eyes on the Lincoln Tunnel. You get the idea.'

So basically, seven clusters of cameras across approximately four miles of waterfront. Importantly, one was at the Christopher Street Pier, where Jack first spotted his mystery woman — or so he claimed. 'I'm surprised the coverage is that spotty,' I said nonchalantly.

'How is that possible?' Melissa asked. 'This is post-nine-eleven New York City.'

'And it's also the real world,' Carl said. 'Times Square? Rockefeller Center? Grand Central? We got those places locked down tight. But what jihadist plotting from a hellhole in Afghanistan gives a rat's ass about the Hudson River greenway? As it turns out, though, we'll have a bunch more cameras along the west side in the next month or so.'

'To respond to the shooting?' I asked.

'Nah, a couple weeks ago, one of my idiot counterparts gave a walk-through to some *New York* magazine reporter who was interested in CompStat. Guess she started asking about surveillance cameras or whatnot, so he tries disabusing her of her paranoid fantasies about twenty-four/seven eyes in the sky. He specifically used the Hudson River Park greenway as an example, telling her exactly where we do — and don't — have cameras. I tell you, some people got squash for brains.'

'So did this article get published?' Again I did my best to sound nonchalant.

'Oh, yeah. The bosses weren't happy. You know, it's a catch-22. If we say we've got it all under control, people complain about the loss of privacy. But here this dumb guy was trying to say, *No, it's not like that*, and the story gets twisted into, *How safe are we?* You can't win.'

'And did the article mention the actual camera locations?'

'Oh, the specifics were definitely there. Trust me, if we weren't union, that guy would be out on his ass.'

So not only were we missing video coverage of the football field, but whoever shot Malcolm Neeley could have been counting on exactly that.

I had Carl play footage from different cameras at sporadic intervals. I wanted to bury my actual inquiry among several others, just in case Scott Temple asked Carl what I seemed to be looking for.

After about forty minutes of skimming footage, I asked him to pull up the Christopher Street Pier cameras from the morning Jack saw his missed moment. I hoped that with luck, we'd get one quick glimpse of a woman in a fancy dress walking in and out of the frame with a basket.

But that's not what we saw. Melissa started to point at the screen, but I tapped her arm gently as a signal to wait.

I let the tape play a few more minutes before announcing that I was beat. Feigning fatigue, I told Carl that I appreciated his help, but that I couldn't make heads or tails out of the video without my client, who was on house arrest. 'Is there a way to get it on disc or something?' I asked. 'I can tell you which cameras and time periods we're interested in.' I planned to make them broad enough to feed Temple's opinion that I was on a fishing expedition.

'Well, the ADA did tell me to give you

whatever you wanted.'

As we were leaving police headquarters, zip drive in my briefcase, Melissa asked if we had found what I was looking for. All I had told her was to look for dark-haired women, especially one wearing a party dress.

I gave Melissa a little hug. 'Remember my drunken babble last night? Forget everything I said.'

Despite what I'd led Carl to believe, what we'd seen had surpassed my expectations. Saturday, June sixth, Jack in his T-shirt on his early morning run. And right there on the grass was a woman in a blush-colored gown, bottle in one hand, book in the other. The woman in the grass was real. Jack wasn't lying.

15

The next morning, Einer and I sat with Jack at his dining room table, huddled around Einer's laptop, searching the video footage from the waterfront for additional sightings of the missed-moment woman.

Einer hit Pause. 'Take a look here. Is that her?'

A voice broke through on the speakerphone. 'Wait. Who are you talking about?'

Thanks to the byzantine rules governing Jack's release, Charlotte had to dial in. Plus, Jack couldn't have an Internet connection. The legal team was allowed to go online but, without a wireless network, we had to use my cell's personal hotspot, which wasn't breaking any records for speed. Somehow Einer and Charlotte had figured out a way to connect their computers remotely so Charlotte could see whatever was happening on Einer's screen, but she still missed out on other information, like Einer's finger pointing to a woman with an umbrella passing Chelsea Piers the morning before the shooting.

Jack shook his head, and Einer continued to play the tape.

'Who were we talking about?' Charlotte asked again.

'It doesn't matter,' I said, annoyed by the cross talk. 'Jack said it wasn't her.'

So far, the only sighting we had of the woman

we were still calling 'Madeline' was the one I'd found yesterday. A few minutes after Jack had passed her on his morning run, Madeline packed up her picnic, turning to the camera just enough to permit Einer to grab a still shot of her face from the footage. In theory, it was a decent enough image that someone might recognize her.

Charlotte had been running that photograph on the front page of the Room website since last night. She had blurred the background so no one would connect what all the 'Roomers' were calling 'Who's That Girl?' to the shooting at the piers. A couple of smaller media-focused websites had picked up the link, wondering why the Room was so curious about the 'lady in the grass,' or to debate the ethics of conducting an online hunt for an anonymous woman. Charlotte was sifting through the hundreds of (mostly smart-assed) responses she'd received, but so far none of the tips had panned out.

Meanwhile, Jack continued to watch surveillance video, hoping to catch a glimpse of Madeline on another day, in a different place, on her way to the football field — anything.

As disappointment began to set in once again, I tried to remind myself that we were lucky to have the initial missed-moment contact on video. Jack's description of seeing the woman would have sounded ludicrous to the police after he was arrested. The video proved that he'd been telling the truth, at least about seeing her in the first place. It also helped bolster his explanation for carrying a picnic basket into the park the day

221

Malcolm Neeley was shot, and coming home without it.

Charlotte gave us the flavor of some of the tips coming into her website. *That's your mother after I kicked her out of bed last night. My next ex-wife. Send her my way when you find her.* 'I've always known that my site caters to the worst of humanity, but damn, I'm starting to hate my readers. I do have a few more people for Jack to look at, though. I'm sending them to you now.'

So far, Charlotte had not heard from anyone claiming to be Madeline, but she had gotten a few legitimate messages from people who thought they might know the woman. In those instances, she was doing her best to get a first and last name and then to aggregate online photos of candidates for Jack's review.

While waterfront footage continued to play on Einer's laptop, I used mine to open the incoming messages from Charlotte.

I turned the screen toward Jack as Charlotte continued to speak. 'The third woman seemed like she could be a match, but the rest didn't really look right to me. But you're the one who saw her in person.' Charlotte could not see Jack's face fall as he clicked through the photographs.

As he pushed the laptop back toward me, I saw his eyes suddenly light up. 'Hey, you. Didn't hear you come in.'

Buckley's high-waisted denim shorts and cap-sleeved blouse looked like an outfit I would've worn at her age. 'I guess today's therapy session has me walking on air,' she said

222

in a sugary-sweet voice.

I suppose if I'd seen a therapist as a teenager, I would have poked fun at it, too.

'Hey, kiddo,' Charlotte called out from the speaker.

'Hey. I don't want to be negative, but I hope you're working on some other defense than finding the woman in that picture. I mean, it seems like a total long shot.'

Charlotte insisted she was on top of it. 'Since we don't really think Madeline herself is behind this, someone must have hired her. I've got a bunch of temp workers pulling up casting and escort sites, looking for a match.'

Charlotte had told me about the strategy this morning. It was a waste of her time and money, but I knew not to argue with her. She loved Jack and needed to help however she could.

Three hours later, we were no closer to identifying Madeline, and we all needed a break. When Einer and I were packing up to leave, Jack asked me to stay behind. He led the way to the kitchen and poured two glasses of orange juice.

'Remember how it was such a splurge to get the real stuff instead of in a can?' he said as I sipped.

'Being poor sucks.'

He smiled. 'So . . . Buckley.'

'I didn't realize how plugged in she was to the evidence.'

'Neither did I. I think she just heard enough to realize that we're looking for a potential witness. She's good at filling in the blanks. She's also apparently good at telling people things that they

223

probably don't need to know. The pictures in my closet?'

'Oh, please. No big deal.' I did my best to sound like I had forgotten all about it.

'Buckley said she told you about the fight Molly and I had when she found them.'

'Really, Jack. It's fine. We don't need to talk about this.'

'Okay.'

I could tell he wanted to say more. I took another sip of my juice.

'It was just an argument,' he said. 'Buckley was still in grade school. It probably seemed like a big deal to her at the time. Other kids' parents were getting divorced. But it was nothing. I loved Molly very much.'

'Of course. You don't need to explain.' Damnit. Did I sound disappointed? Did I actually *feel* disappointed? 'I'm sorry you lost her so early, but I'm happy that you had that time together. Some people never find that.' I never found that. 'At least from what I read, she seemed like a really good fit for you.'

He looked down and nodded. 'After you, Molly was the only one. I never even dated anyone in between.'

I downed the rest of my drink and handed him the glass. He walked me toward the door, stopping at the table that marked the beginning of the danger zone for his electronic monitor. I reached for the doorknob but then turned back. 'Why didn't you call me?'

'I did. Or Buckley did, when I was arrested.'

'No, I mean before. After Owen died. When

you went to the hospital, or after. Why didn't you ever call me?'

'I told you — I just couldn't.'

'I just wanted to know you were okay. I knew you hated me but — '

'I never hated you. I could never — ' I heard his voice break.

'Then why?' He stared at me helplessly, but said nothing. 'Jack, I felt so fucking guilty.'

He cleared his throat and his eyes suddenly hardened. 'So, wait, Olivia: was the hardest part not knowing if I was okay, or that you had to feel guilty for what you'd done? Because maybe not calling you was my way of being cruel right back at you. To let you wonder. To let you think that maybe I wasn't actually okay and never would be. Is that what you want to hear? There, now you know why I never called.'

I stepped toward him and he pulled away. 'Just go.'

We were interrupted when Einer stepped into the kitchen. 'Charlotte just called again. She found her. Your scary, crazy friend actually found Madeline.'

★ ★ ★

'Did you get the pictures yet?' Charlotte was on speaker.

I watched a blue circle spin at the top of my browser window. 'It's taking a while to load.'

'Did someone finally recognize her?' Jack asked.

'Yes,' Charlotte said, 'but it wasn't a tip from

225

the Room. Remember how I said I hired some temp workers to go through websites? Well, I might've understated the size of the effort. I made a list of every single escort, modeling, and casting site I could identify in New York City. And I hired a *shit ton* of eyeballs — and not just normal temp workers. I hired models and actresses and casting agents — people who are good at face recognition. Whatever, you can tell me how amazing I am later. The point is: we found her. Do you have it yet?'

When the website finally appeared, the banner promised 'New York Companionship 24/7' and a 'diverse array of absolutely stunning beauties,' all at rates ranging from $800 to $2,000 an hour. I could imagine the kind of variations that might affect the price.

As I scrolled down, I found the promised array, displayed three per row, in various states of undress.

'Who are we searching for?' I asked.

'Helen. Scroll down. They were thoughtful enough to alphabetize.'

I found her about halfway down the page. Her damp, dark brown hair skimmed the top of her breasts, which were clearly visible beneath a white, wet tank top. Soaking wet, and yet somehow her makeup was perfect.

'That really does look like her,' Jack said next to me. 'She was dry, obviously, and didn't have all that eyeliner on. But that could definitely be her.'

I clicked on the photograph, and my browser did its spinning-wheel churn again before opening to a 'Helen' page, with six more photographs. Jack pointed to one where her back was to the camera, her skirt lifted to reveal an impossibly perfect bottom. 'I really think that's her.'

'You saw her *butt?*'

'No. Her profile.' Helen was looking at the camera over her shoulder. 'I mean, I can't be sure, but it's a lot closer than anyone else you've shown me.'

'The only problem,' I said, 'is that, given the way online prostitution works, if we call for a date with this Helen, some other sexy brunette will show up.'

Charlotte sounded proud to be yet another step ahead of me. 'Which is why I already made a little phone call to the so-called escort service. I got Helen's real name for less than the cost of whatever it is that they call 'the round-the-world treatment.' I'm sending you another picture.'

The incoming e-mail showed the same woman looking considerably more refined.

Jack let out a gasp. 'Oh my God, that's her.'

Charlotte's voice was beginning to crackle in the speaker connection. 'That's one of her professional head shots as aspiring actress Sharon Lawson. Guess she hasn't had her big break yet. I have a home address in Staten Island.'

I asked her to give me the details so I could follow up.

'Nope. I'm the one with the minions. If you're going, I'm going. I'll pick you up in ten.'

★   ★   ★

227

After Charlotte clicked off the phone, Jack shook his head and laughed. 'I'm picturing Charlotte bookmarking that escort site for future purposes.'

I was glad that the good news had gotten us past the tension that had been mounting before Charlotte called. It felt like everything was falling into place. If this Sharon Lawson turned out to be 'Madeline,' and someone hired her to catch Jack's eye, we might actually be able to prove Jack was framed.

'I probably shouldn't get my hopes up, right? Whoever did this had to have been smart enough to cover their tracks.'

'I know, but we don't have to prove who's actually pulling the strings.' We only needed to make it feel plausible that strings were in fact being pulled. After Jack was arrested, that feat felt impossible. Now I was finally starting to picture the beginning of a defense. Max Neeley hated his father, was searching for independence, and would now control the Sentry Group after his father's death. And by all accounts, he was smart — the kind of smart someone would have to be to orchestrate Jack's setup.

'You really think Max Neeley did this?'

'It's not our job to figure that out. I just have to sell it as a possibility.'

'God, is it crazy that I feel bad about doing this to him if he's not actually guilty? For him to come out of that household in one piece is pretty remarkable after everything his father put him through.'

A text appeared on my phone. It was

Charlotte. *I'm here.* How in the world did she get downtown in ten minutes?

As I packed my laptop into my briefcase, I told Jack not to feel bad for Max. 'He's alternative suspect number one right now. And either way, he's free of his dad and has an entire hedge fund to himself.'

Outside, Charlotte had pulled in front of Jack's building in a shiny, white Porsche Carrera.

'No Barbie?' I asked, steadying myself as I crawled into the low-slung seat.

'If we have to cross the Verrazano, we may as well have some fun.'

★ ★ ★

Sharon Lawson's home looked like the setting of *All in the Family*, the right half of a side-by-side row house, complete with a thick, squared-off hedge beneath the windows.

Charlotte beat me to the punch when the door opened. 'Sharon, we have a role to discuss with you. It's a follow-up to your gig at the Christopher Street Pier.'

'What gig on the pier?'

'You know — with the champagne and the basket.'

I saw panic in Sharon's face, quickly replaced by an actress's composure. I stuck my hand out, complete with business card, hoping it would keep her from slamming the door. 'Ms. Lawson, we need to talk to you, or the police will.'

I never should have let Charlotte inject herself into this. Maybe she would have had a chance of making a connection on her own, or I could have done it with my usual approach. But the two of us together were a mess. The door was beginning to close. Charlotte stuck her black canvas tennis shoe in the door. 'A man's life is at stake!'

The door jerked opened again. 'Fucking Emin! He's the one, right?'

I tried again to salvage the situation. 'It doesn't matter how we found you.' Charlotte had indeed bribed a man named Emin at the escort service for Sharon's real name and address. Emin had also confirmed that a cash client had booked Sharon for an 'all-night date' that would have included the early morning when Jack spotted the girl in the grass. Emin did not, however, know the identity of the client or the location of the date. 'We need to know who hired you to go to Christopher Street Pier.'

'I don't know what you're talking about.'

'If you're afraid of discussing the escort business — '

She stepped onto the porch and shut the door behind her. 'Of course I'm afraid. I'm twenty-nine years old and have two children and can barely afford the rent for the roof over our head. I can't believe greedy Emin sold me out. He's the one who found me at an audition and told me this was an easy way to make money on the side. No one was supposed to know. Fine, I guess my secret's out. But I have no idea what you're talking about with some stupid picnic basket.'

'We have surveillance footage,' I said, locking eyes with her. 'We don't have any interest in exposing anything about your life. In fact, there was nothing illegal about this particular job. Someone hired you to sit on the waterfront — dressed to the nines, reading a book, waiting for a man who'd be jogging by. He's in trouble now. You're the only one who can help us understand what really happened. We need to know who hired you.'

'I don't know how many times I can say this: whatever you're talking about has nothing to do with me.'

'Emin confirmed you were hired for the entire night,' Charlotte insisted. 'June fifth.'

'I remember that night. I was at a hotel on Central Park South, if you must know.'

'What hotel?' I asked.

'Essex House, okay? That's all I can tell you. I'm sorry, maybe there's some other woman who looks like me. Now, please, go. I don't want my boys to hear any of this.'

She closed the door once more, this time for good. Charlotte started to knock again, but I shook my head, knowing it was futile.

I had looked up Sharon Lawson the actress online. She had minor guest roles on a number of television shows filmed in New York: *Gossip Girl*, *Law & Order*, *The Good Wife*. Last year, she starred in an off-Broadway play. But New York was no longer a city where artists could pay the bills with a side job waiting tables, especially if the artist had two extra little mouths to feed. On the other hand, I noticed she'd been wearing hundred-dollar yoga pants on the porch and had what appeared to be a relatively new Lexus SUV

231

in her driveway. Maybe she only told herself the money was for her children.

I pulled out my phone to snap a picture of her license plate. It was a long shot, but we could check parking garages near both Essex House and the waterfront to figure out where she'd been before Jack's missed moment.

My phone vibrated in my hand before I had a chance to take the picture. It was a reporter from *Eyewitness News* named Jan Myers. She said she was calling for a comment on Jack's case.

'We're under a gag order,' I said. 'You know that.'

'Well, I'm not, so I always give every party the opportunity, regardless.'

'What's there to comment on anyway? Max Neeley's interviews? Of course it's understandable that a shooting victim's son would be looking for quick answers.'

'Ah, I guess the prosecutors haven't told you yet. Sorry to be the one with bad news.'

It was far worse than bad.

A homeless man named Francis Thomas had arrived at the Downtown Men's Center during this morning's downpour, a shopping cart full of possessions in tow: clothing, cans and bottles, books, a soggy picnic basket. Inside the picnic basket was a Glock .45 — the same kind of gun used in the waterfront shootings.

16

Charlotte double-tapped the horn of her Porsche, but I remained planted in Sharon Lawson's driveway, trying to convince Jan Myers to sit on the story.

I was having such a hard time controlling the tone of my voice that I couldn't even process the information Jan had given me. According to this Francis Thomas person, he found the basket 'by the water' on the same day Malcolm Neeley was shot, though he wasn't sure where. If he even noticed the gun inside, he wasn't able to explain that to the police.

'I can promise you a good exclusive down the road, Jan.'

'*Down the road?*'

'You know I'm good for it.' Even as I was trying to negotiate this one reporter's silence, I was thinking through the possibilities. If Jack was framed, whoever did it knew he was bringing a picnic basket. Jack claimed to have left it just outside the football field. The shooter could have dropped it inside. The theory still worked.

Nevertheless, the basket's discovery was a game changer. Until now, arguing that Jack was framed was just one of many potential options for our defense. There were far safer bets. I had a good chance of getting the GSR evidence suppressed as the fruits of an illegal arrest. Without the GSR, the prosecution was toast. But even if I got the GSR evidence suppressed, the discovery of the murder weapon in a picnic basket that I had a feeling would look just like the one Jack was carrying before the shooting meant that our only option was to argue that he was framed.

'Sorry, no can do,' Jan said. 'Besides, the word's out. I'm not the only one who's got the story.'

'Supposedly we have a gag order.' As I paced behind Sharon Lawson's Lexus SUV, I noticed the curtains part on the aspiring actress's front window. Something about her was bothering me, but I had to deal with Jan first. 'Who's your source? Just a hint: the police or the DA?'

'I was only calling for a comment, Olivia.'

'Is it Max Neeley?' I didn't really think Scott Temple would intentionally leak information, but as a victim's family member, Max could very well be getting inside information from the police. 'Did it ever dawn on any of these reporters he's courting to ask him why he pushed his father's will into probate only two days after he died?'

There was a long pause at the other end of the line. 'You're always interesting to talk to, Ms. Randall. Sounds like you'd have a lot to tell me if you weren't so damn ethical.'

I hit End and then snapped a picture of Sharon Lawson's license plate. The frame around the plate was one of those freebies from the dealer, a place called New York Universal Auto World, which, according to the print on the bottom half of this rickety piece of plastic, catered to 'good people, bad credit.'

When I looked back at Sharon Lawson's house, the curtains were closed. I had no idea if she was a good person or not, but I was certain she knew more than she was letting on.

★ ★ ★

Charlotte turned the stereo volume from stadium blast down to regular-person loud when I got into the car. 'You know she's lying, right?'

I reached over and hit the Power button. 'I need to figure out how to prove it.'

For the next ten minutes, I did my best to block out Charlotte's chatter about all her plans — more money for Emin to wear a wire, blanketing the waterfront with minions armed with photographs in search of witnesses, bribing or blackmailing Sharon for the truth.

She was right: we needed Sharon to come clean. Even if she didn't know who hired her, we'd finally have a narrative: dream woman in the grass, missed-moment post, the 'meet me at the football field' e-mail, the shooting. Beginning, middle, and end. It was a complicated, fascinating story — the kind that jurors love. How many times had I heard jurors say after an acquittal that the defendant's version sounded too bizarre to make up? 'Did you notice that?' Charlotte was saying.

'Huh?' I had tuned her out.

'I said she looked like you. Sharon-slash-Helen. She looked like a younger, thinner, hotter you.'

235

'Love you, too, Charlotte.'

'No, I'm serious. Kind of interesting that Jack's dream woman looks like you, not Molly.'

'And the other day, you said Tracy Frankel looked like a younger, more strung-out me. I'm pretty sure you think every straight girl with black hair looks like some version of me.'

But as I listened to her continue to rail about her certainty that Sharon Lawson was lying, I leaned back in my seat, closed my eyes, and pictured myself barefoot, drinking champagne on the waterfront at the crack of dawn, flirting with some nice-looking, harmless jogger. His dream woman did seem more like me than Molly.

By the time I returned to Jack's apartment, I was exhausted. As soon as Jack saw my face, he said, 'I'm afraid to ask.'

As I delivered the news about Sharon Lawson, Jack fell into the sofa and stared up at the ceiling. I launched into my usual spiel — all the time left before trial, we were only just beginning to investigate, etcetera — but Jack cut me off.

'I gave a writing class at a prison a few years ago. One of the inmates wrote an essay about why, after fifteen years of maintaining his innocence, he planned on telling the parole board how remorseful he was about his crimes. Turns out you don't get parole if you don't accept responsibility, so if he needed to be contrite for something he never did, that's what he was going to do. He said to me, *In is in, and out is out. I just want to be out.* I want this to be over, Olivia. I can't go to prison. I was only in

236

jail for a few days, and I thought I was losing my mind again. I won't be able to make it. Promise me you'll do whatever you can to help me.'

'Of course,' I said quietly. This conversation wasn't making it easy to break the other piece of news. I told him about the call from Jan Myers with *Eyewitness News*. When I mentioned the gun inside the picnic basket, his eyes flickered with confusion.

'They're waiting for ballistics,' I said.

'That's insane. How is that possible?'

I walked him through the explanation I'd been selling to myself since the reporter's phone call. Madeline's e-mails had instructed Jack to bring the picnic basket to their meet-up. For all we knew, the shooter had been expecting Jack to stick around longer than he had. Maybe the plan was to shoot Neeley and then shoot Jack, too, making it look like a murder-suicide. But when the downpour started, Jack had left. The shooter may have figured it was now or never. When he left, he saw Jack's picnic basket and slipped the gun inside.

As I laid out my theory for Jack, I realized what had been bothering me about Sharon Lawson. Charlotte had told Sharon that we knew about the gig at the waterfront with the champagne and the basket. But when Sharon denied being the woman in the video, she said she knew nothing about a 'stupid *picnic* basket.'

Were there other kinds of baskets? Maybe not, but it seemed like a strange detail for her to add. Or maybe I was grasping at straws.

As I left Jack's building, I pulled out my cell

phone and looked at the most recent photograph: a snapshot of Sharon Lawson's license plate, complete with the name of her car dealer. I called information and asked for the phone number for New York Universal Auto World.

And then I got really, really lucky.

★ ★ ★

At exactly nine o'clock the next night, my cell phone rang. It was the doorman; Helen was coming up. I had no idea what Sharon Lawson's skills were as a hooker, but so far she earned five stars for promptness.

I rose from the sofa and straightened Don's tie on instinct.

Einer swatted my hands away. 'Jesus, Olivia, he's a grown-ass man talking to a prostitute, not some kid going to the prom.'

Don pulled the tie off and threw it on the coffee table. 'I'm not even a real john, and you two still have me feeling like a letchy old man. Are you sure we couldn't have figured out some other way?'

I was sure. Charlotte and I had spooked Sharon when we'd shown up at her house unannounced. She'd never answer her door for us a second time. I reassured Don that we weren't doing anything wrong: We were paying her more than her going rate for sex in exchange for a simple conversation. We had already agreed that we wouldn't stop her from leaving, not physically at least. And all three of us were here to witness the interaction, just in case she was tempted to level any false allegations against us.

Einer and I ducked into my kitchen. We couldn't see Sharon-slash-Helen but could hear the conversation in the living room clearly. The initial introductions were as innocuous as a housecleaning visit: Hi, I'm Helen. I'm Don. How are you doing tonight? I'm fine, how are you? And then things got X-rated quickly.

'I think you know how I'm doing,' she said. 'I'm horny. Isn't that why you asked me here?'

I would have thought that a thousand dollar a night whore would bring hotter dialogue than a late-night Skinemax flick, but poor Don was clearly mortified. 'Um, actually — I think we should talk for a little while.'

'Yeah? Is that what you like? Talk? What do you want me to talk about?'

I heard steps and a thud, then couldn't resist any longer. I had to peek. Don was scurrying across my sofa while Helen tried to straddle him.

'You know what I like?' Don asked, standing up and folding his hands protectively in front of his nether regions. 'I like cars.'

'Yeah, baby?' Helen was twirling her long brown hair, kicking one leg back and forth flirtatiously. 'What kinds of things do you like to do when you're behind the wheel?'

'I don't like driving cars as much as knowing about them. Or the business of them.' Don was no longer acting like an embarrassed gentleman. 'Like the kind of business that would sell cars to good people with bad credit. The kind of place that would call itself New York Universal Auto World. The type of business, Sharon, that would lease a luxury SUV to a single mother of two with no steady documented source of income only on the condition that she have a GPS installed in case the car needed to be repo'd.'

She started backing up toward the door. 'How do you know my name? What do you know about my kids?' Her face fell when I stepped from the kitchen. 'How many times do I have to say it? I don't know anything.'

'You told me you were at the Essex House for that all-night date I asked about. But your car dealer's GPS tracker says otherwise. You were at the Quik Park on Bleecker and Washington.' It was the closest discount lot to Christopher Street Pier. 'You arrived just before six thirty in the morning and left a little after seven, not long after a man named Jack Harris completed his usual loop around the pier.'

'I don't want anything to do with this.'

'It's too late for that, Sharon. You can either talk to us now, or I can issue a subpoena to the escort service.' No, I couldn't subpoena the escort service, but hookers and actresses don't know that. 'If you cooperate with us, I can at least try to keep the fact of your side gigs as quiet as possible. How someone found you for the job doesn't matter. What we need to know is how you wound up at the pier that morning. Who hired you?'

'I have no idea. It was all by e-mail. The guy said it was a prank he wanted to play on a coworker. I didn't ask any questions. He told me to wear something fancy. The basket was there waiting for me. I was supposed to read a book.

When the guy ran past me, I was supposed to look interested — a little flirty.' She slumped down into my sofa and ran her fingers through her hair. 'And that's all I know, I promise.'

Einer stepped from the kitchen, but I shot him a look that sent him ducking back out of sight. I didn't want to scare Sharon off again. 'You said *the guy* hired you. What do you know about him?'

'Nothing. I mean, I guess I don't even know it was a guy. It was all by e-mail. They left cash in the basket for me — enough to cover the whole night — under a bench a little south of the pier.' I already knew that cameras didn't cover that spot, and we hadn't seen anyone carrying a picnic basket in any of the footage. 'I wasn't happy about the arrangement but I figured I could check easily enough when I arrived and leave if it didn't pan out. I got paid two grand for an hour's work.'

'And you really thought that was someone's version of a practical joke?'

'Do you know the kind of dough weird people have in this city? I have a friend who got paid ten thousand dollars to clean some dude's condo in her underwear. It's like Monopoly money for perverts.'

'What about after the shooting?'

'Why do you think I was so freaked out when you came to my house? Right after I heard about the shooting, I was thinking, wow, I was just there a couple of weeks ago — you know? But then when I read about the shooter carrying a picnic basket, I e-mailed the person who hired me, like: what the fuck's going on? All I got back was an error message saying the account was closed. I don't know anything else, and I'm terrified.'

'What was the e-mail account?'

She fumbled through her black patent leather clutch purse and pulled out an iPhone. The e-mail address she read aloud was the same one Madeline had used to tell Jack to meet at the waterfront the morning of the shooting.

17

The march toward a criminal trial is slow but never steady — fast and frenetic at the beginning, followed by a long period that would feel almost normal if not for the pending charges, followed by the ramp-up toward trial.

Three weeks after we confirmed that someone had hired Sharon Lawson to pose as 'Madeline,' the frantic stage was coming to a close. The July Fourth holiday had come and gone, and we had spent the weekend at the office, hoping to come up with some theory that might persuade or cajole or embarrass the district attorney into dismissing the case against Jack before we all hunkered down for what would be a long, slow fight.

The larger of the two conference rooms in the Ellison & Randall law firm was devoted completely to Jack's defense. The entire table, the sideboard, and half of the chairs were blanketed by boxes, files, and documents. Two mobile whiteboards were covered with multiple colors of ink.

I could not hear myself over all of the competing voices.

'We have to pare this down. We need a clear narrative.' That was Don. Don was all about narrative.

'Seriously, Olivia. I've looked at this shit fifty times and have no idea what we're missing.'

Einer, sitting on the floor, surrounded by documents.

Jack — conferencing in via speakerphone — was saying, 'I don't know if I'm comfortable dragging the other victims into this.'

'Fuck Gothamist.' That was Charlotte, who was obsessed with online coverage of the case. 'They're accusing me of using the Room to spread pro-Jack propaganda. It's not propaganda if it's true.'

Einer held up a high five for Charlotte, which she returned. 'You tell 'em, Martina Navratilova.' A month of antagonistic banter, and somehow Charlotte was fonder of Einer than she'd ever been of me.

'Quiet, I can't think.' I was determined to send everyone home in the next hour. Charlotte, unaccustomed to being shushed, shot me a glare. I turned to her first. 'Can you back off a little on the Room posts? The last thing Jack needs is a backlash from other media sites.'

She didn't look happy, but she didn't argue, either.

'Einer, I promise you, there is something in those boxes that's worth finding.' I had been pushing Scott Temple to provide discovery earlier than was technically required. In response, he had shipped over seventeen large boxes of documents to our offices two days earlier. We had quickly figured out that six of them were duplicates of documents the police had seized from Jack's home office, including all of his materials regarding the civil case against Malcolm Neeley. But the others went well beyond the obvious discovery I would typically expect. In addition to the usual witness statements, the medical examiner's findings, and crime scene photographs, the prosecution had included hundreds of pages of records like phone logs, credit card and banking statements, and other documents with no clear connection to the case.

Chances are, Temple was fucking with me for nagging him for early discovery. But my gut told me there was another side to the story.

If I had to guess, there was Brady material there — evidence that would help our case, which he was required to turn over — but he'd buried it among several boxes of paper to make me work for it. I told Einer to keep digging.

'Olivia, I swear to you, I've looked at everything. My eyes can't make something magically appear if it's not there.'

'Yes, actually, they can. Get some index cards and put the name of every document on a separate card. Rearrange them in different patterns — first by type of document. Then by the people the documents connect to — Jack, Neeley, the other victims. Look at everything in a new way. Now, on to narrative: Jack and Don, you seem to be arguing about the message I should be sending to the DA's office.'

'Our story is too complicated.' Don gestured toward the ink-covered whiteboards. 'Keep it simple: tee up Sharon Lawson and the Madeline e-mails to show that the same person hired Sharon for the missed moment and then sent Jack to the waterfront that morning as a

245

sacrificial lamb. That's all you need to do. It's intriguing. It plants the seed that there's another side to the story, and shifts the burden back to the state to figure out who's behind that e-mail address. Everything else — it might be Max, it might be another co-plaintiff, it might be related to Malcolm's hedge fund, maybe the other victims had enemies — it's all speculative, and way too complicated.'

Through the speakerphone, Jack was saying, 'Hello?' And 'Can you hear me?' like a sheepish schoolboy at the back of the classroom, fighting to be heard over the gunner in the front row. 'Plus I'm really not comfortable pointing the finger at these other people. I mean, they can't *all* be guilty. Some of those co-plaintiffs have been totally on my side since all this happened. And then dragging the other two victims through the mud — '

'No one's dragging anyone through the mud,' I said.

'Well, okay, but pointing out that one of them was homeless and one had a drug conviction — it's just . . . so unseemly.'

I flashed back to all the times that Jack would lecture me for being so impatient when lines were long, service was slow, or any number of things didn't happen on what he called 'Olivia time.'

'Oh, for fuck's sake,' I snapped. 'You can't afford to be the nice guy right now. What happened to telling me to do whatever I needed to keep you out of prison, Jack? Murder defendants don't get to be *polite*.'

'It's not polite. It's basic human decency. Can we at least agree to leave out the other victims?'

'Jack — '

'Jesus H., Olivia. Did you forget that my wife — my daughter's mother — is also a murder victim?'

'Okay, time out,' Don said. 'I agree we can't think about other people's feelings right now. But, Olivia, we do need to think about how this is going to play with the DA, and eventually the jury. If you're pointing the finger at everyone but Jack, it feels desperate. You told Charlotte we didn't need a media backlash — well, you could trigger one if you're perceived as trashing the victims. That's what I meant about a clear narrative. Just stick with Madeline — or Helen, or what's her name?'

Einer, Charlotte, and I all spoke in unison. 'Sharon Lawson.'

'Stick with that,' Don said. 'We have her affidavit. Someone hired Sharon specifically to look for Jack on his usual running route. Same e-mail address as whoever told him to go to the sports field the morning of the shooting. The prosecution needs to explain that or they can't win. Reasonable doubt's all we need.'

Don was right. The missed-moment and subsequent e-mails were complicated enough. Anything else was information overload.

I looked again at the rows of boxes filling the office.

Something was in there that Scott Temple was hiding. I needed to find out what it was before I told him about Sharon.

★ ★ ★

By the time I left work, it was after ten o'clock. I knew I should go home, but I was feeling antsy and wanted a drink. I hailed a cab and automatically gave the driver the address for Lissa's.

He had driven two blocks when I said, 'Actually, drop me at Grand and Baxter instead.' He sighed even though the route was the same.

'Where am I stopping?' the cabbie asked as we approached.

'That place with the red pillars on the right.'

Unless you've been a woman who walks into a bar late at night by herself, you have no idea how it feels. It shouldn't feel like anything. This city is filled with single adults, busy adults, tourists and businesspeople traveling alone. No one cooks. People are out more often than they're home. Men show up on their own at bars and restaurants, and no one gives them a second thought. I tell myself it's the same for me. But I know it's not, not to the people who see me scanning for a place to sit. Probably not to me, either.

Tonight, my eyes were scanning for more than a chair. I was certain that I'd find the face I was looking for. I don't know why I bothered to feel disappointed when my hopes weren't satisfied. It had been a shot in the dark. But now that I was here, I still wanted a drink. I spotted one empty seat at the bar, with a half glass of wine on the counter and a cloth napkin folded across the back of the stool. That was bar-speak for smoke break. Until the human chimney returned, I could stand here in the meantime to get the bartender's attention.

I had ordered a Hendrick's martini up with a twist and was listening to the rattle of shaken ice when I felt someone brush up next to me.

'You're stealing chairs now?'

I caught a whiff of lingering cigarette smoke, and turned to see Scott Temple. My gut hadn't been off after all.

'Just ordering an end-of-the-day libation.'

'Would that be a bad day or a good day?'

Funny how that works. Whether everything goes right or nothing goes your way, booze always seems like a good idea.

He pulled out the barstool and offered it to me. 'After you.'

I accepted and took a generous sip of my martini. 'I didn't know you smoked.'

'I don't, but every once in a while, with the drinks — old habits, I guess. The bartender lets me bum them off her. Now why do I have the feeling bumping into each other isn't pure coincidence? You and I have had some pretty meaningful conversations here.'

'Sometimes a cigar is just a cigar, and sometimes lawyers need gin near the court-house.'

'You're fishing for information, aren't you?'

'You're acting like you have information you want me to catch.'

'Sure, why not? Today I spoke to one of your client's fellow plaintiffs in the Penn Station suit. His name's Jon Weilly.'

I did my best to act unconcerned. 'You don't think jurors have also said things in anger?' I asked. 'You have to be desperate if that's the best you've got. I was hoping you might tell me why you sent over seventeen boxes of discovery, months before trial.'

His eyes were already glassy but he took another sip of his wine. 'I love it. A defense attorney bitching that I sent over *too much* evidence.'

'I'm not some rookie, Scott. If you flood me with irrelevant evidence, I know you're hiding something. You may have technically complied with the discovery rules, but you can only get so cute before a judge calls you out on your shit.'

'I'm not sure what you want here, Olivia. I've told you from the very beginning that our case is tighter than you think, but you won't believe me.'

'Is the slam-dunk evidence in those boxes? Because, if so, I don't see it.'

'Your request was for *Brady* material — that's the exculpatory stuff, remember?'

So I was right. Scott may not have turned over everything, but something that helped Jack was buried in the avalanche of paper spilled across our conference room. 'Give me a hint. A little help for both of us. I don't rat you out to the judge, and you tell me what's hiding in those boxes.'

'You know that story about the frog and the scorpion? The scorpion bites the frog even though it means they'll both die. The frog says, 'Why?' and the scorpion says, 'It's in my nature.'

You're a defense attorney. In my book, that makes you the scorpion.'

'Except you're the scorpion for assuming you can't trust me. You know I don't vouch for clients unless I mean it. And I know you want to get convictions the right way. This hide-the-ball stuff might be par for the course for your office, but not you. You're too good for this.'

He pulled out his wallet, dropped a couple of twenties on the counter, and drained the rest of his wine.

'It's always a tough call, Olivia.' His hand squeezed my forearm. 'I'll talk to you later.'

I left fifteen minutes after Temple, my martini softening the edges of my anxiety. I pulled up Einer's number on my cell once I hit the sidewalk, and hit Enter.

'Hey.'

'You still going through the discovery?' I asked.

'I'll say yes if I'm supposed to, but do you know what time it is?'

I looked at my watch. Five minutes past midnight.

'Some of the documents are phone records, right?'

'Yeah, a bunch. The LUDs from both of Neeley's homes and his cell. And Jack's cell, of course. Plus call records for the Sentry Group. I told you: they flooded us with paper.'

'Whatever they're hiding, it's got something to do with the phone records.'

'How do you know that?'

'I just do.'

It's always a tough call, Olivia. That was my hint.

★ ★ ★

I jerked at the sound of my own cell phone on the nightstand the next morning.

Barely morning: 10:45. It was Einer.

'Hey. I was just walking out the door.'

'I don't know how you had magical information at midnight, but your inner soothsayer was right. All those boxes of paper, and somehow you nailed it. It was in the phone records. The incoming calls to the Sentry Group, to be exact.'

'Please don't tell me that Jack called him.' When I first learned that the police had pulled incoming calls to the Sentry Group, I had assumed they were looking for evidence that Jack — true to their stalking theme — had phoned Malcolm Neeley. But Jack had assured me that there would be no such evidence. And I was sure that whatever the prosecution was hiding in those boxes would help us, not hurt.

'No, thank God,' Einer said. 'I can't believe I missed it, but the list of calls is *long*. The Sentry Group records are only for the main switchboard, so I was paying more attention to Neeley's home and cell phones. And the records only have the phone numbers on the other side of the line, not the name of the caller or anything.'

'I got it. Just tell me.'

'You ready? In this very long list of incoming calls to the Sentry Group during the week before the shooting, three of them came from the same number.' He rattled off ten digits. 'You wanna take a guess? Because, trust me, there's no way you'd ever guess — '

'Einer!'

'It's Tracy Frankel. That number belongs to the cell phone found in Tracy Frankel's purse after she was killed at the football field with Malcolm Neeley. She was calling the Sentry Group. Now does that blow your mind, or what?'

18

Two days later, I showed up at Judge Amador's courtroom during his afternoon motions docket.

'Well, good afternoon, Ms. Randall. I didn't see you on the list. To what do I owe the pleasure?'

'Something has come up in the Jack Harris case, Your Honor. You oversaw his bail hearing? It's a touchy discovery issue that I thought you might be able to oversee informally if you have the time.'

Amador had his clerk call Scott Temple to see if he was available. Five minutes later, Temple walked into the courtroom, a legal pad in hand. 'Very mysterious,' he whispered as he joined me past the bar.

'Predictable is boring,' I said. I felt bad for what I was about to do to him, but it was all part of the job.

*   *   *

'Your Honor, I'm here to request a subpoena for the phone records of Tracy Frankel.'

The judge squinted. 'Remind me again of who that is?'

'She was one of the other victims — the youngest one, the female.'

'Oh, of course. I should have realized. I'm sorry. What is this all about?'

Temple gave me a worried look.

'We believe the phone records are Brady material, but have serious doubts about the prosecution's willingness to disclose it voluntarily. Unfortunately, after a week spent reviewing several boxes of unlabeled and unorganized documents produced by the People, we finally realized that they had intentionally buried important and exculpatory evidence that should have led them on their own to obtain the information we're requesting.'

'What kind of evidence are we talking about?'

Temple opened his mouth, but I jumped in before he could answer. 'The prosecution hid concrete evidence linking two of the shooting victims, namely, direct proof that Tracy Frankel phoned Malcolm Neeley's hedge fund, the Sentry Group, three times in the week before the murder. Just as I said at the bail hearing, there is another side to the prosecution's story. Their case rests entirely upon my client's supposed animosity toward a single victim — Malcolm Neeley — with the other two victims caught in the wrong place at the wrong time. That's why the prosecution tried to bury any connection between Tracy Frankel and Malcolm Neeley.'

'How exactly did they bury it?' the judge asked.

Temple finally found a chance to jump into the conversation. 'Your Honor, this is a completely unnecessary conference. If Ms. Randall had simply called me — '

'Given her allegation, perhaps she doesn't agree, which is why I asked my question.'

'They produced nearly twenty boxes of unsorted documents,' I said. 'A few of the pages listed incoming calls to the Sentry Group. We had to read every line of every page of every document multiple times before we finally realized that one of the phone numbers on the list belonged to Tracy Frankel's cell phone.'

Judge Amador tapped his eyeglasses on the bench while he processed the information. 'Mr. Temple, a yes or no question: did you know this?'

'To our knowledge, there are no direct communications between any of the victims — '

'Yes or no: did you know that Tracy Frankel's phone was used to call the Sentry Group three times in the week before the shooting?'

'Yes, but — '

'Not another word. I've seen this from your office before, Mr. Temple. You flood the other side with a bunch of garbage hoping they can't separate the wheat from the chaff. The defense made it quite clear at the bail hearing that other people may have had a motive to kill either Mr. Neeley or perhaps one of the other victims. A link between two of the victims — two people who, until now, appeared to share no connection whatsoever — could clearly be relevant to the defense. Do I seriously need to spell that out for you?'

'That's not necessary, Your Honor.'

'So what do you have to say for yourself, Mr. Temple? How is the way you've handled the disclosure of this information consistent with a prosecutor's ethical obligations?'

256

'If I may, Your Honor — '

'Of course you *may*. I just asked you to speak. I really want to know how you can justify this.'

'I understand that the defense would like to portray this as some kind of smoking gun — '

'Bad analogy, Mr. Temple.'

Scott took a deep breath and tried again. 'I believe Ms. Randall used the words 'important' and 'exculpatory,' but I would not agree with either description. This was a long list of incoming calls, not to Mr. Neeley's direct line, but to the general company switchboard. More than thirty employees work in that firm. Tracy Frankel could have been calling any one of them.'

'Does Ms. Frankel have an *account* with Sentry Group? I did not get the impression that she was a big mover and shaker in the finance world.'

'No, Your Honor. But Ms. Frankel had a prior conviction for drugs, and there are indications that she struggled, let's say, financially. It is no secret that people who work in finance sometimes have interactions that involve drugs and perhaps other activities, such as prostitution.'

'So you're saying that your victim was either selling drugs or sex to someone at the Sentry Group?'

'No, I didn't say that.'

'Right, because you don't know. Am I correct?'

'Yes, that's correct.'

'And that's exactly why you were hoping Ms. Randall and Mr. Ellison would not put two and two together and force you to deal with this inconvenient piece of evidence. I get it. But I don't like it, and if I had to guess, Mr. Temple, you wouldn't have done things this way if it were totally up to you.'

'It's *not* how I dealt with it, Judge. I had a private conversation with Ms. Randall just two days ago. I basically told her to look at the phone records.'

'You *basically told her?* What does that mean? I must have missed that phrase in law school.'

Temple turned to me to save him, but I looked away. Just as I anticipated, he was trapped. To defend himself by saying he gave me a tipsy hint at a bar would be to admit that he'd been intentionally elusive in the first place.

'We could have been better about organizing the discovery,' he finally said. 'But I think it should be noted that we produced disclosure far earlier than required. This case was arraigned less than a month ago, and no trial date has been set.'

'Mr. Temple, tell your bosses I'm not impressed. Now, Ms. Randall: what exactly are you asking for?'

I was ready to go. 'A subpoena for Tracy Frankel's cell phone records. Our hope is to turn up witnesses who may know more about a connection between Ms. Frankel and Mr. Neeley, perhaps a common enemy. Or, possibly, a link between Ms. Frankel and someone at the Sentry Group who may have had a motive to harm Mr. Neeley. I don't want to speak prematurely, but one employee in particular stands to gain a significant financial benefit and apparently even made threats against Mr. Neeley.'

Judge Amador was waving a hand, telling me

not to get ahead of myself. I didn't tell him that my comments were intended for an entirely different audience.

Temple glared at me while the judge signed the subpoena I had prepared. He barely waited for Amador to step from the bench before turning to leave. 'Just like I said, Olivia, it's in your nature. You're a goddamn scorpion.'

When I walked out of the courtroom, I saw Jan Myers from *Eyewitness News* sitting on a bench just outside the door, tucking a small recorder into her purse.

She smiled at me as I passed.

★   ★   ★

Jack didn't bother with a greeting when he opened his apartment door.

'We talked about this, Olivia. Malcolm Neeley was a horrible person, but I don't want to vilify the other shooting victims.'

Jan Myers had worked quickly, already reporting the shocking news that one of the other waterfront victims had been calling Neeley's hedge fund in the days prior to the shooting. She was a good journalist. She'd find out about the terms of Neeley's will and Max's Princeton disciplinary hearing soon enough. Walking the edge of the gag order, I had told Jan that an after-lunch trip to the fifth floor of the courthouse might be worth her time. She'd owe me next time.

I set my briefcase down and followed Jack into the living room. I explained that we started

259

looking into Tracy only after her phone number appeared in the Sentry Group phone records.

'Jack, remember telling me that in is in, out is out, and you just want to be out? I promised to do everything possible to keep you out. I can't ignore this kind of evidence.' I was not about to check with him every single time I followed up on a lead.

'That girl is dead, Olivia. Her family is mourning her. And now there are pundits on television speculating about all kinds of scenarios, most of them insinuating that she somehow brought this on herself.' Jack was pacing, and his eyes were darting around the room. I was wishing that the police had cut off his cable in addition to his Internet connection.

'You've been telling me ever since you were arrested that something truly bizarre was going on. These phone calls back that up.'

He pressed his face into his palms. 'I don't know how you do this for a living. It's like the truth doesn't even matter anymore.'

'Do you want to be in, or do you want to be out? Because if you want to be out, you should be thanking me for the crap I pulled for you today at the courthouse.'

* * *

I joke that I only eat at five restaurants, but the real number is two. Lissa's, because it's home, like stopping by the school dining hall. And Maialino because the food is delicious, I can usually score a seat at the bar, and it's only two

260

blocks from my apartment.

At Lissa's, I was never alone; I had Melissa, and usually Don, too. And at Maialino, I was alone. And when I was alone, I could sit and think about things like how I'd treated Scott Temple and whether it made me a bad person or a savior.

After an unmistakable hint that some overly perfumed woman move her purse, I assumed an unoccupied buffer seat between two couples and ordered a dry martini. The bartender's name was Travis. He told me once he was from Kansas. He moved here for some kind of interest in art, I think. As usual, he stopped by every ten minutes or so for some small talk so my iPhone wasn't my only dinner company.

I had just finished the bucatini and was ordering a replacement for my Barolo when I felt a hand on my back. It was Ryan. Here's another thing about eating at only two restaurants: it makes you easier to find than the average person. Ryan never dropped by Lissa's. If he wanted to bump into me under the right circumstances, this was the place.

Ryan, as always, was beautiful. There really was no other word for it. When the gods were handing out genes, they gave him a perfect bundle of smart and sweet and cunning, without any of the pretty-boy smarm. He could take home anyone, probably even the cared-for, coupled-up women next to me. But whenever he looked at me, I felt wanted.

'Hey you.' His hand remained on my back. 'I get it. No more texting you in random intervals.

But please don't treat me like I don't matter.'

I finished my last sip of wine. His wife must be gone again.

'Do you want me to go?' he asked. 'I thought you might want to celebrate. I saw your story on the news. You put that prosecutor through the wringer.'

As Travis refilled my glass, I ordered one for Ryan. I didn't want to be alone.

★ ★ ★

Two days later, Don, Einer, and I were at Lissa's. We were desperate for a change of scenery, so Melissa had allowed us to take over her biggest table at the back of the restaurant for a long working lunch.

The discovery that Tracy Frankel had been calling the Sentry Group in the days before the shooting had reinvigorated our efforts. We were even more certain that the police had only skimmed the surface of what was really going on. With a little more evidence on our side, we might actually be able to get Jack's case dismissed.

Einer took an enormous bite from his hamburger. 'You guys are the experts, but on TV, this is where Viola Davis would be all, *I found a hooker who was hired to set my client up*. Drop the mic. Season cliffhanger.'

Don and I had already talked about the option of going to Scott Temple with the information we had gotten from Sharon Lawson, but agreed that we weren't ready yet. Without more evidence, Scott would simply argue that Jack had been the one to hire Sharon to pose as 'Madeline,' hoping that the video proof of her existence would work in his defense.

But now that we'd connected Tracy Frankel to the Sentry Group, we might have a shot at figuring out who hired Sharon and why. Whoever framed Jack must have wanted both Tracy and Malcolm dead, and then shot the third victim because he was a witness or to make the killing seem more random than it was.

Ever the teacher, Don took the time to explain the logic to Einer. 'The DA's not going to dismiss the case just on our say-so that *someone* framed Jack, with fifteen different theories as to why. So here's the big question: How do we use these phone calls to put some bones on the third-party theory? Einer, you're sure we didn't miss any other calls in Tracy's records that we can link to Malcolm Neeley?'

Within a few hours of Judge Amador's signing the subpoena, AT&T sent us a list of three months of Tracy Frankel's incoming and outgoing calls. The three calls to Sentry Group the week before the shooting were the only ones to Neeley's hedge fund, but Einer had been working on identifying the other people Tracy had spoken to.

'No other calls to or from Neeley's cell phone or either home number. She actually didn't have that many contacts, in or out.'

'But she had more than zero,' Don said. 'Do we know who they were? Maybe one of her friends could explain the connection.'

Einer had the documents on the empty seat

next to him. 'I have almost every number identified. Her parents. Her older sister, Laura. A guy named Double Simpson — that's his actual legal name, believe it or not. A source at the department tells me Double's a low-level drug dealer by all indications.'

Don leaned forward. 'Maybe the dealer had some kind of beef with Tracy and wound up shooting two bystanders in the process?'

Einer shook his head. 'He spent that morning in custody for a probation violation — nonpayment of court fees. And that brings us to miscellaneous: takeout Chinese two blocks from her apartment, a cheap hair salon a few blocks from that. And then three calls, all back-to-back, two weeks before she died, to some hoity-toity shoe store in Soho called Vala. I paid a visit — the shoes were fugly, like made for Little Bo Peep.'

'And — ?' I asked.

'And no one there knows anything about Tracy Frankel. One of the salesgirls vaguely remembered someone calling multiple times with the wrong number — like too stupid to realize they're just dialing the same digits over and over again. So I assume that may have been Tracy.'

I was impressed that Einer had taken the time to make an in-person visit. He was clearly determined not to miss something else. 'But Tracy didn't dial a similar number afterward?' That was the usual response to dialing incorrectly.

'No. And that's it except for a couple of blocked numbers and a payphone in Prospect

Heights. Those are dead ends.'

'Okay, so we still have no idea who she was calling at Sentry.'

Melissa dried her hands with a white kitchen towel and plopped down in the seat next to me. 'Consider me on a break.'

'Perfect timing,' I said. Melissa frequently served the role of mock jury. She may have been only a sample size of one, but bartenders have a talent for figuring out how real people think. Melissa could consult fifteen fictional jurors running around in her head anytime she wanted. 'Malcolm Neeley had stopped seeing the married woman he was having an affair with. Maybe Tracy Frankel was the new girlfriend? A jealous boyfriend finds out?'

'Neeley goes from a high-society missus to a twenty-year-old druggie?' Einer said. 'Big change in type.'

'Maybe not a girlfriend, exactly,' I said. 'It's not unusual for a woman with drug problems to supplement her income with prostitution.'

Don shook his head. 'She'd have more phone calls.'

Melissa raised a hand. 'And a trick at seven in the morning? Only married dudes do that. Nope, I don't buy it.'

Just as Scott Temple said, the Sentry Group housed more than thirty employees. Tracy could have been calling any one of them. Coincidences do happen.

But one particular Sentry Group employee had already been on our radar. 'It has to be Max. He's obviously unhappy that we're looking for other people with a motive to kill his father. And we know from his ex that he wanted to get out from under his father's control. He benefits far more from Malcolm's death than anyone else. He inherits everything, including control at the Sentry Group. And, I'm sorry, I don't care how drunk he was, you don't talk about shooting your father in his sleep unless there's some serious underlying hatred.'

Melissa jumped in without missing a beat. 'So if the Tracy girl was calling Max — then . . . what?'

I shrugged. 'He's in love with his ex-girlfriend, Amanda, but can't be with her because of Daddy. Guy his age still needs to have sex.'

'So Tracy was his no-commitment hookup,' Don said. 'But wants more.'

'Maybe,' I said, turning over the possibility in my head. 'Tracy gets a little too pushy. Three calls in one week, at the company phone. No other calls between them, meaning they're not a regular item. Maybe he picked her up at a bar one night. Or off the street. But it wasn't supposed to be a *thing*. She takes a business card from his wallet, starts calling work. She's now a problem.'

'Two birds with one stone,' Melissa said. 'If Max was planning on taking out his dad anyway — '

I smiled. My jury of one had come to the conclusion all by herself. That meant the story felt real. I'd used people before as alternative suspects, but this one was actually guilty. Two Neeley sons, both of them killers.

19

I knew from Tracy Frankel's one interaction with the criminal justice system that she had attended multiple private high schools and then managed to secure an expensive private defense attorney when she got caught as an eighteen-year-old trying to buy heroin from an undercover officer in Washington Square Park. But there's a difference between rich kids and *rich* kids.

The Frankel family home turned out to be a brick townhouse on East 76th Street. Approximately five thousand square feet on the Upper East Side, complete with an elevator and servants' quarters.

Given the cotton smock of the woman who answered the door, I took an educated guess that she was not one of Tracy's family members. 'Hi. I'm looking for Joanne Frankel.' Tracy had given her mother's name as her emergency contact when she was arrested.

The woman closed the door without comment and soon a younger woman took her place. 'Tracy's not around anymore, so you can lose this address — ' Looking me up and down, the woman apparently decided that I didn't fit her expectations for a person inquiring about Tracy. 'Wait. Who are you?'

'Olivia Randall. I'm a lawyer. I'm here about Tracy Frankel?' I quickly replayed Einer's rundown of Tracy's phone records. 'Are you perhaps her sister?'

She was in fact Tracy's sister, Laura. Her mother, Joanne, was also home. Her father, Eric, was at work at his commercial real estate management job.

Once I explained who I was, Joanne made it clear that I had *some nerve* showing my face at the family home. I apologized for their loss, knowing how shallow the sentiment sounded. As I had countless times before, I did my best to make it appear that our interests aligned. 'I know it seems out of place for me to be here, but there's some evidence I don't think the prosecution has brought to your attention. They've portrayed Tracy as a random victim caught in the cross fire, but this is what we've learned.' I spelled out the phone calls from Tracy's cell phone to the Sentry Group. 'Your daughter wasn't just . . . collateral damage. I want to find out the truth about why she was killed.'

It was straight out of a Lifetime movie. But I could tell from Joanne's quick response that it was working.

'When they told me she was at the waterfront at seven in the morning, it didn't make any sense. I don't think Tracy has woken up voluntarily at that hour since she stopped believing in Santa Claus.'

'Can you think of any reason why she would have called the Sentry Group?'

Joanne looked away. 'My daughter was flawed. She had — problems.'

Laura reached over and grabbed her mother's hand. 'What my mother's trying to say is that my sister was an addict — a junkie. We don't know why she was at the waterfront that morning, but assume it was related to her substance abuse.'

'You don't have to be so harsh,' Joanne said, pulling her hand away. 'Yes, Tee had her issues. That's what Tracy always wanted us to call her. For reasons I never understood, she decided in the sixth grade that Tracy was too much of a boy's name. I tried to tell her that Tee sounded too much like tee-tee. She would giggle, but thought the nickname was cute. Sort of street tough, I guess. I never did quite warm to it. One of many, many mistakes, I suppose. But, yes, as I was saying, Tee had her issues, but I always thought they were temporary. She just needed to find the right school. She did really well at one of them, was it Halton Girls'? I don't remember. Anyway, she had that teacher who got her into her poetry. She even talked about applying to a writing program. But then it became clear that it was all just a crush on an older man. It was always about men for her. She was such a kind soul but so reckless.'

I caught Laura the sister in an eye roll. Time to get the conversation back on track. I changed the subject to Tracy's phone calls to the Sentry Group. 'Forgive me if I'm saying anything to upset you, but this seems too coincidental. We're worried that perhaps the police have missed an important explanation for the reason your daughter was shot.'

Joanne was shaking her head. 'Do you have children?'

'No,' I responded.

'My husband loves Tee as much as I do — *did*, I suppose. More, if I had to say so. But when you have a child consumed by addiction, there are no clear right answers. I wanted to give her the world. To make her so happy that no drug could possibly compete. But Eric was all for tough love after Tracy was arrested. We hired the lawyer to keep her out of prison, but that was pretty much it for him. He cut her off. She moved to some crappy walk-up in Brooklyn.'

'So you have no idea why your daughter may have called the Sentry Group?'

'I wouldn't say *no* idea.'

'*Some* idea,' I said.

'Yes, if I had to guess. She was — ' Joanne reached for her daughter's hand again. 'An addict, as Laura said. Tee had even stolen from us in the past. Once we stopped letting her inside the house, I suspected she'd find other ways of raising money. That's what drugs can do to a person.'

I couldn't imagine what it would be like to be a mother who suspected that her daughter was turning tricks to support her drug habit. I tried one more time. 'You never heard her mention Malcolm or Max Neeley or anyone else at the Sentry Group?'

Joanne Frankel shook her head. 'I know I'm too smart to believe your answer to this question, but are you really telling me that someone other than Jack Harris killed my daughter? This isn't just some stunt you're pulling for your client? If it is — please, just leave us out of it. It's not right to put us through this if what you're saying isn't true.'

'I'm a hundred percent certain the police don't have the full story about why your daughter was killed.' I rose from my chair, leaned forward, and placed my hand on her wrist. 'You take care of yourself, Mrs. Frankel.'

I was on the sidewalk, using my phone to pull up the app for an Uber car, when Tracy's sister, Laura, walked outside.

'Thank you,' she said.

'For what?'

'Not promising more to my mother than you could deliver. I think she's yearning for some miracle explanation about Tracy's death. Like she's not just some random piece of garbage caught in the cross fire.'

'I don't think any human being is garbage.'

'And I suppose that's how you're able to be a criminal defense lawyer. I don't know why my sister was calling the Sentry Group, but I do know more than my mother. The last time I saw Tracy, I gave her my hundredth lecture about going to rehab. Taking some classes, just to get on a routine. Trying to get her life straight. And she told me that I didn't need to worry. She had a plan. Some guy was going to take care of her. I assumed at the time she was full of shit. But now that you're asking these questions, I have to wonder — she said she had, quote, *a finance guy on the hook*. She talked about going to Costa Rica, then getting a nice apartment in Soho.'

'Did she tell you anything about him? Maybe he was at a hedge fund?'

She shook her head.

I used my phone to pull up a photograph of Max Neeley. 'What about this guy? Does he look familiar?'

'Isn't he the son? The one giving all those interviews?'

Of course she recognized him. 'Did you ever see him with your sister?'

'No, but she cut me out years ago. I feel like my sister spent her whole life chasing a new rock bottom.'

* * *

I finished up a proofread of my memo about the visit to the Frankel house and e-mailed it to Einer with a request that he add it to the file. At the round table in my office, I was surrounded by stacks of documents and pages and pages of handwritten notes.

It had been nearly a month since Jack was arrested. Thanks to the early document dump from the DA's office and multiple investigators paid by Charlotte, I had far more information than I'd normally have at this point, but I had no idea what other evidence the prosecution might be sitting on.

I leaned back in my chair and envisioned the trial if it were held today. My expert opinion? Coin toss.

Without eyewitnesses, the case against Jack was circumstantial. I had a strategy to attack every single piece of evidence, but my attacks were jabs, not knockouts. For every challenge I raised, the prosecution would have a rebuttal.

Reasonable doubt or not? Fifty-fifty.

Why was Scott Temple so confident? Was I missing something, or was he holding something back? Tracy Frankel was the wild card. Why in the world had she been calling the Sentry Group?

I stopped turning pages when my office phone rang. It was Einer from the front desk. 'Max Neeley's here. Should I call security?'

★ ★ ★

Even though I had told Einer that I was sure everything was fine, I took the precaution of meeting Max up front instead of bringing him back to my office.

The second my heels hit the tiled reception area, he walked toward me and jabbed a finger in my face. 'Lady, I'm going to sue your ass off. Do you have any idea how much money you're costing me?'

'Your finances aren't my first priority, Mr. Neeley. And if you don't calm down, this conversation is over.'

He took a step back, but his hands remained balled into fists. 'You don't think I know what you're doing? You told that judge that Tracy Frankel may have been calling someone at the Sentry Group with a *financial motive* to kill my father? It took five seconds for Gothamist to quote anonymous sources that Dad wouldn't help me start my own fund. I had finally gotten that asshole Frederick Gruber back in line, and now he's talking about pulling his money again. Our phones have been ringing off the hook. The press has been digging around for details about my father's will from the probate court. Now they're starting to ask about that bullshit back in college. Not to mention, you're accusing me of murdering my own father. What kind of person are you?'

'Are you done?'

'No, you have to stop this.'

'I don't *have* to do anything except defend my client. Why was Tracy Frankel calling you?'

'The DA tells me Jack Harris is the killer and that your job is to twist the facts around and confuse people. Leave me out of it, lady, or I will use every last dollar I have to sue the shit out of you for defamation. You think you're the only one who can dig up some dirt? How would you like it if I started leaking stories about you to the press?'

'Again, Mr. Neeley, are you done?'

'No, I'm definitely not done. You'll be the first to know when I am.'

He slammed the door so hard on his way out that I thought the glass might break.

'Are you okay?' Einer asked.

I told him I was fine.

★ ★ ★

I had finally regained my composure when Einer knocked on my office door again. 'Sorry to bug

you, but a process server was just here. I think
you need to see this.'

THE PEOPLE OF THE STATE OF NEW YORK v.
JACKSON HARRIS, defendant.
PEOPLE's motion for reconsideration of bail.

I knew Scott Temple was angry with me for
embarrassing him in court, but I had not
anticipated this.

★　★　★

I was ready to call it quits for the day, but felt
obligated to tell Jack about the bail motion in
person. I had just gotten the all-clear from Nick
the doorman when I saw a familiar face heading
in my direction in Jack's lobby. It was Ross
Connor, Owen's former partner on the NYPD.
    'The last I heard, you made it pretty clear you
wanted nothing to do with my client.'
    He held up both palms. 'Just here to see an old
friend, Olivia.'
    'That's bullshit. He's on house arrest. He
doesn't let anyone up without police approval.
No friends allowed. Just ask Charlotte.'
    'Damn. Charlotte, that's right. Remember that
time I tried haunching on her after way too many
shots of whatever we were drinking? I thought
she might clamp my balls in a vise, but instead
she just started laughing. Talk about brutal.'
    I wasn't going to be distracted by humor. 'Is
this about the bail motion?'
    The question appeared to confuse him.

275

'That's over and done with it. He's home, so kudos to you.'

'You came here as law enforcement, Ross. Otherwise, you couldn't have come at all.'

'Fine, you caught me. I thought I might have better luck with Jack than the stranger who questioned him when he was arrested.'

'While he has murder charges pending? I'll go to the judge.'

'And if you do, I'll say that ever since you came to see me, I've been thinking about him. How close we used to be, when his brother was around. Felt I owed it to him — or maybe just to Owen — to come. How will it look if you rat me out for that?'

'You're unbelievable. You just admitted to a defense attorney that you're willing to testi-lie.'

'Just calm down, okay? I gave it a shot, but your boy didn't even say anything incriminating. No harm, no foul.'

'He didn't incriminate himself because he's innocent. Has the job tainted you so badly that you can't even entertain the possibility that the department screwed up?'

'Do you want to keep yelling at me, or do you want to know why I bothered to come here?'

'We've established that you came here to question my client. As for your reasons, you've already decided whether to share them with me or not.'

He pretended to mull it over for a few seconds. When he spoke, he put his hands in his pockets and looked at the ground. 'So after you stopped by my office, I kept thinking about when

I came here to tell him about Molly. And those condoms fell out of his bag, and he started acting all spooked.'

'I think you said it was awkward. Now it's *spooked*?'

'I kept going back to that moment where Jack freaked out. I couldn't stop thinking about it. So I called the medical examiner. They autopsied all of the Penn Station victims. Standard procedure for homicides. Turns out Molly had a hysterectomy.'

'So maybe they used condoms for some other reason.'

'Married people don't use condoms — period. But especially not when they're done having babies.'

He was right, of course, as a general matter. Not to mention the fact that Jack was carrying the condoms around in his bag. So if Jack was cheating on Molly at the time she was killed, how did that affect the current case against him? It didn't. I said as much to Ross.

'You're missing the point. Trust me, on the job, I've seen plenty of men with side pieces. I thought if I told him what I knew, he might drop the facade and tell me the truth about what really happened with him and Neeley. I asked him point blank: did you do it? No luck, but it was worth a shot.'

'I think that's called a violation of his Sixth Amendment right to counsel.' Even as I spoke the words, I remembered the various times I had also tried to get Jack to open up to me in the last month. About his hospitalization. His feelings about Malcolm. Us. Jack had specifically told me that Molly was the 'only one' after me. Had there been others during his marriage?

'I'm telling you, Olivia. You don't know that guy the way you think you do.' He was shaking his head as he walked away.

Jack didn't bother with a hug or any other greeting when he opened his apartment door. His back was already to me as he walked down the front hall. 'I didn't know you were coming by.'

He was obviously still upset that I had leaked the information to a reporter about Tracy's phone calls, but, in typical Jack fashion, was sulking instead of telling me he was angry.

'I figured we hadn't talked for a couple of days, and I want to keep you up to date. How about you? Anything to report on your end?'

'Ha-ha. I can see it now, my next book, *A Diary from Home Confinement*. Riveting stuff.'

Apparently I was going to have to ask him about Ross Connor's visit. I made myself comfortable on his sofa. 'This is a crazy question,' I said offhandedly, 'but I could have sworn I saw Owen's old partner leaving your building.'

'Oh, yeah, I guess I did have one break from routine. Man, I can't believe you recognized him. Ross Connor, after all these years.'

'I've always been good with faces. So what did he want?'

Jack shrugged. 'Just to see how I was holding up. He went through corrections and got approval to come by and everything. Pretty nice

278

of him, don't you think?'

All those times I had lied to Jack, it had never dawned on me that he might be the better liar. This was masterful.

'I guess so, but he's also a cop. He didn't ask you about the case?'

'Nah. Just shooting the breeze. A little awkward, I guess, but still — it's the thought that counts, right? So, you said you have an update?' It was a nice pivot. Just like that, no more Ross Connor talk.

As I told him the information I'd gotten from Tracy's mom and sister, I was struggling to keep my thoughts straight. If Jack had cheated on Molly, did it change anything about his case? Maybe he was only lying about the reason for Ross's visit to avoid the awkward topic of an old infidelity. But once again, I was wondering whether I'd been too quick to assume Jack was innocent.

I forced myself to focus on what mattered: Tracy's connection to the Sentry Group. 'My best guess is that she was looking at Max — or maybe Malcolm — as a potential sugar daddy. If it was Malcolm, she might have been at the waterfront to meet up with him when Max killed his father. Or if she was seeing Max, he may have sent her there to get rid of them at the same time. Two for one. Either way, it plays into our theory that Max Neeley's the one behind this.'

'I know we've been throwing Max's name around, but do you really think he did this?'

I thought about the contempt Max had revealed in my office. At the time, I thought I was looking into the face of a killer. But maybe his anger was a perfectly natural response to our not-so-subtle suggestions that he had killed his father. 'More likely him than you, right?'

If Jack sensed my suspicions in the question, he didn't show it. 'Jesus, what a family. Neeley trained his mentally ill son to use guns as if it were any other hobby, like it was golf or scuba or coin collecting. He made the other one hate him so much that he was driven to murder. Malcolm Neeley blamed those boys for their mother's death. His own stories about the ways he tried to parent them are like a handbook on how to screw up your kids. Ticking time bombs, the both of them.' He shook his head. 'So is that it?'

'No, I'm afraid not.' I slipped a copy of the People's motion to reconsider bail from my briefcase and handed it to him. The title of the motion was self-explanatory.

When Jack looked up, he tried to hand the papers back to me as if that would make them go away. 'But I haven't done anything wrong. Honestly, I find myself staying feet away from the door when I open it, even for you, just in case I accidentally set it off.'

'They're not saying you violated your release conditions. They're alleging that you shouldn't have had them from the beginning. Basically, the state's saying the court got it wrong from the get-go.' The hearing was in three days.

'You sound awfully calm.'

'It's just Scott Temple wanting a second bite at the apple. Without new evidence, I'm sure the judge will keep the status quo. So unless you know something I don't know . . . '

'So okay, then. I'm sure it will be fine.'

I said good-bye like it was any other visit, promising to contact him with new developments. I placed one foot in front of the other, through his apartment, down the hallway, into the elevator. The second the doors closed, I felt myself tremble.

Golf. Scuba. Coin collecting. Those 'stories' Malcolm Neeley had told about his parenting had come straight from Malcolm's deposition — the one that Jack swore to me he had never read.

* * *

That night, in bed with Ryan, I was starting to doze off but couldn't stop thinking about Ross Connor and Jack. 'Do you know any married men who use condoms?'

'With their wives?' He laughed.

'I'm serious. And this isn't about you and Anne. It's for one of my cases. A married man had condoms in his briefcase: what does that mean to you?'

'I'd say, sure, it's just birth control. Not every woman wants to be pumped full of hormones. But in his briefcase? Wouldn't they go from shopping bag to nightstand?'

'Plus the wife had a hysterectomy.'

'Then that dude was stepping out.'

I of all people knew that having an affair didn't make you a murderer. But it did make you a liar.

281

Jack had lied about his fidelity to Molly. He had lied about Ross Connor's visit to the apartment. And he had lied about having read Malcolm's deposition, which meant that he knew long before the shooting that Malcolm could be found at that football field every Wednesday morning. What else was he lying about?

Ryan kissed me on the shoulder, crawled out of bed, and began getting dressed. 'You realize next month, we'll have known each other two years?' I asked. Ryan had called me after not making partner. Preston & Cartwright always breaks the bad news at the end of August.

'I've known you a lot longer than that. I was one of the many summer associates who was terrified of you years before.'

'This wasn't supposed to go on for two years.'

He was standing next to my bed, his shirt half buttoned, being beautiful. 'I'm happy. I thought you were, too. If anything, I wanted more. You were the one who — '

'I know. I don't want more. But I also don't want . . . this. We need to stop.'

'We tried that before, remember? And it was my own *wife* who asked you to come back.'

'It wasn't supposed to be for two years. She didn't know what else to do, Ryan. You were sad and damaged and convinced you had failed at work and therefore had failed as a provider, and for some reason, I made you feel better. But you're not damaged anymore. You need to go home.'

'Anne's okay with us.'

'Well, I'm not. Not anymore.'

'So, what? This is good-bye?'

'Yes,' was all I could say. I didn't think it would be this hard. I was never supposed to care about him.

He leaned over and kissed me on the forehead. 'You're a better person than you give yourself credit for, Olivia. Don't forget that.' He touched my hair one last time and left.

When he was gone, I blocked his number and then deleted it from my phone. When I say good-bye, I mean it.

20

I was back at my conference table, thinking about all the same evidence I had reviewed yesterday. How could everything look so different today?

Yesterday, I thought we had a good shot at explaining the GSR on Jack's shirt. I had multiple witnesses who would confirm that Jack had gone to the West Side gun range a few times in the months before the shooting. And I'd get an expert to explain that residue could in fact linger on fabric for long periods of time. But now I was picturing those same witnesses on the stand. Though they weren't positive, they seemed to recall Jack wearing T-shirts — as if he was trying to fit in — and not the checked collared shirt in question. And then there was the added problem of Jack not having any writing to prove that he'd gone to the range for research, instead of training to kill Malcolm Neeley.

Same thing with the Madeline e-mails. I could tell a jury that someone else had suggested the football field for the meet-up, but Scott Temple would have a field day on cross-examination. Because the e-mails were anonymous, I couldn't prove Jack didn't send them himself. Same thing with whoever hired Sharon Lawson to pose as 'Madeline' on the waterfront.

Then there was Jon Weilly, the co-plaintiff Temple planned to call to the stand. With more specific questioning than I'd been willing to risk, the prosecution had refreshed Weilly's memory of hearing Jack say he hoped Malcolm Neeley would someday learn how it felt to have a gun-happy madman ruin his life. I would argue it was just a comment made in anger; the prosecution would call it evidence of intent.

The murder weapon turning up in the very basket Jack had carried to the waterfront? Was it literally a smoking gun, or even more evidence that Jack was framed?

Like every circumstantial case, every piece of evidence had two sides.

The case looked different today from yester-day because I was no longer on the side that believed Jack. And it wasn't just the case evidence I was seeing in a new light. In ten years as a defense attorney, I had never encountered a crime as calculated as this one. Hiring a prostitute to pose at the pier. Telling Charlotte about the sighting, knowing how much she loved missed-moment posts. Working the camera coverage to his advantage. Sending e-mails to himself as 'Madeline,' using a location from what was supposedly his favorite book, all to create an explanation in the event someone happened to see him at the football field where Malcolm Neeley could be found every Wednesday. A person doesn't suddenly become that cunning and manipulative.

How had I failed to recognize that part of him?

When his father died, did Jack come to me because he really thought of me as an important part of his life, or did he use his father's death as a way to get closer to me? I thought about all the times he tried to convince me that he loved me just the way I was. Was that real, or was being 'the good one' his way of trying to control me? I had spent the last twenty years feeling guilty for what I'd done to Jack, but maybe my gut had been telling me that something was seriously wrong. He had tricked me into spending five years with him.

When Buckley first called me to the precinct, Jack had pleaded with me to take his case instead of passing it on to another lawyer. *You know I didn't do this, but some other lawyer won't.* He had counted on me being blinded by my own guilt.

I heard a knock at the office door, and Einer poked his head in. 'Sorry, I know you didn't want to be interrupted, but Charlotte's here. She wouldn't wait in the lobby. I think she was too uncomfortable with our sexual energy. She insisted on coming back here.'

'It's fine.'

As Charlotte slipped past Einer, he said, 'I could turn you if you gave me a chance.'

'Dear boy, I would *break* you.'

Once the door was closed, she made herself at home in my chair behind the desk.

'So what's up, Charlotte?'

'The DA's about to revoke Jack's bail, and Jack says you haven't returned his calls all day. What the fuck do you think is up?'

'I've been busy.'

'Nice. Well, now I know why Jack's wondering

if he needs a different lawyer for this bail thing. What's going on, Olivia?'

So when Jack first got arrested, he only wanted me. Now that I saw the truth, he was ready for someone else. 'Maybe he should switch counsel. He could probably get an adjournment. Buy himself some more time.'

'You're really going to drop him? Are you even allowed to do that after what I've paid you?'

'Really, Charlotte, this is about your money? Remember why you guys pushed me to take this case from the beginning? Because I knew Jack, so I'd believe him and work harder for him. Well, I don't believe him anymore.'

'Will you just tell me what's going on? Jack said he messed up and lied to you about someone coming to the apartment, but you've got him so trained only to talk to his lawyers that he clammed up after that. Did someone mess up his bail by coming over? Jack can't control that.'

'Do you remember Ross Connor? Owen's old partner?'

'Drunk gropey Irish boy who tried jamming his sloppy tongue down my throat at Bowery Bar?'

'That'd be the one. I tried to get him to vouch for Jack at his bail hearing, and it led to this whole conversation about Ross thinking Jack has a secret side to him. He said that when he went to tell Jack that Molly was killed, Jack dropped his book bag and condoms fell out. But now Ross has found out that Molly couldn't even have children anymore. He went to Jack's apartment hoping he'd say something incriminating.'

'Because of a suspected affair? I hear some people cheat, and it doesn't make them murderers.'

'The point is, Jack lied to me, and not just about Ross's little social visit. It's bad, Charlotte. Seriously bad.'

She rose from my desk and sat next to me at the conference table.

'I've had some girlfriends over the years, a couple of them who were really pretty great. But I'm not sure I've ever loved anyone the way I love Jack. The way I loved Owen.'

'You guys are like siblings.'

'Not *like* siblings. We are *family*. Except better — truly connected. But Jack's not perfect. No one is. We both know that Owen wasn't.'

I turned and caught her intense gaze. She knew. I had never told anyone except Melissa the complete story of what happened that night.

That Seiko Jack found on our bed? If he'd looked a little closer, he would have recognized it. The watch belonged to his brother, Owen.

Owen had been with me. Only once, and not for very long. There had always been a silent recognition that we were more alike than Jack and I. Jack even mentioned once that his brother and I had the same kind of energy in the way we talked and moved. We may have looked at each other too long across the table a few times, but neither of us had ever even mentioned the possibility of an attraction.

He stopped by unexpectedly after testifying at

288

the courthouse. I'd just gotten the final rejection letter on my applications for a federal judicial clerkship. It was a plum job, practically a requirement in some circles. It also would have been a reason to bump the wedding for another year. I let Owen console me, and then made it very difficult for him to stop. Like I had convinced myself about Gregg, *it just happened*.

That's how Owen was able to meet Jack so quickly after his distraught phone call. Had he come clean with Jack? Or had he just nodded along as the two of them drank into the night?

I still had no idea. All I knew was that six hours after Owen ran out of our apartment saying he couldn't believe what we had done, he died in a car accident. For the next month, I would sleep on the sofa because I couldn't bring myself to climb back into that bed.

'How did you know?'

'Owen came to my apartment that night, after you guys — *ugh*. He was frantic, completely out of his mind. I was pissed as hell, screaming at him for letting himself become yet another notch in your very busy belt. Jesus, Olivia, what the fuck were you thinking? I always had a feeling you were messing around on Jack, but his brother?'

'I know.' I had nothing else to say for myself.

'And then Jack called Owen's cell phone, needing someone to talk to. I should have stopped Owen from going. He'd already had three drinks at my place, plus whatever he had with you — and I knew Jack was going to want to drink, too. Owen would have been drunk as a

289

skunk by the time he was driving home. The police somehow managed to leave that out of the reports.'

'Does Jack know?'

She shook her head. 'At least, not from me. I've never told him, and I never will.'

'Thank you.'

'It's not for you. It's for him. That's not something he needs to learn about his only brother. You know why I never liked you with Jack?'

'Because you and I are so much alike?' I gave her a small smile, which she actually returned.

'You never really understood him. You treated him like a one-dimensional character — the sweet, preppy guy who loved you more than anything. But Jack's always been more complex than you realized. He loved his parents, but they did a fucking number on him, because that's what all parents do. His dad was always angry — resentful that he didn't have more to give his family. And his mom was always trying to keep the peace. It made Jack learn how to be passive. It's why he's always got to play the good guy. It's not healthy. Everyone's got to be bad on occasion. Don't you realize that he was drawn to you because you let him be a little bit naughty? The condoms Ross Connor saw? Jack had affairs. Multiple.'

'I can't picture that.'

'He loved Molly — don't get me wrong. It's like Molly was to Jack, as Jack was to you. Does that make any sense?'

Unfortunately, it did. I had known in my head

290

that I should be devoted to Jack. That I should love him and marry him and grow old with him. But we never actually felt *right* together. Being with him was so much work, like I was constantly pretending to be a nicer, better, more generous person than I really was. 'This sounds awful, but our relationship was so — '

'*Uninspired?* That's what Jack said to me once about his relationship with Molly.' Charlotte began to fiddle with a pen on the table. 'Eventually third parties got involved — no one that really mattered, but who filled the gap in his life with Molly and Buckley. It's kind of ironic: you always thought Jack was too nice for you, but he always had an edge, a darkness, that he didn't show you.'

'How dark? Dark enough to kill three people? Because, I've got to be honest, Charlotte: I think that's what we're looking at.'

'That's why I came here, Olivia. To tell you, I honestly don't know if Jack did it or not. The minute Buckley pulled out Jack's laptop at my apartment, I thought, maybe somewhere deep in her unconscious, even she knows it's possible her father did this.'

'You're the one who's been telling me the whole time that it's ridiculous to even imagine Jack hurting another person.'

'Because I wanted you to help him. I still do. And I was probably lying to myself, too. But I'm not blind; I've seen the evidence trickling in. The reason I'm here is because I've thought about it: Jack could tell me he did this horrible thing, and I'd still fight for him to my last breath. I'm not talking about excusing him. I'm talking about supporting him. I still love him, and I need to know that you're still fighting for him.'

What she was saying would probably sound crazy to someone who wasn't a criminal defense lawyer, but I knew exactly what she was talking about: the parents, spouses, and siblings who came to understand their loved ones were guilty, who helped them get through the court process, who visited in prison. People don't stop existing just because they've done something terrible.

'I don't know, Charlotte. I've been lied to by clients, but this is Jack. It feels personal.'

'That's because it is. You owe him, Olivia. Help him however you can.'

★ ★ ★

I woke to the sound of people screaming at each other. My left ear, resting on my pillow, was killing me. I slipped my hand beneath my cheek. I had fallen asleep with my earbuds in, repeat episodes of *Law & Order* still playing back-to-back on my iPad.

It was four in the morning. A half-empty bottle of wine was open on my nightstand. I resisted the temptation to pour another glass.

There was a reason I had jammed those earbuds in. Without the distraction of a television show, I kept hearing the clash of competing voices in my head. Ross Connor, saying Jack had a dark side. Scott Temple, telling me that Jack was playing me. Then the sound of Jack, begging me to do what I could to keep him out of prison.

292

Followed by Charlotte, saying that I owed him.

I pulled out my earbuds, sat up, and opened my nightstand drawer. I found the black velvet box at the very back, covered in dust. I hadn't looked inside it for years. I pulled out the watch first and placed it next to the clock. The necklace was tangled but I managed to smooth out the chain and slip it around my neck. It was Jack's present to me for my twenty-first birthday, the first time I'd ever received a little blue box with a white ribbon.

I had returned his mother's ring to Charlotte after the breakup, but these things I'd kept: the watch because how could I return it, and the necklace because I wanted it. The tiny silver clasp locked on the second try, still a familiar maneuver after all these years.

I rolled onto my back, closed my eyes, and ran the tip of my index finger around and around the infinity-shaped pendant. Over the last twenty years, my relationship with Jack had been condensed down to a single day — no, the single moment when he had walked into the apartment and seen the evidence that would finally convince him to leave. But there had been all those other moments when he had stayed.

★ ★ ★

The last time I saw my mother in person was during winter break of my senior year in college. It was January third. I remember the date because Dad put her in the emergency room with internal bleeding in the early hours of the

New Year. The next-door neighbor called me on the second because she thought I 'ought to know.' From what she'd heard, the emergency room had called the police, and my father was in custody.

I had to max out one credit card and dip into another for a full-fare ticket on the earliest flight the next morning. I would have spent ten times more if necessary. Jack insisted on coming with me. I suspected it was the only time in his entire friendship with Charlotte that he asked her for money.

When I got to the hospital, I found my mother watching *Wheel of Fortune* in a shared room. She turned her bruised face away the second she saw me. 'Thought you were staying in New York for the holidays.'

'Marla called.'

'Of course she did. Does your father know you're home?'

'We came straight here from the airport.'

'He picked you up all the way in Eugene?'

'No, Jack came with me. We rented a car. He's in the waiting room.'

'Still got him fooled, do you?' She winced from the pain of a chuckle.

'Marla told me Dad got arrested.'

'Got out last night.' My father had always managed to confine the proof of his violence to our home. Naively, I had thought that his getting arrested meant that he would actually stay in jail for more than a day.

'The nurse told me they sent in a social worker to talk to you about options. Support

294

groups. A part-time job. Pretty soon, I'll be in a position to help. You can do this.'

'You've got to stop being so judgmental, Olivia. I don't know where you got that from.'

'Mom, I'm not judging you. I'm trying to help.'

'No, you're telling me once again how to live my life. I've never heard of a child so convinced she's better than her family.'

It escalated quickly, the way these things always did with my parents. Within minutes, she was screaming that I should mind my own damn business and telling me to 'go back to that school of yours.' She got so loud that her roommate pressed the call button, and I was asked to leave so 'the patient could get her rest.'

When Jack woke up alone in the motel that night, he asked the clerk where to find the nearest bar. He found me playing quarters with two guys in blue jeans and work boots. I was to the point of grabbing the glass before waiting to see where the coin landed.

Jack had thrown some bills on the counter and turned the empty glass upside down. 'Let's go home.'

My drinking buddies rose from their stools, begging to differ, but something about the look in Jack's eyes made them back down. Had they seen his dark side?

At the motel, Jack held my hair in the bathroom until I had nothing but dry heaves. He washed my face and helped me into bed. As he wrapped his arms around me, he whispered, 'I'm so sorry, Olivia. I understand you now. I know you. And I love you, forever.'

In the morning, we flew back to New York. I pretended not to remember anything after leaving the bar, and we never talked about that trip again. Five months later, he proposed.

★ ★ ★

I spent the next hour flipping from one side of the bed to the other. The second the clock clicked to five o'clock, I took off the necklace, jumped up, and pulled on a pair of jeans.

The office was pitch black. I was careful to lock the door behind me immediately.

I hit the lights and headed straight to the conference room, where an entire wall of brown boxes stood, threatening to tumble. I scanned the Sharpie notes I had scrawled on the ends of each box. 'Penn Station.' I pulled that box from beneath the one resting on top of it. It contained everything Einer had been able to compile about the Penn Station shooting.

I had skimmed the contents a couple of weeks earlier, and then quickly packed them up again because it was so upsetting. The video surveillance showing the entire shooting had never been released, but the media had published several still photographs from the scene. Thirteen dead bodies. Others splattered with blood. Some victims still alive, crawling, appearing to beg for help.

Inside these boxes was a way for Jack to not spend the rest of his life in a cell, even if he was guilty.

I hadn't gotten Jack's psychiatric records yet, but an insanity defense was out of the question. In New York, we'd have to prove that Jack lacked 'substantial capacity' to appreciate either the nature of his conduct or the fact that his conduct was wrong. The problem was, Jack obviously went to great lengths to hide what he did, proving that he knew what he was doing and that it was wrong.

But if I could show that Jack acted under an 'extreme emotional disturbance,' he would be convicted of manslaughter instead of murder. Plus, the jury would weigh the reasonableness of an extreme emotional disturbance claim from the perspective of a person in the defendant's situation 'under the circumstances as he believed them to be.' Last year, a woman had gotten an EED verdict when she claimed that she killed her child to save him from being tortured by his father. Even though she offered no proof that the father had ever hurt the child, what mattered under the law was that *she* believed the child would be tortured and that a painless death was the better alternative.

The facts *as Jack believed them to be*. Jack believed that Malcolm Neeley had neglected his son Todd, and nurtured his antisocial tendencies to the point where the father was to blame for the deaths that occurred at the son's hands.

I was already picturing our arguments in court. Scott Temple would claim that the photographs from Penn Station were inflammatory, but the jury would need to see them to understand Jack's psychological reaction when the civil suit against Malcolm Neeley was dismissed, stifling the one hope he retained for justice.

He could serve as little as five years. The judge would probably sentence him to more given the other victims involved, but it was still better than a life sentence for murder.

I had represented far worse people for doing even more horrible things. Jack might be guilty, but I could still help him.

*　*　*

I set the photographs aside and began flipping through the police reports. The first four pages were devoted entirely to a list of the victims — some dead, some wounded; some female, some male; birth dates and races listed; last known addresses and phone numbers. Their next of kin.

Molly Buckley Harris. W/F. DOB 8-5-73. NOK: Jackson Harris, 212-929-4145, 177 W. 13th St.

It's a funny thing. When you're tired, general cognitive ability drops. There's scientific evidence to back that up, no question. Because you're slacking off, some other part of your brain — the base, the lizard, the id, whatever you want to call it — tries to compensate. Eighty-five percent brain-dead, fifteen-percent instinctive genius.

Maybe if I had slept more than three hours, I would have missed it. But I was exhausted, so my inner lizard kicked in. What my eyes might normally have skimmed past became a magnet drawing my full attention.

The phone number listed for Molly Buckley Harris's next of kin. I'd seen that phone number before.

21

Three hours later, I appeared at Jack's apartment door in one of my best suits — a slate Armani — a black coffee in hand for me, cream and sugar for him.

'This is a nice surprise.'

I never had returned his phone calls yesterday. 'It's officially been a month since you've worn that state-provided jewelry on your ankle. I figured I should be here when the police come by for your home inspection.' In theory, the visit was a routine monthly appointment to monitor the equipment and sweep for any obvious violations of release conditions, but with the prosecution trying to pull Jack's release, I assumed they might be looking for problems. 'I brought caffeine.'

I held out a cup, but his hands were occupied by the two ties that he held up at either ear. 'What do you think? A or B?' One was blue with white and red stripes, the other red with blue and white stripes.

'Either indistinguishable white-boy tie is fine.'

'Got it. We'll go red.'

As he looped the silk around his collar, I led the way into the living room and set his coffee on an end table. 'Have you ever noticed how things that seem like big decisions turn out not to be? Do you pick red or blue? And then you just get used to something and never think about it again.'

'I'm one hundred percent positive that I never cared about the contrast between those two ties. I think I bought them at the same time because they were on sale.'

'Right. But for all you know, red or blue could look totally different to the police officers who come here to check you out. Blue is honest, red is cynical, or vice versa.'

'Seriously? You can't possibly think this is going to make me feel better.'

'Sorry, I'm just rambling. The check today is no big deal. But, just in case, wear the blue one. It's perceived as calming. There's research, actually, by overpaid jury consultants. My point is that sometimes we make decisions without really making them. Like, there's a ton of articles out there about the number of people who have decided to give up landlines. It's a huge cultural shift. Political polling even gets thrown off because some of the pollsters only call landlines and miss out on all the younger people who are cell only.'

'That's a far cry from red versus blue ties.'

'I know. But what I mean is that sometimes you decide things accidentally. Like Einer mentioned a few weeks ago that I was the rare forty-something-year-old who was cell only. But I never consciously made the decision. In the old days, I had a shitty apartment with a home phone because everyone automatically set up a phone account when you got an apartment. And then when I finally had some money in my pocket, I moved into a not-shitty place a few blocks away, and I just never hooked up a phone.

Before I realized it, anyone who needed to find me called my office or cell. I ended up being one of those people who didn't have a home phone number, just a mobile.'

Jack was adjusting the blue tie. Double Windsor. It looked good. He was one of those men who looked better at forty-four than twenty-four.

'So, you don't have a landline, either,' I said.

'Uh-uh.' His tie was straightened. He was now fiddling with his hair in the mirror above the fireplace.

'But you've lived here since — what — 2001?'

'Yeah, right after Buckley was born.'

'So that's what I don't understand. No one was cell phone only in 2001. But now you don't have a landline. It's one thing to never get around to hooking it up. But at some point, you actually took the time to call Verizon and tell them to disconnect your phone. Why? To save thirty bucks a month?'

He had moved on to taming a stray eyebrow. 'We never used it, I guess. I really don't remember.'

It was the same breezy tone he'd used when he lied to me about Ross Connor's attempt to interrogate him: *Oh, yeah, I guess I did have one break from routine.* When I'd asked him about making a threatening comment about Neeley: *Did I?*

'Now that I can tell when you're lying to me, I can't help but wonder how many times I missed the signs.'

He turned away from the mirror and faced

me. 'Go ahead and ask the question, Olivia.'

'It's not a question, it's a fact. Tracy Frankel's phone records — Einer thought she dialed the wrong number to a Soho shoe shop three times in a row. But he was wrong. Tracy was trying to call *you*.'

He punched the side of a fist against the edge of the mantelpiece. 'This is just like you to dance around the issue for ten minutes, setting up some kind of test that's impossible for me to pass. Can't you just talk to me like a normal human being? It's not what you think. I didn't do this.'

My legs were shaking as I rose from the sofa. I had never seen Jack like this. 'I saw your face when the ADA read Tracy's name at the arraignment. I thought you were freaked out because she was so young, but you recognized her name.'

Jack opened his mouth but nothing came out.

'By the way, you're on your own for this inspection,' I said, dropping my cup in his office garbage can. 'And once the police are gone, I'd spend the rest of your time coming up with an explanation for why Tracy would be calling your old number. I figured this out, and it's pretty obvious that Scott Temple did, too. The bail hearing's in two days. You're going back to jail.'

* ★ *

I exited the elevator to find Nick the doorman buttoning his blue blazer around his thick torso. 'Good morning, Miss Randall. Normally I see

303

you here when I'm on my way home.'

'I'm the early bird today, I guess. Hey, Nick. Do you mind if I ask you a question?' I rifled through my briefcase until I landed on a manila file folder, and then plucked out an eight-by-ten printout. 'Have you ever seen this woman before?' It was Tracy Frankel's booking photograph from her one drug arrest.

'Um — maybe? She looks familiar, I guess.'

'Do you mean from the newspaper?' I prompted. The media coverage of the shooting had been so focused on Jack and Malcolm Neeley that Tracy Frankel's and Clifton Hunter's photographs were rarely shown. But they had been featured in a few articles. 'Something about the shooting down at the waterfront?'

Nick looked left and right, monitoring the lobby traffic before speaking in a hushed voice. 'We're under strict directions from the co-op board not to gossip about Mr. Harris's . . . *situation*. Let the justice system do its thing, you know? Not for the neighbors to be all up in his business.'

'Sure. That sounds sensible.'

I was heading toward the revolving door when Nick called out behind me. 'You know what? Come to think of it, now that you mention Mr. Harris, I do remember where I've seen her. She came here looking for him once, or maybe twice.'

I turned around and pulled the picture again from my bag, laying it on the marble counter before Nick. 'This woman? She came looking for Jack Harris?'

'Yes. It was a while ago. You know, before the, uh — '

'Situation?'

'Yeah, exactly. But not long before, because I remember she wasn't wearing a lot of clothes, you know? So it was hot out already. I described her to Mr. Harris, and he made it clear that I should ask her to leave if she came back. I thought maybe she was some bad-influence friend of Buckley or something, but it's not my place to ask. Oh, wait, that's right — yeah, it's coming back to me. After he said tell her to leave if she comes back, I saw her one more time, talking to Buckley on the street, but she never showed up again, not that I saw. That was the end of it. Does that maybe help Mr. Harris with his . . . you know?' he whispered.

I thanked Nick effusively for his help, but, no, it was definitely not helpful to Jack's case.

Jack had an affair with one of Buckley's friends? No, Tracy was four years older, an entire generation in teen years; I couldn't imagine a connection between them. There was another explanation.

The second I hit the sidewalk outside Jack's building, I called Don. He picked up immediately. 'That former client who works at CUNY, the one who told you that Tracy Frankel only enrolled in one class before dropping out? Any chance you can call him? We need him to look up Tracy's college application. Her mother said she bounced around from school to school.'

'What exactly are you looking for?'

305

'A list of every school she went to, hopefully with the dates.'

'That's a tall order.'

'And don't say anything about this to Jack or Charlotte yet.'

'Okay. Am I allowed to ask what's going on?'

'Jack's been lying to us this entire time.'

★　★　★

By the time I got to the office, Don had the information I'd asked for. 'I got hold of my guy at CUNY. I've never heard of any of these places, but I'm no expert on schools for rich, troubled city kids.' He handed me a sheet of paper. 'What the hell's going on?'

According to her one and only college application, Tracy had attended three high schools: the French School, Halton Girls' School, and the Stinson Academy. 'It's a connection to Jack. Or at least it might be.' I showed him the crime report from the Penn Station shootings, listing Molly's next of kin as Jackson Harris, along with his phone number. 'Remember how Einer said Tracy called a shoe store in Soho three times? It bugged me at the time because if it had been a wrong number, she eventually would have called someone just one digit off. But she didn't. She was trying to call Jack. The shoe store number used to be Jack's landline at home, before Penn Station.'

Don looked confused. 'And why would Tracy Frankel be calling him?'

'My guess is for money. She was an addict,

306

and her parents had cut her off.'

'What am I missing here?'

'I think Tracy was blackmailing Jack. I just need to make a phone call to confirm it.'

★ ★ ★

I called the last high school Tracy had attended.

The headmaster at the Stinson Academy sounded nothing like a headmaster. No snoot or toot. In a heavy Bronx accent, John DeLongi confirmed that he'd been what he preferred to call the 'head coach' at Stinson Academy for eleven years.

'Oh good. That means you'll probably be able to help me. My name is Olivia Randall, and I'm one of the lawyers representing Jackson Harris.'

'Oh my. Well, that's certainly been in the news.'

'Yes, that always makes our job interesting. We're gathering background information in the event we decide to put on character evidence. Of course one aspect of Mr. Harris's good character is the volunteer work he's done discussing literature and writing with kids.'

'I'm no lawyer, but is that really the kind of thing a court will look at in a murder trial?'

I flipped the bird at my phone. Just give the information! 'Well, as I said, we're just collecting background for now. I assume that if the time came for it, someone there could tell the court about the work Mr. Harris did at the Stinson Academy?'

'Yeah, sure, no problem. I mean, he hasn't

come around for — I don't know — two or three years, I guess, but, yeah, he was very generous with his time. Our students need modes of teaching that go beyond the traditional. With creative outlets, they can see that not everyone has the same cookie-cutter, billion-dollar jobs as their parents, and that's okay.'

'So, just to confirm, Jack Harris volunteered with his writing workshops during the 2011 to 2012 academic year?'

'Well, that's quite specific. Just one second and I can check this fancy machine here. Yep, sure enough, that was his last visit.'

I now knew for certain how Jack had met Tracy Frankel. I hung up the phone and took the seat next to Don in the conference room.

'I'm still completely confused,' he said. 'Jack knew Tracy? How does this fit into his case?'

'Jack and Tracy weren't the only people at that high school.' I found a copy of Malcolm Neeley's transcript from the Penn Station civil suit on the table. I flipped to page forty-two. 'Look. Right there.'

Don followed my finger to the critical sentence: *Let's talk next about your son's move from the Dutton School to the Stinson Academy.*

★ ★ ★

I remembered that Amanda Turner worked at a high-end PR firm in the Flatiron District. I took the liberty of showing up unannounced.

The security guard at the front desk made a

quick call, and minutes later, Amanda — perfect hair and makeup — stepped from the elevator.

'Max has made it perfectly clear that I'm not supposed to talk to you,' she said.

'Please,' I said, 'I can call you to the stand if necessary — Max, too — but something has come up in our investigation. It's important. Doesn't Max want to know the truth about his father's murder?'

Amanda let out a sigh. 'Do you know what it's like for him to be the crazy shooter kid's brother, the one with the stupid asshole father? But Malcolm being a bad person doesn't justify what Jack Harris did — '

'Please, just one question about Max's brother, okay? You told me that Todd was pining over a girl before the shooting at the train station. Was that another student at the Stinson Academy?'

'Seriously? This is what you're worried about?'

'I think it matters, yes.'

Amanda waved at an attractive blonde who whisked through the lobby toward the elevator, then stepped toward me and lowered her voice. 'Yes, it was some girl he knew from the Stinson Academy. We never actually met her. Todd would talk about how beautiful she was, and — this is mean — but no beauty was going to give Todd the time of day. Max and I called her his imaginary girlfriend.'

'Did Todd at least say what she looked like?'

'Um, a little, but again, we'd sort of goof on it. He said she had dark hair and pale skin and looked like something out of a fairy tale. She was a couple of years older, I think.'

'Do you remember anything else about her?'

'Not really. But I remember he called her Tee. That's all I know.'

* * *

I was disappointed when Buckley answered the door at Jack's apartment.

'Is something wrong?'

For a teenager, the girl's people-reading skills weren't too shabby. 'Just need to run something by your dad. Sorry for not calling.'

'He told me the DA's trying to put him back in jail until trial?'

'It's typical bluster,' I said. 'The legal equivalent of trash talk. The DA is just trying to panic us into a plea deal.'

I was lying through my teeth but didn't know what else to tell her. She walked me into the living room, and Jack emerged from the back of the apartment, his hair still damp from a shower.

'Guess all pop-ins are unannounced when you're on electronic monitoring.'

I wasn't about to apologize. 'Can we talk for a second?'

He gave Buckley a look that had become shorthand for 'beat it.' She couldn't be within earshot if we were going to preserve attorney-client privilege.

The second we were alone, I said two words: Tracy Frankel.

'I don't know why she tried to call my old number.'

Still lying. 'This whole time, you've been saying it was *so unseemly* to point out that she was a drug addict. *Basic human decency.* You are so full of shit, Jack. You didn't want us digging into Tracy's background because you were afraid we'd come right back to you. I called the Stinson Academy. You taught one of your workshops while she was a student. Tracy's mother told me she had a crush on a poetry teacher. The condoms that Ross Connor saw. It all makes sense now; she was one of your girlfriends.'

I saw Jack's gaze move toward the back of the apartment. Even with a life sentence on the line, he was worried about his daughter finding out he was a cheater.

'I screwed up, okay?' He sat on the sofa and gripped his knees with his fingertips. 'It was a few times, and it was colossally stupid.'

Finally. 'So what happened, Jack? Did Tracy get a little too clingy after Molly died, calling you at home, talking about becoming the next Mrs. Jackson Harris? So you dropped her cold and disconnected your phone, and thought you'd gotten rid of her. But fast-forward, and now Mommy and Daddy won't pay her bills. You're in the news, a beloved widower and plaintiff in a multimillion-dollar lawsuit against a hedge fund manager. Suddenly you're back on her radar.' I was pacing, my words flowing quickly. I could see every part of the story I was telling. 'She calls the old number three times in a row, then starts showing up at your building. And when you don't give her what she wants, she moves on to another target. She wasn't calling the Sentry

Group for Max; she was calling Malcolm. She was going to tell him everything she knew about you. And now she and Malcolm are both dead.'

'You really think that? You think I could do something like that?'

Yes, after all these weeks, with all this evidence, I finally did.

Jack could see the answer to his question in my eyes. 'I disconnected our phone line because she kept calling me after Molly died, and I just couldn't even look at her without feeling sick. Then she showed up at the building a couple of months ago. She was blackmailing me.'

'I found a witness who saw Tracy talking to Buckley. Was she threatening to tell your daughter, too?'

Jack shot another look toward the back hallway. 'She doesn't know anything. Tracy asked her for directions or something, and then told me she'd met my daughter. Yes, she threatened to tell her everything.'

'This wasn't just about your affair with a seventeen-year-old girl,' I said. 'This had something to do with Penn Station. Your lawsuit. Why else would Tracy go to Malcolm Neeley?'

When I first realized Tracy had been trying to call Jack, I had assumed that it had something to do with an affair. But once I connected them both to the Stinson Academy, I had seen the common link to Todd Neeley. He had also been a student there, in love with an older girl named Tee, with dark hair and pale skin.

'She saw the lawsuit in the paper. She cornered me when I was coming out of my

312

building and said, 'I wonder what Mr. Neeley would think if he found out that you had a role in the shooting, too?' I honestly never made the connection until then.'

The connection. I felt the links in the chain beginning to form, but I still hadn't managed to hook them together. 'Todd found out about you and Tracy.'

Jack nodded. 'He was obsessive. I guess he followed Tracy around enough that he saw her get in my car.'

'And Penn Station?' I asked.

'The witnesses said Molly was talking to Todd before he pulled out the gun. Everyone assumed she had seen something — some kind of gesture or a flash of the weapon, or maybe heard him say what he was about to do. She was the heroic teacher, the one who tried to talk him out of doing it.'

'But Tracy told you otherwise,' I said, 'when she showed up this summer.'

'At first, I had no idea what she was talking about,' Jack said. 'But then she tells me that she knew Todd from school. When he asked who her boyfriend was, she actually told him — that's how she was. Bold. Reckless. And smart enough to figure out the truth. I should have told you, but I was afraid no one would believe me. I mean, falling for some girl who threw herself at me — '

'Really, Jack?'

'She did,' he said. '*Repeatedly.* But you're right; she was seventeen years old. I don't know what the hell I was thinking. I was — I wasn't

313

happy with Molly. I always had one eye open, looking for something else — someone else. You of all people should understand.'

It was a low blow. 'That's not the same. I wasn't a teacher sleeping with a teenager.'

'No, you were just fucking my brother.'

I felt myself flinch. All these weeks, he had acted like he had forgiven me. I had convinced myself he didn't know it was Owen. 'Jack — '

'I helped him pick out that watch.' His voice sounded distant. 'Nice enough to be presentable, cheap enough to take an occasional beating on the job.'

I searched his face for some explanation for why he hadn't said anything earlier, but his eyes were dead. I had no idea who I was looking at.

'You keep accusing me of lying?' he said. 'The biggest lie I've told was that I don't blame you for what happened. Of course I do. I called him so I could beat the crap out of him. But when he walked into the bar, I realized I'd have no one else. I wasn't going to let you take away the only family I had left. I wallowed all night about you, but never said what I knew. That's why he drank so much, because of what you made him do.'

'I didn't *make* him do anything.' I stopped myself, knowing that he was manipulating me again. He'd been saving up this moment for when he really needed it. 'You have no idea how much I've punished myself, but don't try comparing that to what you've done.'

'It's exactly the same, Olivia. Don't you see that? You didn't put Owen behind the wheel, but the circumstances you created — that all three of us created — did. I may have set all this in motion, but I didn't pull the trigger. Todd followed Molly from the apartment that morning so he could expose my affair with Tracy. Knowing Molly, she didn't believe him. She always thought the best of me, even when I didn't deserve it. Todd must have moved on to Plan B and pulled out the guns. That's why there was a pause after they spoke; he'd been trying to get her to see the truth about her husband. Molly died because of me — because I cheated on her with some screwed-up teenager, and she refused to believe it.'

I was not going to let him use Owen to keep lying to me. 'There's no way you were going to allow Tracy to tell the world this information.'

His expression shifted again. 'Well, I definitely wasn't going to let her shake me down.' His voice was stronger now, his fists tucked under his arms. I had never seen Jack this aggressive. This was the same guy who used to eat food he didn't order rather than point out a waiter's mistake. 'I was terrified, but made it absolutely clear I'd rather be exposed as some adulterous creep than let her control me for the rest of our lives. I assume that's why she was calling the Sentry Group — to tell Malcolm what she knew, for a price. When the prosecutor said her name at my arraignment, I literally felt like I was going to vomit. But I swear to God, Olivia, I have no idea who killed them.'

'It does work out very well for you that both of them are dead.'

'And that's why I couldn't tell you, don't you

see that? You never would have believed me.'

He was right. And I still didn't.

★ ★ ★

I was hailing a cab at the corner when I heard someone call out my name. I turned to see Buckley walking toward me.

'Wait, don't go,' she said as a taxi started to roll in my direction. I waved off the driver.

'What's up, Buckley?'

'You have to help my dad. You promised.'

This was the last thing I needed to deal with right now. 'You're not supposed to eavesdrop on us. It's attorney-client privilege. The prosecution could make you testify. Do you understand that?'

She flinched as my words got louder, as if she'd never been scolded before.

'I didn't eavesdrop. I could just tell something was wrong after you left. Dad almost ran after you, and I had to remind him about the monitor.'

'Well, that's good then. Go back home.'

'Are you going to be able to keep him out of jail?'

She couldn't possibly believe I had an answer to that question. Her brow was furrowed, and she looked like she was about to cry. This was about more than sensing that 'something was wrong.' She had definitely heard something.

'You've been following your father's case. I know you've seen pictures of Tracy Frankel.' She'd been staring at Tracy's mug shot on Charlotte's iPad right before Jack came home on

316

bail. 'Why didn't you say anything?'

Buckley might think of herself as smart, but she was sixteen years old, and I'd learned a skill or two as a lawyer. I let my question sit between us. If my suspicions were wrong, it was a non sequitur. If not, she'd eventually reply.

'I — she just came up to me on the street. She asked me where she could find a WiFi connection.'

'Are you sure that's all she said?'

'Yeah, she was some stranger on the street.' Buckley was looking at the sidewalk, tapping one foot nervously. She may have thought Tracy Frankel was a random woman last month, but she certainly knew more now. If I had to guess, she'd heard my entire conversation with Jack. 'Did I screw up? I didn't say anything about recognizing her because I thought it would look bad for my father. I was confused.'

Maybe some part of her had known all along that her father was guilty. I heard my cell phone chime in my purse. I held up an arm toward an approaching cab before she could argue.

'It's fine, Buckley. Just go back home. I'll see you at the bail hearing. Everything's under control.'

I waited until she reached her lobby before climbing into the cab. The driver had already started the meter. 'Are we going somewhere or not?'

If he hadn't been so snarky, I might have ignored the buzz of my phone. Instead, I made a point of checking my screen before closing the door. It was a text from Einer: Jack's medical records from the Silver Oaks Psychiatric Center had finally arrived. Einer was leaving them in my office.

I dropped my briefcase in one of the guest chairs and headed straight to the small box that had been added to the chaos of my conference table. I recognized Einer's handwriting on the note dropped on top: *Finally! Maybe something in here to help an EED claim?*

Extreme emotional disturbance. Manslaughter instead of murder. Einer had picked up some legal knowledge over the years.

I grabbed the letter opener from my desk and used it to cut through the tape around the box's edge. I pulled out a three-inch stack of files and placed them in front of me. As I did a cursory flip through the pages, I saw references to all the grief Jack had suffered in just a few years. His mother's death when he was just a teenager. His father a few years later. Then Owen. I caught my own name a few times.

The notes were roughly in reverse chronological order. It was going to be a long night. I flipped to the very back page to start from the beginning.

The initial intake notes were dated six days after Owen's car accident. They resembled every scribble I'd ever seen my own physicians make — completely illegible.

When I realized what I was reading, I saw the file begin to shake in my hands. I looked away, and then forced myself to check to see whether I'd somehow misunderstood. I needed — I didn't know what I needed. To get out of here.

To have never taken that phone call from Buckley. To be someone else.

I moved to my desk, opened my browser, and searched for 'Robin Scheppard doctor.' Jack's psychiatrist was still at Silver Oaks. According to the hospital website, Dr. Scheppard had attended the U.S. Military Academy at West Point and Boston University School of Medicine before completing her residency at Walter Reed Army Medical Center.

I picked up my phone and dialed the phone number listed on the website. 'May I please speak with Dr. Robin Scheppard?'

An hour and a half later, I was pulling a Zipcar rental off I-95 in Stamford, Connecticut. When I passed the brick wall with a discreet sign that said Silver Oaks, I turned into the hospital parking lot and came to a stop.

As I reached for the stack of folders on the passenger seat, I clicked on the car's dome light. I looked one more time at Jack's intake form, knowing that the words wouldn't have magically transformed during the drive from New York.

Ptx presents requesting inptx hosp. 'Thinking of possibility' of killing gf after death in fam.

Jack had checked himself into the hospital because he had found himself thinking about killing me.

22

Dr. Robin Scheppard met me at the reception desk with a chilly handshake — both literally and figuratively. 'Thank you so much for seeing me after hours, Doctor. And on such short notice.'

She led me to an office that felt more like a cozy study than a medical office. 'So, Ms. Randall, I reviewed the release that Jack Harris signed. It does authorize me to speak to you directly, but this is certainly unusual.'

'I'm aware. But Jack's on trial for murder, and we have an important hearing tomorrow. I only got his medical records today.'

'Does this mean Jack is pleading insanity? Surely testimony from a doctor who has treated him more recently would be more helpful. I haven't seen him for — it must be twenty years. I was barely out of my residency.'

'So you remember him.'

'Of course. But I assure you, my notes will be far more complete than my memory at this point.'

'I want to know your reaction when you heard that your former patient had been arrested for murder. That won't be in your notes.'

'No. But I can't imagine why it's relevant, either.'

'Because you saw him when he wasn't well. You'd know better than anyone whether the current charges seem like the kind of thing his illness could lead to. I'm not asking you to testify, Doctor, or even your medical opinion per se. I'm asking you simply as a person who knew a side of Jack that no one else ever saw: how did you respond to the news when he was arrested?'

'Well, as long as we're clear that that's what you're asking, I was shocked. When Jack was a patient here, he was initially unresponsive, with severe depression. Even when he started to communicate, he was stoic. If there were any concerns about violence, it was more about self-harm. He presented as someone who may never have had any onset of mental illness had it not been for this tremendous reaction to grief.'

'His brother's death.'

'Yes, that. But grief can be cumulative, even over years, especially to a personality that might be described as fragile. His mother's death when he was a teenager, followed by his father's death a few years later. Then his brother. And a breakup, which I believe you know about?'

'Yes, I'm that Olivia Randall. The one he thought about killing if I read your notes correctly.'

Her face went blank momentarily. 'It's funny. I had actually forgotten about that.'

'Seems pretty significant to me, and not especially funny, but I'm the one he wanted to kill.'

She shook her head. 'If I had ever taken his comment about hurting you seriously, I would have been obligated to do something to protect you. But the very fact that he chose to come here — simply because the thought even crossed his mind — made me think that the last thing he wanted was to harm others.'

'But on the other hand, you also can't tell me with any certainty that Jack's innocent, can you?'

'Of course not, and you know that. Maybe this will help: I had a reporter call me a few months ago. She was covering a murder case where a seemingly nice, normal college student came up with an extensive plan to kill a fellow student over some slight grudge. Because I've testified in numerous homicide trials, she wanted my insight about how a quote-unquote normal person can come to commit cold-blooded, premeditated murder.'

'And?'

'I've spent a good number of hours of my career talking to people who admit to being murderers. These seemingly normal people tell me how it starts small. They get fired from their job, or dumped by their husband, and they begin to wish some kind of bad upon the person responsible — typically, that the world will come to see the person for what they really are. And when karma or fate or whatever doesn't come through, the seemingly normal person starts to think, 'What if they died?' And that turns into, 'What if I killed them?' And eventually, 'How would I do it?' and 'Would I get away with it?''

'That doesn't sound normal to me.'

'Really? Many people, if they were being honest, would admit to having thought about it. It's all hypothetical, mind you — just a fantastical and devilish daydream. But what happens psychologically is that the seemingly normal person is now becoming conditioned to the idea of killing, no different behaviorally than a dog hearing the doorbell over and over again. It's no longer shocking. So the idea develops. And for most people, the idea remains exactly that. It stops right there. But for others, those thoughts become a training ground. And then when something happens to trigger and heighten the emotion toward the contemplated victim, the conditioning kicks in. *Bam*. The person kills. And it may seem premeditated because the thoughts were there all along. But they only became real at that second.'

'And you're saying that Jack is like most of these people, where it all remained hypothetical.'

'Clearly. You're still alive, aren't you?'

★ ★ ★

Once I was on I-95, I listened to the hum of the Toyota Corolla, tires against concrete, my own breathing. It was almost like meditation.

I replayed the doctor's tutorial in my head. *For most people, the idea remains exactly that.* When the thoughts were about me, Jack had made them stop by locking himself up for a year. *But for others, those thoughts become a training ground.* By the time he came to hate Malcolm Neeley, Jack no longer had the luxury of inpatient treatment. He had a daughter to take care of. *So the idea develops.*

Jack knew where Malcolm Neeley could be found on Wednesday mornings. He could research information about surveillance along the Hudson River. Find the magazine article detailing the location of the cameras. He was a gifted novelist. He knew how to tell a story. He would know that truth could be stranger than fiction. He would know that the story of a mysterious beautiful woman would seem too bizarre to be a lie. How had he described it to Detective Boyle? Surreal, like he was narrating a tale for a reader.

I pictured him at the firing range, learning how to shoot a Glock. Driving to Jersey to buy one on the street. Opening a temporary e-mail account to hire Sharon Lawson. Telling her where to sit, right where a camera would catch a fleeting glimpse of the lady in the grass. I imagined him pulling the gun from the basket, aiming it at Malcolm.

Or had he shot Tracy first? The woman who looked like a younger me.

Tomorrow, Scott Temple was going to try to put Jack back into custody. I had seen what Jack looked like after only a couple of days in jail. And I had seen how anxious Jack was to know one way or the other whether he'd be convicted. I knew exactly how the uncertainty of the future, combined with pretrial incarceration, could change a defendant's fortitude. Once Jack was in jail awaiting trial, he would become the kind of client who'd plead guilty just to get it over with.

What did I still owe him?

★ ★ ★

At 9:52 the next morning, the courthouse elevator doors opened. From the hallway outside

324

Judge Amador's courtroom, I saw Charlotte, Jack, and Buckley, side by side in a row. I'd grown accustomed to the picture, like a three-person *American Gothic* — two grim, worried faces, Jack the unreadable pitchfork in the center.

Jack was having a hard time maintaining eye contact with me. 'I was wondering whether you'd even show up.'

'I'm your lawyer, Jack.'

I fought for clients all the time, even when I knew they were guilty. It wasn't my job to know the truth. That didn't change just because my client was Jack Harris.

When I walked into the courtroom, Scott Temple was already at counsel table. He shot me a sideways glance as I crossed the bar, and then continued to look at his notes.

'Can we talk about why we're here?' I asked. I wished Don was here to ask the question, but he had texted me to say he was stuck in Judge Gregory's courtroom and might be a few minutes late.

'The way you talked to me before pulling me in here on a so-called Brady violation? The frog and the scorpion, Olivia. No more side deals.'

Scott had always been one of my best resources at the DA's office. I may have resolved to continue working for Jack, but I did regret burning a friend on his behalf.

'He hasn't violated any of his release conditions, Scott. I really don't understand why we're here.'

'Because you ran over that incompetent ADA

Amy Chandler at the original bail hearing. The case against your client is a lot stronger than you know. It's time we got that on the open record.'

I turned to face the galley and realized the media were here. I recognized Jan Myers, along with reporters from the *Times, Daily News,* and *Post.* Max Neeley had just walked in, hand in hand with his ex-girlfriend Amanda Turner. She looked at me blankly, clearly not wanting me to show any sign of recognition.

I heard a door open at the front of the courtroom, and Judge Amador walked out of chambers in his robe. The bailiff called us to order.

* * *

'I see familiar faces,' the judge said. 'The People are moving to revoke bail? What's the alleged violation?'

Temple rose from his chair. 'If I can clarify, Your Honor. This is a motion to reconsider your original decision to grant bail in the first place. At the time, Your Honor concluded that Mr. Harris was not a flight risk, in large part because our case did not appear particularly strong. I take responsibility for that, Your Honor. I should have attended personally to present evidence that the arraignment ADA was not aware of.'

'Correct me if I'm wrong, ADA Temple, but isn't that Mr. Harris right there? If so, the house arrest appears to be working. What exactly is the problem here?'

'The problem, Your Honor, is that although the People have already complied with our

326

obligations to disclose exculpatory evidence, eventually we will need to disclose additional information that will make the strength of our case quite clear. We believe that once this happens, Mr. Harris might indeed be motivated to flee.'

'Well, we wouldn't want that. What exactly is it that you'd like me to know that I didn't hear at arraignment?'

Temple was starting to talk about the deposition transcript found among Jack's files, revealing Malcolm Neeley's habit of going to the football field on Wednesday mornings, when I interrupted. 'This is clearly an attempt to get around the gag order, Your Honor. The courtroom is filled with reporters. I have no idea what evidence Mr. Temple thinks he has, but he's trying to advertise it to the jury pool before I'm able to rebut it.'

As if on cue, a voice erupted from the galley. I turned to see Max Neeley on his feet, Amanda grabbing his hand, trying to return him to his seat. 'Judge, I deserve to have a private lawyer intervene on my behalf. Jack Harris's lawyer has continually slandered me in these proceedings.'

'Okay, everyone.' Judge Amador was banging his gavel. 'In chambers, lawyers only. Go on home, reporters. You, too, Mr. Neeley. There's nothing to see here.'

★   ★   ★

Amador unzipped his robe and took a seat at his desk. 'Okay, kids. What exactly is going on? Does this have something to do with our last hearing miraculously ending up on *Eyewitness News* even though the courtroom was empty?'

Temple was having a hard time not looking smug. 'You're a very smart man, Your Honor.'

'All right, let's cut to the chase. Ms. Randall, I think you probably leaked something to the press the last time you were here. Mr. Temple, I suspect you haven't exactly been tight-lipped with Max Neeley, who must have a publicist working for him at the rate he's giving interviews. Enough. I'm not letting this motion be used as a run around my gag order.'

I thanked the judge, but he said, 'Not so fast. I took a huge risk releasing your client given the severity of the charges. I think we all know Amy Chandler's not exactly the sharpest knife in the DA's kitchen, so if she didn't give me the full picture the first go-round, I want to hear it now.'

I had been expecting Temple to lay out the evidence of Jack's affair with Tracy Frankel. What he actually had was far, far worse.

Judge Amador looked like a high school student trying to understand advanced physics as Scott Temple brought him up to speed. The prosecution had established at arraignment that Jack had a motive to kill Neeley, was at the waterfront the morning of the shooting, and tested positive for GSR, but now Temple was explaining the rest of the story: the missed-moment post, the Madeline e-mails, and the homeless man who'd found the picnic basket containing the murder weapon.

'I might officially be a loony tune,' Amador

said, 'because I think I followed all that. But I'm afraid I still don't see your point, Mr. Temple.'

'The point is that Jack Harris has been absolutely clear that the only reason he went to the football field that morning was because this woman Madeline told him to. So naturally we were interested in finding this Madeline person to confirm or disprove Mr. Harris's story.'

I had been waiting until we knew more to tell Scott about Madeline, but now it was obvious he'd known all along. I tried to breathe evenly as Temple explained that 'Madeline' had used an account with an anonymous service called Paperfree.

'The Paperfree address was used not only to *respond* to the missed-moment post and contact Jack Harris, but also to hire a prostitute to pose as Madeline in the first place.'

Amador took off his glasses. 'You finally lost me.'

I had no way of stopping Temple as he detailed the e-mails between the anonymous Paperfree account and an online escort. 'Though the escort used a pseudonym on the escorting website, we have now identified her as a woman named Sharon Lawson. She has invoked her Fifth Amendment right to counsel, but we know from the e-mail messages that the person using the Paperfree account told her precisely where to sit, to bring champagne and a picnic basket, and to read a book called *Eight Days to Die*. She was given a photograph of Jack Harris and instructed to try to catch his eye as he passed.'

This was the evidence that I had planned to

use to save Jack. Now Temple was the one presenting it. I had managed to intimidate Sharon into signing an affidavit, but she hadn't bothered to update me with the fact that the prosecution had located her, too.

'And from the People's perspective,' Judge Amador asked, 'what was the point of all that?'

'So that Jack Harris could then tell his best friend Charlotte Caperton about his desire to see this woman again. She then wrote a missed-moment post that this fictitious person 'Madeline' responded to, which gave Harris an explanation for being at the waterfront the morning of the shooting. In the event no one believed him, he had the e-mails and even surveillance camera footage of Lawson to back up his story.'

Temple handed the judge and me a thin stack of stapled pages.

'This is an affidavit from Paperfree.com.' It would have been nice to have Einer here to translate, but I could tell from Scott's confident demeanor that what I was looking at wasn't good. 'It includes a list of IP addresses used to log into the e-mail account in question. Almost all of them are public WiFi connections — Starbucks, a hotel lobby, NYU, and a fro-yo shop. Importantly, they're *all* within walking distance of Harris's apartment.'

As I watched Judge Amador nod, I realized why Scott Temple had been so confident, when I thought the evidence was so equivocal. As a prosecutor, he could get information from sources that would never cooperate with a defense lawyer — sources like e-mail providers. The DA's office would have gotten a subpoena for Jack's e-mails, and then Madeline's, within hours of his arrest.

For weeks, we'd been convinced that someone had framed Jack. Would I have figured out the truth earlier if I'd known that all of the Madeline messages were sent from Jack's neighborhood? I thought I saw a pang of sympathy as I caught Scott Temple's eye. He had tried to warn me. Scott had been right. I was the scorpion.

'Then take a look at paragraph seven,' he said. 'See that IP address there? It's a one-time log-in, for less than a minute. It's the one and only time anyone ever logged in to the Paperfree account from a nonpublic Internet connection. That IP address belongs to Jack Harris's Verizon FiOS account.'

Amador peered over his reading glasses, first at Temple and then at me. He didn't need to use words. A few numbers in an affidavit had just changed the entire case.

'Your Honor, this is a lot of technical information all at once,' I said. 'I'm going to need an opportunity to consult with an expert.'

'Nice try, Ms. Randall, but we all know what we're looking at.'

'I don't understand why the prosecution didn't provide this information earlier. I've been pressing Mr. Temple for discovery.'

Temple was ready with an explanation. 'Initially, because we hadn't yet identified Ms. Lawson. The escort service was less than cooperative. Even now, we're continuing to work on an immunity agreement with Ms. Lawson so she will testify, but in light of recent . . . unusual circumstances with the press, we decided we needed to reassess Mr. Harris's detention status.'

Amador was fiddling with the edges of a motion on his desk. 'I take it the People are arguing that this makes your case stronger, which gives the defendant a greater incentive to flee?'

'Yes, but there's more,' Temple said. 'The day of the shooting, police seized a desktop computer from Jack Harris's office. A forensic analysis of that computer reveals no online use at the time of this one log-in to the Paperfree account, nor any evidence that the computer was ever used to access Paperfree's website.'

'You're starting to lose me again,' the judge said.

'An IP address covers an entire WiFi network, not just one computer,' Temple explained. 'Put simply, Your Honor, a different device was used to check the Paperfree account from Mr. Harris's wireless connection. Mr. Harris has spoken at various writing workshops about his practice of writing on one computer — his desktop, the one police seized — and confining his Internet use to another, his laptop. However, we found no such laptop in his apartment when we executed a search warrant, and have been unable to locate it since.'

Judge Amador's brow furrowed as he turned in my direction. 'I think we can all agree this is quite different from what I heard at the original bail hearing. A stronger case, plus indications of hiding or destroying material evidence.'

'Your Honor, this is the first I've heard of any of this. Again, I need time to respond.'

'That's fine, Ms. Randall, but, at this point, I don't think your client will have the luxury of living at home while you prepare. Maybe you two should talk.'

★ ★ ★

Whatever empathy Temple had felt for me in chambers had dissipated by the time we hit the hallway. 'Don't say I didn't warn you, Olivia. Harris is a sociopath. He hired you as his lawyer for a reason. You were so sure he was innocent, you may as well have been a rookie.'

I told him he was overplaying his hand, and that he was the one who should have been paying closer attention. 'Someone — probably Max Neeley — went to maniacal lengths to frame my client. Is it any surprise that they'd access this e-mail account from spots near Jack's home, even logging on once to Jack's home network?'

'Are you even listening to yourself at this point? You're saying he can't be guilty because he looks too guilty? You're too good for that, Olivia.'

'And you were too good to slip phone records into a truck full of documents, but that happened. You buried Brady material.'

'You know what? You're right. I should have told you about Tracy Frankel's number being in those LUDs. It's just a weird fucking fluke; she was probably selling dope to one of Neeley's employees. But I didn't tell you, and I got nailed for it. So now I'm showing you everything. We've got Harris solid. You know he was in a psych ward? Only someone bat-shit crazy could come up with something this elaborate. But he fucked up one time — one log-in to his fake e-mail account.'

'If he's so maniacal — '

'Yeah, yeah, yeah, I know, it's too stupid a mistake so it must be a frame job. Save it. I ran the same theory past our IT expert. Here's the thing. Paperfree? If you leave it open on your browser, it will automatically update every few minutes. So Harris is being all sly with his anonymous e-mail account, sneaking off to Starbucks and hotel lobbies to check it, but then forgets to close the browser. He comes home. The laptop automatically connects to his home network. And then the account refreshes. Voilà. He fucked up. And then he realizes that the laptop refreshed his account, so, lo and behold, the laptop goes missing. I won't even ask whether you knew. I assume he threw it in the Hudson before the shooting.'

I was trapped. The truth about the laptop would be a problem for both Charlotte and Buckley, and wouldn't do anything to help Jack. That IP address wasn't going away.

'Let me talk to my client.' There was no way around it: Jack was going back into custody to be held pending trial, where he'd be convicted.

★ ★ ★

334

We found an empty jury deliberation room at the end of the hall and closed the door. Don had shown up while I was in chambers, so didn't know any more about this morning's developments than Jack.

Jack's eyes darted between us. 'What's going on? You guys were back there a long time.'

'And I just spoke with the prosecutor one-on-one as well. It's not good, Jack. The judge is not going to let you remain at home pending trial.'

He winced. 'Did they find out about me and Tracy?'

I shook my head. 'That, I would have been prepared for. This, not so much. It's an affidavit from Paperfree.' I handed him the copy Temple had given me. I pulled off the bandage in one fell swoop. 'I might have been able to explain the WiFi connections in your neighborhood, but you logged into that e-mail account from your own IP address. Only once, but it's the nail in your coffin, Jack.'

'My IP address?'

'Yes. From *your* apartment. And your wireless connection has a password, so it's hard to argue that this is one more part of the conspiracy. A jury won't buy it.'

His face went blank. It was the same unreadable expression he'd given Buckley when he heard Tracy Frankel's name at arraignment, then again when he heard about the GSR evidence moments later. At the time, I thought he was worried about how his daughter was handling the hearing.

Now I understood that the facial expression I had seen was panic. He'd looked at Buckley to see if she recognized Tracy's name. And he was surprised by the GSR because he had probably washed his hands after the shooting, but didn't realize that residues could remain on his shirt.

This time, there was no recovering. He was caught.

'So what do I do?'

'You'll be booked today.' Judge Amador hadn't made a final ruling, but I was certain he'd already made up his mind. I had a plan, but it wasn't going to change the facts. 'We'll withdraw as counsel. It will at least buy you some time before trial. I can say it was a conflict of interest to represent you in light of our previous relationship.'

'But it wasn't,' Don said. 'You even checked with the state bar. You don't owe anyone your reputation, Olivia.'

'You're the one who taught me it's always about the client. Jack might get a better plea offer with another lawyer.' I didn't think Temple would intentionally punish Jack because of decisions I had made, but sometimes prosecutors act unconsciously.

'Stop talking about me like I'm not here!' Jack was gripping the edge of the table in front of him. 'If I start all over again with another lawyer, that will just give the DA more time, too, right? And with more time, they might find out about Tracy.'

He was right. As of now, Temple still thought Jack was a widower obsessed with the man he

336

blamed for his beloved wife's death. If he had only killed Malcolm Neeley, Jack would be a hero in some people's eyes. But if the police found out about his affair with Tracy Frankel, any possible sympathy would be gone. 'It's definitely a risk,' I said.

'And I'm going to be convicted anyway, aren't I?'

I looked at Don. We were both on the same page. 'Yes. Your best shot is to go for manslaughter based on what the law calls extreme emotional disturbance. We'd present all the Penn Station evidence — '

Jack was already shaking his head. 'No, I don't want that, not when I know the truth. If I hadn't been involved with Tracy, Todd never would have followed Molly to the train station. Or if I hadn't duped her — if she had actually believed Todd when he told her about my affair — all those people . . . ' His voice trailed off.

'It's your only chance, Jack.'

'Well, then I don't have a chance. I want to change my plea. Go tell the prosecutor.'

'I can ask for an offer, Jack, but you're rushing things.' Yesterday, I had wanted to lock him in a cell myself. Now the desire to help him felt surprisingly natural. 'Is this just about them finding out about Tracy? I think Buckley already knows — '

'It's not about that, okay? Don't you get it? I did it. I did every single thing that prosecutor said. Why do you think I kept telling you to find the woman in the grass?' As if startled by the volume of his own voice, Jack stopped talking and took a seat in one of the chairs around the deliberation table. When he spoke again, it was with control — confident and clinical, like a doctor reporting a diagnosis. 'I *knew* there'd be video footage of her. I knew, because I told her exactly where to sit. And I told Charlotte how seeing that woman had me opening my heart again, knowing it would send her off on some online search for romance. I even told everyone who would listen that I loved *Eight Days to Die*, all because — guess what? — it had a scene set at the football field.'

As Jack continued to document his plan's ingenuity, I felt like I was inside a bubble, hearing him through a filter. His voice was clear, but in my head, the world was silent, as if I could hear my own heartbeat.

I was finally sure: Jack was guilty.

When we returned to the courtroom, I let Jack make his way to Charlotte and Buckley on his own. I didn't think it was my place to be there when he broke the news.

Scott Temple was waiting at counsel table. 'You ready to go back on record?' He lowered his voice. 'It's good that he's talking to his daughter first. I think it's pretty clear which way the judge is going, and the officers will take him into custody immediately. Let me know if they need a couple extra minutes.'

'You're a good guy, Scott Temple, even when you're trying to be a hard-ass.'

'Just figuring that out?'

'Look, I know I made some bad calls on this one, but we need to talk — '

338

I heard a loud thud behind me and turned to find Buckley on her feet, pushing her way past Charlotte and her father into the aisle of the courtroom. Jack reached for her wrist, but she jerked away. He caught up to her, and pulled her into a tight hug. Her arms were locked at her side, but she rocked against his weight. 'No, you can't. No.' She just kept saying no, over and over again, then locked eyes with me. 'You were supposed to help him. What did you do?'

Charlotte stood next to them awkwardly, and then wrapped her arms around Buckley, too. The girl was barely visible as the two of them held her.

Judge Amador stepped from his chambers. As he took in the scene from the bench, I thought it might be the first time I had seen a judge at a loss for words.

He signaled to the court reporter that we were not yet on the record. 'What are we doing here, Counselor?'

Scott let me have the first — and as it turned out, last — word for the day. 'We're ready for you to rule on today's motion, Your Honor. And we'll be in discussions about a non-trial resolution of the case.'

As expected, Judge Amador ordered that Jack be taken into custody. It took nearly forty minutes for officers to arrive at the courtroom to take him away, a delay I attributed to some maneuvering by Scott Temple.

Two weeks later, even though I told him I thought I could get him a better deal if we waited, Jack pled guilty.

THE PEOPLE OF THE STATE OF NEW YORK   )
v.   )
JACKSON HARRIS.   )

Before the Hon. William Amador
For People: Scott Temple
For Defendant: Olivia Randall

BY COURT:
I understand we're here on a change of plea.

BY MS. RANDALL:
That's correct. The defendant will be entering a
plea of guilty to three counts of second-degree
murder.

BY MR. TEMPLE:
One more condition, Your Honor. In light of the
defendant's prior, adamant denials, the People
have requested as part of negotiations that Mr.
Harris provide a detailed factual basis for these
charges to put to rest any kind of doubt the
victims' families or the public might have about
his guilt.

BY COURT:
And this is acceptable to the defendant as well,
Ms. Randall?

BY MS. RANDALL:
Yes, Your Honor.

BY COURT:
Very well, then. Mr. Harris, please state your

actions that give rise to the charges against you.

BY DEFENDANT:
Thank you, Your Honor. Roughly three years
ago, my wife, Molly, was murdered during the
Penn Station massacre by a boy named Todd
Neeley. For reasons that are detailed elsewhere,
I blamed the killer's father, Malcolm Neeley, for
his son's actions. When a civil suit against Malcolm Neeley was dismissed, I came up with a
plan to kill him. On June 17, I shot Mr. Neeley
two times. I also shot two other people who
were in the vicinity. I later learned that they
were Tracy Frankel and Clifton Hunter. To say
that I regret my actions sounds hollow, but I do
regret them. It's almost like I can't believe
I actually did this. But I did. I did this, and I
want to say with all sincerity that I'm sorry,
especially to the families of Ms. Frankel and
Mr. Hunter. No one else was supposed to get
hurt.

BY COURT:
Is that satisfactory to the People, Mr. Temple?

BY MR. TEMPLE:
No, Your Honor. The defendant went to elaborate lengths to make it appear that someone
else had framed him. Though the parties have a
joint sentencing recommendation, I do not want
a situation where Your Honor hears facts that
might be beneficial to the defendant — the
tragic loss of his wife and expressions of contri-
tion — without hearing the rest, including the

extensive planning that went into these murders.

BY COURT:
Mr. Harris, can you tell me more about the preparation for these crimes?

BY DEFENDANT:
I know it seems like planning, but at the time, it felt like a fantasy, like I was making up a plot in my head. I knew from a deposition in the lawsuit that Mr. Neeley went to the waterfront football field every Wednesday morning before work. Not long after that, I read a review of a book called *Eight Days to Die* that mentioned a scene set at the football field. So I bought the book and started telling people how I loved it and was even checking out some of the New York settings, so maybe if I went to the football field and confronted Neeley, I could use the book as an excuse for running into him. But then it would just be my word without any backup. A friend had told me about people who start up online relationships using false identities. I came up with the idea of making myself appear to be a victim of one of these scams, where my supposed love interest would be the one to tell me to go to the football field. I wrote a chain of e-mails back and forth with this nonexistent person. I even hired a woman to pose as her in case anyone doubted that she was real. Is that enough, Your Honor? The point is that I'm guilty and take complete responsibility for my actions.

BY COURT:
I'd say that's quite complete. Mr. Temple?

BY MR. TEMPLE:
That's fine.

BY COURT:
The change of plea is accepted, and I understand that we are proceeding straight to sentencing. Is there anything either party would like to add before I reach a decision?

BY MS. RANDALL:
Just that you follow the joint sentencing recommendation, Your Honor.

BY COURT:
Very well. Mr. Harris, I am accepting your change of plea, and you are hereby convicted of three counts of second-degree murder. It is the judgment of this court that the defendant is hereby committed to the custody of the New York State Commission of Correction for twenty-five years to life.

23

Jack's front door was propped open by a stack of books. I managed to weave a path through the clutter to find Charlotte in the back hallway, yelling at someone in Buckley's bedroom not to 'linger on the panties. Don't think I didn't see you.'

'Movers are all ex-felons,' she muttered.

I was pretty sure that wasn't true, but Charlotte needed something to yell about today. Jack had been sentenced two weeks ago, and she was already breaking down his home.

'Not wasting any time, are you?' Seeing Charlotte in the midst of open boxes and Styrofoam peanuts reminded me of the day she came to our apartment to pack Jack's things.

'If it were up to me, I'd pay the maintenance for the next twenty-five years. But Buckley's therapist says it's for the best. As long as she's running back and forth between here and my place, she'll keep telling herself it's temporary. Sounds like a crock of shit to me, but for once, I'm doing as told.' Charlotte's voice mail summoning me to the apartment hadn't explained the timing of the move. 'I was starting to wonder if you were going to come.'

Charlotte's message had also asked whether I wanted the old photographs of me and Jack, the ones he kept in his closet. It took me hours to decide that, yes, I did want them. I had no idea why, other than that the thought of them being thrown down the trash chute with coffee grounds and greasy takeout containers made me break down in tears in my office.

She went to the dining room and handed me an envelope. I tucked it into my briefcase and pulled out a much larger envelope for her. 'Mostly I wanted to drop these off.' They were guardianship papers. Until Buckley reached the age of majority, Charlotte would be the legal equivalent of her parent.

She muttered a thank-you, and then I handed her something else, a black velvet box. She peeked inside and then closed it. She didn't ask for an explanation. After all these years, I could finally return Owen's watch to someone he really loved. I kept my necklace.

I started to leave, and then turned back. 'Jack tells you everything. He always has.'

'Not this time. He confessed to you before me.'

'But you knew he was guilty. When you came to my office about Ross Connor, you made it sound like you'd support Jack one way or the other. But you already knew.'

'I had my suspicions when you first realized Tracy had been calling the Sentry Group. I never knew her name, but Jack told me he screwed up. Some high school girl he slept with years ago had turned up at the apartment trying to blackmail him. And remember how I said Tracy looked like a young version of you? With the exception of Molly, everyone Jack ever fell for looked like you. I even asked him about it. Tracy was the girl, all right, but he insisted he was innocent. I guess some things are just too horrible to admit, even to your best friend.'

Until the prosecution had dropped the IP evidence on us, Jack had said the same thing to me — admitting to the affair with Tracy but insisting that he was framed. I had never seen a defendant change his position so quickly.

Charlotte was pulling books off the office shelves and stacking them in boxes. 'I'm the last person who should be doing this. I can't throw anything out. I keep thinking that he'll want it later. But there is no later.' She paused on one of the books. 'Oh, man, what should we do with this? Save it or burn it in the street?'

She held up a copy of *Eight Days to Die*.

'I hate to tell you this, but there's probably a market for that on eBay. They call it Murderabilia — sick fucks who collect souvenirs from criminal cases.'

'I don't think I can hold on to this,' she said. 'Can you please take it? Don't even tell me what you do with it. Give it to your sad little boy Einer, or something.'

'Sure.' She handed it to me, and then, for perhaps the first time since I'd known her, she hugged me with both arms. She was a good hugger.

'You did your best for him,' she said. 'Thank you for that.'

I told her to take care of herself.

★ ★ ★

346

Melissa waved at me from behind the bar. She somehow managed to see every corner of the restaurant simultaneously.

She reached for a martini shaker, but I asked for a glass of prosecco instead.

'Look at you getting all classy.' She hit the nasal hard for the word 'classy.' 'Seriously, Livvie, you look good.'

'Thanks.' I had finally been able to sleep through the night a few times in the last week. Yesterday, I had even gone to the gym for the first time in months.

I had just started to tell her about my conversation with Charlotte when we heard a glass break at the back of the restaurant, followed by loud voices. Melissa threw her bar towel on the counter. 'I knew I should have kicked those drunk douche bags out. Hold on a sec.'

While she left to do crisis management, I reached into my briefcase, retrieved the photographs Charlotte had given me, and flipped through the collection. When I first found them in Jack's apartment, these scenes felt like yesterday. Now even that moment felt like it was a lifetime ago.

As I slipped the envelope back into my briefcase, I saw Jack's copy of *Eight Days to Die*. Like that old child's game of hot potato, I had accepted it from Charlotte and now had no idea how to get rid of it.

I couldn't remember the last time I'd read a novel. I scanned the back cover. A woman has scheduled her own death in eight days. What does she do with her remaining time?

I flipped to the final chapter of the book to confirm my suspicions. Yep, her scheduled death was an execution, and all those scenes that preceded it were memories supplemented by imagination. This is why Melissa would only watch movies with me if I promised not to yell out my theory about the ending.

I took another sip of my prosecco and looked for Melissa. She had her hands on her hips and was scolding a hipster with a soda-fountain mustache and skinny jeans. It was no contest; the only issue was how long it would take for her to get him to leave without more breakage.

I opened the book again, this time at the beginning. On the title page was a handwritten inscription.

3/18 To the best dad a girl could ask for. Happy Birthday, Old Man. Love, Buckley

I had finished a short first chapter before turning back to the inscription. At his plea colloquy, Jack said he bought this book after reading a review that mentioned the scene at the football field, but it had been a birthday gift from his daughter. It was a tiny discrepancy, but I couldn't stop looking at that inscription.

Buckley. She heard and saw everything that happened in that apartment of theirs. Her parents' fights. My conversations with Jack. She may have told me that Tracy Frankel had only asked for directions, but what if Tracy had told Buckley everything? She'd been at the apartment by the time the police arrived for her father, but where had she been the morning of the shooting? The freight elevator, unlike the one her father had used, had no cameras. She could have easily slipped in and out of the building, while her father assumed she was still sleeping in her bedroom.

I pulled my laptop from my bag and used my phone hot-spot to jump online. I pulled up the website for Paperfree and found the link to reactivate a closed account.

Enter e-mail address: mlh87@paperfree.com

The 'Madeline' account, the one used to make it appear that a stranger had beckoned Jack to the football field.

Enter password.

I'd typed Jack's so many times that my fingers nearly moved on muscle memory to jack<3smollybuckley.

But that wasn't the password I was interested in. I thought about Jack's explanation at the First Precinct: 'Jack loves Molly and Buckley. It was an easy way for all of us to remember our passwords when we first set up the accounts. Molly's was Molly loves Jack and Buckley. And so on.'

And so on. That many years ago, Jack and Molly would have set up their daughter's password, too. And like most people, she may have continued to use that same password for everything, even an account no one was supposed to trace to her.

I sounded out the words mentally as I typed:

buckley<3sjackmolly

349

Enter.

I realized I was holding my breath as a circle turned on my screen. I let myself exhale with relief when I got an error message. *Your e-mail address and password do not match an account that can be reactivated. Try again if you think you have made an error, but, remember, there is no password retrieval for an account that has been closed.*

I was about to close my computer when I decided that if I was chasing paranoid theories, I might as well be thorough.

Enter password. Buckley<3smollyjack.

Another error message, followed by another try. Enter password. Buckley<3smomanddad

Congratulations. Your account has been reactivated. We hope you and your paperfree account have a long and fulfilling relationship.

24

ABOUT FOUR YEARS LATER
AUGUST 10

I found myself looking at my watch, even though I'd only been here twenty minutes. 'Here' was the Greenhaven Correctional Facility. Despite the name, there was nothing correctional about it. This was a maximum-security prison, former home to 'old sparky,' when New York used to electrocute people.

The first time I visited Jack at Greenhaven, I'd stayed more than an hour. I was officially still his lawyer, so the guards gave me relatively free rein.

In the last two years, Jack's only other visitors, according to the prison staff, were Charlotte, Buckley, and Jack's editor, who was pressing him to write a memoir. I knew that as long as he was in prison, he would never write about his case.

'So, I take it your answer's still the same?' I asked.

Today was the four-year anniversary of his guilty plea. Every year, on this date, I had made the drive to Greenhaven to try to convince him to let me work with the district attorney's office to set aside his conviction. But, because Jack couldn't be freed without revealing the truth about who killed Malcolm Neeley, Tracy Frankel, and Clifton Hunter, he refused. I had called the state bar multiple times, trying to find

351

some way around Jack's authorization. The law was clear: I was bound to pursue his interests *as he defined them*. And I had been tempted countless times to say, fuck ethics. But without Jack's cooperation, I had no hope of convincing anyone of the truth.

'I know you don't want to hear this, Jack, but she's not going to be okay.' At least on the surface, Buckley was doing fine, having finished her sophomore year at Brown. 'She can't have a normal life after what happened. You're not protecting her.'

'I am for now.'

For now. That was as much as I'd ever gotten.

I was about to signal for the guard when Jack said, 'You look good, Olivia. Happy.'

'I am, finally.' Unless he noticed the bump last year, he didn't even know about Grace. I saw no reason to tell him. Maybe I was projecting, but I had the feeling he was keeping something from me as well. 'You can tell me anything. You know that, don't you?'

He nodded.

'Will you at least tell me whether she knows that you know?'

He smiled and shook his head. At least she had no idea that I had figured it out. Unlike Jack, I didn't have a maximum-security prison to protect me.

'Not that it's the same, Jack, but in a weird way, I feel like I lost twenty years of my life, because I squandered it. And now I'm free. And someday you will be, too. Call me the minute you're ready.'

352

I tossed my briefcase in Grace's car seat. It was a multifunction accessory.

Once I was behind the wheel, I checked my e-mail. Einer had scheduled four more interviews in the next two days. Lately, I seemed to spend more time as an employer than a lawyer. Don was determined to retire, at least as he defined that term. I knew he'd still have his hands all over every case, but he was insisting that I find a 'me' — a younger lawyer who would eventually become a full partner.

More immediately, Einer was starting his third year of law school, and we needed someone — probably three someones — to begin training to replace him once he graduated.

I hit Reply. *Einer, please cancel all the lawyer interviews. At some point, I'll stop begging, but I refuse to hire someone until you tell me you're going elsewhere. And why would you do that? Ellison, Randall & Wagner has a nice ring to it, don't you think?* Eventually he'd realize it wasn't a pity offer. He was the perfect person for the job.

I was halfway back to the city when my phone rang. It was a familiar number. I could hear the caller clearly through the car's speakers. 'Good news,' he said. 'I didn't think it would happen, but Miller just pled out. I'll get Grace from day care, and was thinking about picking up some steaks for dinner?'

'Have I told you lately that you're a really good husband?'

Only seven months old, Little Miss Grace Randall Temple was in her first weeks of part-time day care. I had never understood those mothers who fret about leaving their children with other people, but now I was one of them, and fortunately I had a spouse who shared my dedication to figuring out a schedule that made sense for all three members of our family.

'Are you okay?' he asked.

My husband, still at the district attorney's office, knew about my annual visits to Jack, but had no idea of the real reason behind them. It was, to my knowledge, the only secret between us.

'I'm good, Scott. Thanks.' As usual, we exchanged I love yous before I hung up.

One of these days I would tell him. I still wasn't certain, but until I heard otherwise, I believed Buckley never meant for her father to be convicted. I had seen her face when I told her about the GSR results. She was devastated, but not for the reason I assumed at the time. At some point after the shooting and before the police arrived at the apartment door, Buckley must have hugged her father. That's why his hands were clean and his shirt was dirty. That was her first mistake.

But even with the GSR, I could have gotten an acquittal. Buckley's big slip was letting their home's IP address show up on a log-in to the 'Madeline' e-mail account. It wasn't Jack's laptop that had been used for those e-mails. It was Buckley's.

Jack had known it was Buckley the moment he heard Tracy Frankel's name among the victims

354

at his arraignment. That's why he had turned to look at her.

Tracy had been stopping by the apartment, trying to shake him down for money. But then Jack's underage mistress made the fatal decision of going to Buckley and telling her that her next stop was Malcolm Neeley.

Jack, in typical fashion, had tried to brush it off, telling his daughter that the girl was just troubled. Confused. He'd handle it. But Buckley wasn't like her father. He was the kind of person who needed to be protected, even if it was by his sixteen-year-old daughter. She, on the other hand, was willing to take care of business.

They both had to go. Killing Malcolm Neeley and Tracy Frankel had allowed the Harris family to maintain the myth. Poor Clifton Hunter just happened to be there.

When you're a criminal defense lawyer, you get used to trying to understand why people do horrible things. I was still trying to understand Buckley. She was a little kid who made her mother take a later train because she didn't wake up on time one day — a day that just happened to be the morning a boy named Todd Neeley opened fire in Penn Station. She saw her father become consumed with Malcolm Neeley, because blaming the shooter's father was easier than blaming his own daughter. And then one day, she realized that if anyone was to be blamed other than her or a mentally ill boy, it was Jack.

She could have left Jack out of it. She knew where to find Neeley on Wednesday mornings.

Luring Tracy there would have been easy — a quick call from a blocked number, asking her to meet to pick up her blackmail money. But Buckley was also angry that her father's infidelity had put them in this position. Maybe she hired the woman in the grass as a test — to see if her father would yet again take the bait of an attractive girl with long, dark hair.

She wanted him to connect enough dots to realize that all of this was his fault. She probably counted on the police to at least question her father, and calling me afterward was almost certainly part of the plan. Forcing Jack to accept help from the woman he'd always loved more than her mother was a nice chunk of the intended punishment. But my best guess is that she never expected him to be arrested, let alone convicted. She thought I'd save him. She pleaded with me to save him.

But four years later, Jack was still in prison, and he knew exactly why. I no longer thought of Jack on a regular basis, but he was in my calendar as an annual event. Every year, I would check.

Author's Note

The Ex is set in the real New York City, with very slight modifications. The football field is a larger, fictionalized version of the sports courts south of Pier 40, and Olivia and Melissa had a more classic college dorm than the actual student housing at Columbia University. Though every legal process in Jack's case is authentic, some of the bumps along the way are not typical of the run-of-the-mill trial. Café Lissa isn't real, but oh, how I wish it were.

Acknowledgments

Writing is a solitary exercise, but the completion of *The Ex* was a collective effort. My editor, Jennifer Barth, is a smart and loyal perfectionist with a careful eye and sharp instincts; she forces me to be a better writer. My agent, Philip Spitzer, remains my biggest champion. NYPD Lt. Lucas Miller, Nic Wolff, and Roy Simon generously allowed me to pick their very impressive brains for information.

I am endlessly grateful for the support I receive at the Spitzer Agency from Lukas Ortiz and Jennifer Woodason; at HarperCollins from Amy Baker, Erica Barmash, Jonathan Burnham, Heather Drucker, Michael Morrison, Katie O'Callaghan, Kathy Schneider, Leah Wasielewski, Erin Wicks, and Lydia Weaver; at Faber & Faber from Angus Cargill and Sophie Portas; and from Jody Hotchkiss.

I'd especially like to thank readers. Until a book is read, a story hasn't really been told. Your imagination is what completes the process, so thank you for sharing it with me. Some of you have gone even further by telling friends about the books, serving as volunteer photographers and tour guides at book events, and acting as informal publicists, advisors, life coaches, and dog trainers in the online 'Kitchen Cabinet' on Facebook, Twitter, and Instagram. I'm humbled and grateful for the support.

Finally, I don't know how I'd stay (relatively) sane without the love, support, and patience of my family and friends. And hey you, Sean: Happy tenth anniversary.

We do hope that you have enjoyed reading this large print book.

Did you know that all of our titles are available for purchase?

We publish a wide range of high quality large print books including:
Romances, Mysteries, Classics
General Fiction
Non Fiction and Westerns

Special interest titles available in large print are:
The Little Oxford Dictionary
Music Book
Song Book
Hymn Book
Service Book

Also available from us courtesy of Oxford University Press:
Young Readers' Dictionary
(large print edition)
Young Readers' Thesaurus
(large print edition)

For further information or a free brochure, please contact us at:
Ulverscroft Large Print Books Ltd.,
The Green, Bradgate Road, Anstey,
Leicester, LE7 7FU, England.
Tel: (00 44) 0116 236 4325
Fax: (00 44) 0116 234 0205